WAYWARD

WAYWARD

BOOK TWO OF THE WAYWARD PINES SERIES

by

BLAKE CROUCH

The characters and events portrayed in this book are fictitious. Any similarity to real persons, living or dead, is coincidental and not intended by the author.

Published by Thomas & Mercer
P.O. Box 400818
Las Vegas, NV 89140

ISBN-13: 9781477808702
ISBN-10: 1477808701
Library of Congress Control Number: 2013906097

For Chad Hodge

ABOUT WAYWARD

An electrified fence topped with razor wire encircles the town of Wayward Pines, which also lies under 24-7 sniper surveillance. Each of the 461 residents woke up here following a catastrophic accident. There are hidden cameras in every home and business. The residents are told where to work. Where to live. Who to marry. Some believe they are dead, that this is the afterlife. Some think they're trapped in an experimental prison. Everyone secretly dreams of leaving, but the few who dare to try are in for a terrifying surprise. Ethan Burke has seen the world beyond. He's sheriff, and one of the few who knows the truth—Wayward Pines isn't just a town. And what lies on the other side of the fence is a nightmare world beyond anyone's imagining.

The mind is its own place, and in itself can make a heaven of hell, a hell of heaven.

—**John Milton, *Paradise Lost***

If you look out at nature, you find that as you tend to see suspended animation, you tend to see immortality.

—**Mark Roth, PhD (Cell Biologist)**

Yesterday is history.
Tomorrow is a mystery.
Today is a gift.
That's why it's called the present.
Work hard, be happy, and enjoy your
life in Wayward Pines!

—Notice to all residents of Wayward Pines (required to be posted prominently in every residence and place of business)

1

Mustin had been watching the creature through the Schmidt & Bender telescopic sight for the better part of an hour. It had come over the cirque at daybreak, pausing as the first radials of sunlight struck its translucent skin. Its progression down through the boulder field had been slow and careful, stopping occasionally to sniff the remains of others like it. Others Mustin had killed.

The sniper reached up to the scope, adjusted the parallax, and settled back in behind the focus. Conditions were ideal—clear visibility, mild temperature, no wind. With the reticle set at 25x zoom, the creature's ghostly silhouette popped against the gray of the shattered rock. At a distance of one and a half miles, its head was no larger than a grain of sand.

If he didn't take the shot now, he'd have to range the target again. And there was a possibility that by the time he was ready to shoot, the creature would have passed out of his sight line. It wouldn't be the end of the world. There was still a high-voltage security fence a half mile down the canyon. But if it managed to scale the cliffs over the top of the razor wire, there'd be trouble. He'd have to radio in. Call for a team. Extra work. Extra time. Every effort would be made to stop the creature from reaching town. He'd almost certainly catch an ass-chewing from Pilcher.

Mustin drew in a long, deep breath.

Lungs expanding.

He let it out.

Lungs deflating.

Then empty.

His diaphragm relaxed.

He counted to three and squeezed the trigger.

The British-made AWM bucked hard against his shoulder, the report dampened by the suppressor. Recovering from the recoil, he found his target in the sphere of magnification, still crouched on a flat-topped boulder on the floor of the canyon.

Damn.

He'd missed.

It was a longer shot than he normally took, and so many variables in play, even under perfect conditions. Barometric pressure. Humidity. Air density. Barrel temperature. Even Coriolis effect—the rotation of the earth. He thought he'd accounted for everything in calculating his aiming solution, but—

The creature's head disappeared in a pink mist.

He smiled.

It had taken a little over four seconds for the .338 Lapua Magnum round to reach the target.

Helluva shot.

Mustin sat up, struggled to his feet.

Stretched his arms over his head.

It was midmorning. The sky steel blue and not a cloud in sight. His perch was atop a thirty-foot guard tower that had been built on the rocky pinnacle of a mountain, far above the timberline. From the open platform, he had a panoramic view of the surrounding peaks, the canyon, the forest, and the town of Wayward Pines, which from four thousand feet above, was little more than a grid of intersecting streets, couched in a protected valley.

His radio squeaked.

He answered, "Mustin, over."

"Just had a fence strike in zone four, over."

"Stand by."

Zone 4 encompassed the expanse of pine forest that bordered the southern edge of town. He took up his rifle and glassed the fence under the canopy of trees, tracked it for a quarter mile. He saw the smoke first—coils of it lifting off the animal's scorched hide.

"I have a visual," he said. "It's just a deer, over."

"Copy that."

Mustin swung the rifle north into town.

Houses appeared—colorful Victorians fronted with perfect squares of bright grass. White picket fences. He aimed down into the park where a woman pushed two children in swings. A little girl shot down the blinding glimmer of a slide.

He glassed the schoolyard.

The hospital.

The community gardens.

Main Street.

Fighting down that familiar swell of envy.

Townies.

They were oblivious. All of them. So beautifully oblivious.

He didn't hate them. Didn't want their life. He had long ago accepted his role as protector. Guardian. Home was a sterile, windowless room inside a mountain, and he had made as much peace with that fact as a man could hope to make. But that didn't mean that on a lovely morning as he gazed down into what was literally the last vestige of paradise on the face of the earth, there wasn't a pang of nostalgia. Of homesickness for what had once been.

For what would never be again.

Moving down the street, Mustin fixed his sight on a man walking quickly up the sidewalk. He wore a hunter-green shirt, brown pants, black Stetson cowboy hat.

The brass star pinned to his lapel refracted a glint of sunlight.

The man turned a corner, the crosshairs of the reticle zeroing in on his back.

"Morning, Sheriff Burke," Mustin said. "Feel an itch between your shoulder blades?"

2

There were still moments, like this one, when Wayward Pines felt like a real place.

Sunlight pouring down into the valley.

The morning still pleasantly cool.

Pansies gemmed a planter under an open window that let the smell of a cooking breakfast waft outside.

People out for morning walks.

Watering lawns.

Collecting the local paper.

Beads of dew steaming off the top of a black mailbox.

Ethan Burke found it tempting to linger in the moment, to pretend that everything was just as it appeared. That he lived with his wife and son in a perfect little town, where he was a well-liked sheriff. Where they had friends. A comfortable home. All needs provided for. And it was in the pretending that he'd come to fully understand how well the illusion worked. How people could let themselves succumb, let themselves disappear into the pretty lie that surrounded them.

* * *

Bells jingled over the door as Ethan entered the Steaming Bean. He stepped up to the counter and smiled at the barista, a hippie chick with blond dreads and soulful eyes.

"Morning, Miranda."

"Hi, Ethan. Usual?"

"Please."

While she started the espresso shots for his cappuccino, Ethan surveyed the shop. The regulars were all here, including two old-timers—Phillip and Clay—hunched over a chessboard. Ethan walked over, studied the game. By the looks of it, they'd been at it for a while now, each man down to a king, queen, and several pawns.

"Looks like you're heading toward a stalemate," Ethan said.

"Not so fast," Phillip said. "I still got something up my sleeve."

His opponent, a gray grizzly of a man, grinned through his wild beard across the chessboard and said, "By *something*, Phil means he's going to take so damn long to move that I die and he wins by forfeit."

"Oh, shut up, Clay."

Ethan moved on past a ratty sofa to a bookshelf. He ran his finger across the spines. Classics. Faulkner. Dickens. Tolkien. Hugo. Joyce. Bradbury. Melville. Hawthorne. Poe. Austen. Fitzgerald. Shakespeare. At a glance, it was just a ragtag assembly of cheap paperbacks. He pulled a slim volume off the shelf. *The Sun Also Rises*. The cover was an impressionistic bullfighting scene. Ethan swallowed against the lump that formed in his throat. The brittle-paged, mass-market edition of Hemingway's first novel was probably the sole remaining copy in existence. It gave him goose bumps—awesome and tragic to hold it in his hands.

"Ethan, you're all set!"

He grabbed one more book for his son and went to the counter to collect his cappuccino.

"Thanks, Miranda. I'm going to borrow these books, if that's okay."

"Of course." She smiled. "Keep 'em straight out there, Sheriff."

"Do my best."

Ethan tipped the brim of his hat and headed for the door.

* * *

Ten minutes later, he pushed through the glass double doors under a sign that read:

OFFICE OF THE SHERIFF OF WAYWARD PINES

Reception stood empty. Nothing new there.

His secretary sat at her desk looking as bored as ever. She was playing Solitaire, laying cards down at a steady, mechanical pace.

"Morning, Belinda."

"Morning, Sheriff."

She didn't look up.

"Any calls?"

"No, sir."

"Anyone been by?"

"No, sir."

"How was your evening?"

She glanced up, caught off guard, an ace of spades clutched in her right hand.

"What?"

It was the first time since becoming sheriff that Ethan had pushed his interaction with Belinda beyond perfunctory greetings, goodbyes, and administrative chitchat. She'd been a pediatric nurse in her past life. He wondered if she knew that he knew that.

"I was just asking how your evening was. Last night."

"Oh." She pulled her fingers through a long, silver ponytail. "Fine."

"Do anything fun?"

"No. Not really."

He thought she might return the question, inquire after his evening, but five seconds of uncomfortable silence and eye contact elapsed and still she didn't speak.

Ethan finally rapped his knuckles on her desk. "I'll be in my office."

* * *

He propped his boots up on the massive desk and kicked back in the leather chair with his steaming coffee. The head of a giant elk stared down at him from its mount across the room. Between it and the three antique gun cases behind the desk, Ethan felt he had the trappings of a country sheriff down cold.

His wife would be arriving at work right about now. In her past life, Theresa had been a paralegal. In Wayward Pines, she was the town's sole realtor, which meant she spent her days sitting behind a desk in an office on Main Street that people rarely entered. Her job, like the vast majority of those assigned to the residents, was mainly cosmetic. Window dressing for a pretend town. Only four or five times a year would she actually assist someone with a new home purchase. Model residents were rewarded with the option to upgrade their home every few years. Those residents who had been here the longest and never violated the rules lived in the biggest, nicest Victorians. And those couples that became pregnant were all but guaranteed a new, more spacious home.

Ethan had nothing to do and nowhere to be for the next four hours.

He opened the book from the coffeehouse.

The prose was terse and brilliant.

He choked up at the descriptions of Paris at night.

The restaurants, the bars, the music, the smoke.

The lights of a real, living city.

The sense of a wide world brimming with diverse and fascinating people.

The freedom to explore it.

Forty pages in, he closed the book. He couldn't take it. Hemingway wasn't distracting him. Wasn't sweeping him away from the reality of Wayward Pines. Hemingway was rubbing his face in it. Pouring salt into a wound that would never heal.

* * *

At a quarter to two, Ethan left the office on foot.

He strolled through quiet neighborhoods.

Everyone he passed smiled and waved, greeting him with what felt like genuine enthusiasm, as if he'd lived here for years. If they secretly feared and hated him, they hid it well. And why shouldn't they? As far as he knew, he was the sole resident of Wayward Pines who knew the truth, and it was his job to make certain it stayed that way. To keep the peace. The lie. Even from his wife and son. In his first two weeks as sheriff, he'd spent most of his time studying dossiers on each resident, learning the particulars of their lives before. The details of their integrations. Surveillance-based reports of their lives after. He knew the personal histories of half of the town now. Their secrets and fears. Those who could be trusted to maintain this fragile illusion. Those with hairline cracks in their veneer.

He was becoming a one-man gestapo.

Necessary—he got that.

But he still despised it.

* * *

Ethan hit Main Street and headed south until the sidewalk and the buildings ended. The road went on, and he walked its shoulder into a forest of towering pines. The murmur of town life dropped away.

Fifty feet past the road sign that warned of a sharp curve ahead, Ethan stopped. He glanced back toward Wayward Pines. No cars coming. Everything still. No sound but a single bird cheeping in a tree high overhead.

He stepped down from the shoulder and set off into the woods.

The air smelled of pine needles warming in the sun.

Ethan moved across the cushiony floor of the forest through spaces of light and shadow.

He walked quickly enough to sweat through the back of his shirt, his skin cool where the fabric clung.

It was a nice hike. No surveillance, no people. Just a man on a walk by himself in the woods, briefly alone with his thoughts.

Two hundred yards from the road, he reached the boulders, a collection of granite blocks scattered between the pines. At the point where the forest swept up the mountainside, a rock outcropping loomed, half-buried in the earth.

Ethan approached.

From ten feet away, the smooth, vertical rock face looked real. Right down to the quartz vein and the bright smatterings of moss and lichen.

At close range, the illusion was less convincing, the dimensions of the face just a touch too square.

Ethan stood several feet back and waited.

Soon, he heard the muffled mechanical hum of the gears beginning to turn. The entire rock face lifted like a giant garage door—wide and tall enough to accommodate a tractor-trailer.

Ethan ducked under the rising door into the dank, subterranean chill.

"Hello, Ethan."

"Marcus."

Same escort as before—a twenty-something kid with the buzzed hair and sharp jawline of a grunt or a cop. He wore a yellow windbreaker, and it dawned on Ethan that he'd forgotten to bring his jacket again. He was in for another freezing ride.

Marcus had left the doorless, topless Wrangler idling and facing back the way it had come.

Ethan climbed into the front passenger seat.

The entrance door thudded closed behind them.

Marcus pulled the emergency brake and shifted into gear as he spoke into a headset, "I've got Mr. Burke. We're en route."

The Jeep lurched forward, accelerating on a single, unmarked lane of pristine pavement.

They sped up a fifteen-percent grade.

The walls of the tunnel were exposed bedrock.

In places, rivulets of water came down the rock and spider-webbed across the road. An occasional droplet starred the windshield.

The fluorescent luminaires blurred past overhead in a river of morbid orange.

It smelled like stone, water, and exhaust.

Between the engine growl and the wind, it was too noisy for conversation. This was fine by Ethan. He leaned back into the gray vinyl seat and fought the urge to rub his arms against the constant blast of cold, wet air.

Pressure built inside his ears, the roar of the engine fading.

He swallowed.

The noise returned.

They kept climbing.

At thirty-five miles per hour, it was only a four-minute trip, but it seemed to take longer. Something disorienting and time-skewing in the face of all the cold and the noise and the wind.

The sense of literally boring up inside a mountain.

The unnerving anticipation of going to see *him*.

* * *

The tunnel emptied into an immense cavern that contained the floor space of ten warehouses. A million square feet or more. A room expansive enough for the assembly of jets or spacecraft. But instead it held provisions. Huge cylindrical reservoirs filled with food staples. Long rows of shelving forty feet high stocked with lumber and supplies. Everything needed to keep the last town on earth running for years to come.

Marcus drove past a door with the word *Suspension* stenciled across the glass. Misty blue light clouded behind the entrance, and it ran an icy finger down Ethan's spine to know what stood inside.

Pilcher's suspension units.

Hundreds of them.

Every resident of Wayward Pines, himself included, had been chemically suspended in that room for eighteen hundred years.

The Jeep jerked to a stop beside a pair of glass doors.

Marcus turned off the car as Ethan climbed out.

The escort typed in a code on the keypad and the doors whisked apart.

They moved past a placard that read "Level 1" into a long, empty corridor.

No windows.

Fluorescent lights humming.

The floor was a streak of black-and-white checkered tile. Every ten feet stood a door inset with a small circular window. No handle, no doorknob—they opened only with a keycard.

Most of the windows were dark.

Through one, however, an aberration watched Ethan pass, the pupils of its large, milky eyes dilating, razor cuspids bared, a single black talon clicking on the glass.

They visited him in nightmares. He'd wake dripping with sweat, reliving the attack, Theresa patting his back and whispering that he was safe at home in bed, that everything would be okay.

Halfway down the corridor, they stopped at a pair of unmarked doors.

Marcus swiped his keycard and they opened.

Ethan stepped inside the small car.

His escort inserted a key into a chrome panel, and when the sole button began to blink, pushed it.

The movement was smooth.

Ethan's ears always popped once during the ride, but he could never tell if they were rising or descending.

It stuck in his craw that even after two weeks on the job he was still escorted around this place like a child or a threat.

Two weeks.

Jesus.

It felt like just yesterday he'd been sitting across the desk from Adam Hassler, Special Agent in Charge of the Seattle field office, receiving the assignment to come to this town and find Ethan's missing ex-partner, Kate Hewson. But he wasn't a Secret Service agent anymore. He still hadn't fully come to terms with that fact.

The only way to know that they had stopped was that the doors opened.

The first thing he saw stepping off was a Picasso, which Ethan suspected was original.

They walked through a posh foyer. No fluorescent lights and checkered linoleum here. It was all marble tile and high-end wall sconces. Crown molding. Even the air tasted better—none of that canned, stale-edged component found in the rest of the complex.

They passed a sunken living room.

A cathedral kitchen.

A library walled with leather-bound volumes that smelled absolutely antique.

Turning a corner, they finally headed down toward the double oak doors at the end of the hall.

Marcus knocked hard twice, and a voice on the other side responded, "Come in!"

"Go ahead, Mr. Burke."

Ethan opened the doors and stepped through into a spectacular office.

The floor was a dark, exotic hardwood with a high-gloss sheen.

The centerpiece was a large table that displayed, under glass, an architectural miniature of Wayward Pines, accurate even to the color of Ethan's house.

The left-hand wall was adorned with the works of Vincent van Gogh.

The opposite wall consisted of a floor-to-ceiling bank of flat-screened monitors. Nine high, twenty-four across. Leather sofas faced the screens that showed two hundred sixteen simultaneous images of Wayward Pines—streets, bedrooms, bathrooms, kitchens, backyards.

Every time Ethan saw those screens he had to stifle an irresistible impulse to tear someone's head off.

He understood the purpose—fully—but still . . .

"That fury," said the man behind the intricately carved mahogany desk. "You flash it every time you come to see me."

Ethan shrugged. "You're eavesdropping on private lives. Just a natural reaction."

"You believe privacy should exist in our town?"

"Of course not."

Ethan moved toward the giant desk as the doors behind him swung shut.

He shelved his Stetson under his right arm and eased down into one of the chairs.

Stared at David Pilcher.

He was the billionaire-inventor (when money meant something) behind Wayward Pines, behind this complex inside the mountain. In 1971, Pilcher had discovered that the human genome was degrading, and he'd privately predicted that humanity would cease to exist within thirty to forty generations. So he built this suspension superstructure to preserve a number of pure humans before the genome corruption reached critical mass.

In addition to his inner circle of one hundred sixty true believers, Pilcher was responsible for the abduction of six hundred fifty people, all of whom, himself included, he'd put into suspended animation.

And Pilcher's prediction came true. At this very moment, beyond the electrified fence that surrounded Wayward Pines, lived hundreds of millions of what humanity had devolved into—aberrations.

And yet, Pilcher didn't own the face he'd ostensibly earned. He was a physically unthreatening man. Five foot five in boots.

Hairless save for the faintest silver stubble—more chrome than winter clouds. He watched Ethan through diminutive eyes that were as black as they were unreadable.

Pilcher pushed a manila folder across the leather-topped desk.

"What's this?" Ethan asked.

"A surveillance-based report."

Ethan opened the folder.

It contained a black-and-white screenshot of a man he recognized. Peter McCall. The man was editor-in-chief of the town paper—the *Wayward Light*. In the photograph, McCall is lying on his side in bed, staring empty-eyed into nothing.

"What'd he do?" Ethan asked.

"Well, nothing. And that's the problem. Peter hasn't shown up for work the last two days."

"Maybe he's been sick?"

"He hasn't reported feeling ill, and Ted, my head surveillance tech, got a weird vibe."

"Like he might be considering running?"

"Perhaps. Or doing something reckless."

"I remember his file," Ethan said. "I don't recall any major integration issues. No subsequent insubordinate behavior. Has he said anything disturbing?"

"McCall hasn't spoken a word in forty-eight hours. Not even to his children."

"What do you want me to do exactly?"

"Keep an eye on him. Drop by and say hello. Don't underestimate the effect your presence can have."

"You aren't considering a fête are you?"

"No. Fêtes are reserved for those who exhibit true acts of treason and try to bring others along with them. You aren't wearing your sidearm."

"I think it sends the wrong message."

Pilcher smiled a mouthful of tiny white teeth. "I appreciate your taking an interest in the message *I* want my sole figure of authority in town to espouse. I mean that. What would your message be, Ethan?"

"That I'm there to help. To support. To protect."

"But you're not actually there to do any of those things. I've been unclear—this is my fault. Your presence is a reminder of *my* presence."

"Got it."

"So the next time I spot you walking down the street on one of my screens, can I expect to see your biggest, baddest gun bulging off your hip?"

"For sure."

"Excellent."

Ethan could feel his heart punching against his ribs with a furious intensity.

"Please don't take this minor rebuke to be my overall impression of your work, Ethan. I think you're integrating nicely into your new position. Would you agree?"

Ethan glanced over Pilcher's shoulder. The wall behind the desk was solid rock. In the center, a large window had been cut into the stone. The view was of the mountains, the canyon, and Wayward Pines—two thousand feet below.

"I think I'm getting more comfortable with the job," Ethan said.

"You've been rigorously studying the resident files?"

"I've gotten through all of them once."

"Your predecessor, Mr. Pope, had them memorized."

"I'll get there."

"Glad to hear it. But you weren't studying them this morning, correct?"

"You were watching me?"

"Not *watching you* watching you. But your office popped up a few times on the monitors. What was that you were reading? I couldn't make it out."

"*The Sun Also Rises*."

"Ah. Hemingway. One of my favorites. You know, I still believe that great art will be created here. I brought along our pianist, Hecter Gaither, for that explicit reason. I have other renowned novelists and painters in suspension. Poets. And we're always looking for talent to nurture in the school. Ben is thriving in his art class."

Ethan bristled internally at Pilcher's mention of his son, but he only said, "The residents of Pines are in no state of mind to make art."

"What do you mean by that, Ethan?"

Pilcher asked it like a therapist might—the question charged with intellectual curiosity, not aggression.

"They live under constant surveillance. They know they can never leave. What kind of art would a repressed society possibly be motivated to create?"

Pilcher smiled. "Ethan, to hear you talk, I wonder if you're fully on board with me. If you actually believe in what we're doing."

"Of course I believe."

"Of course you do. A report came across my desk today from one of my nomads just returned from a two-week mission. He saw a swarm of abbies two thousand strong only twenty miles from the center of Wayward Pines. They were moving across the plains east of the mountains, chasing a herd of buffalo. Every day, I'm reminded how vulnerable we are in this valley. How tenuous, how fragile our existence. And you sit there and look at me like I'm running the GDR or the Khmer Rouge. You don't like it. I can respect that. Hell, I wish it could be different. But there are reasons for the things I do, and these reasons are based upon the preservation of life. Of our species."

"Aren't there always reasons?"

"You're a man of conscience, and I appreciate that," Pilcher said. "I wouldn't have someone in your position of power who wasn't. Every resource I have, every person under my employ, is devoted to one thing. Keeping the four hundred sixty-one people in that valley—your wife and son included—safe."

"What about the truth?" Ethan asked.

"In some environments, safety and truth are natural born enemies. I would think a former employee of the federal government could grasp that concept."

Ethan glanced over at the wall of screens. On one in the lower left-hand corner, his wife appeared.

Sitting alone in her office on Main Street.

Motionless.

Bored.

The screen adjacent to hers showed a camera feed unlike anything Ethan had seen—a bird's-eye view of something flying a hundred feet above a dense forest at a considerable rate of speed.

"What's that camera feed?" Ethan asked, pointing at the wall.

"Which one?"

The image was replaced by a camera shot from inside the opera house.

"It's gone now, but it looked like something flying at treetop level."

"Oh, that's just one of my UAVs."

"UAV?"

"Unmanned Aerial Vehicle. It's an MQ-9 Reaper drone. We send them out every so often on reconnaissance missions. Has a range of about a thousand miles. Today, I believe it's flying south to do a loop around the Great Salt Lake."

"Ever find anything?"

"Not yet. Look, Ethan. I'm not asking you to like all of this. *I* don't like it."

"Where are we going?" Ethan asked as the image of his wife was replaced with the image of two boys building sand castles in a sandbox. "As a species I mean." He fixed his gaze back on Pilcher. "I get what you've done here. That you've preserved our existence far beyond what evolution had in mind. But was it just for this? So a small contingent of humanity could live in a valley under 24-7 surveillance? Shielded from the truth? Occasionally forced to kill one of their own? It's not a life, David. It's a prison sentence. And you've made me the warden. I want the best for these people. For my family."

Pilcher rolled back in his chair away from the desk, spun it around, and stared through the glass at the town he had made.

"We've been here fourteen years, Ethan. There are less than a thousand of us and hundreds of millions of them. Sometimes the best you can do is simply survive."

* * *

The camouflaged tunnel door closed shut behind him.

Ethan stood alone in the woods.

He moved away from the rock outcropping back toward the road.

The sun had already dropped behind the western wall of cliffs.

A crisp, golden quality to the sky.

A night-is-coming chill to the air.

The road into Pines was empty, and Ethan walked down the middle of the double yellow.

* * *

Home was 1040 Sixth Street, a Victorian just a few blocks from Main. Yellow with white trim. Pleasant and creaky. Ethan moved across the flagstones and up onto the porch.

He opened the screened door, the solid wood door.

Stepped inside.

Said, "Honey, I'm home!"

There was no answer.

Only the silent, clenched energy of an empty house.

He topped the coat rack with his cowboy hat and sat down on a ladder-back chair to wrestle off his boots.

In sock feet, he crossed to the kitchen. The milk had come. Four glass bottles rattled against one another when he pulled open the door to the fridge. He grabbed one and carried it down the hallway into the study. This was Ethan's favorite room in the house. If he sat in the oversized upholstered chair by the window, he could bask in the knowledge that he wasn't being watched. Most buildings in Pines had one or two blind spots. On his third trip to the superstructure, he'd gotten his hands on the surveillance schematics for his house. Memorized the location of every camera. He'd asked Pilcher if he could have them removed, and been denied. Pilcher wanted Ethan to have the full experience of living under surveillance so he could *relate to the people under his authority.*

There was comfort in knowing that, in this moment, no one could see him. Of course, they knew his precise location at all times thanks to the microchip embedded under his hamstring.

Ethan had known better than to ask if he could be exempted from that security measure.

Ethan popped the top off the glass bottle and took a swig.

It wasn't the kind of thing he could say to Theresa (with people listening), but he'd often thought that out of all the terrible hardships attendant to their life in Pines—no privacy, no freedom, the ever-present threat of death—this daily milk from the dairy in the southeast corner of the valley had to be the one bright spot.

It was cold and creamy and fresh, with a grassy sweetness.

Out the window, he could see into the next-door neighbor's backyard. Jennifer Rochester knelt over a raised flowerbed, scooping in handfuls of soil from a red wheelbarrow. He recalled her file before he could stop the thought. In her past life, she'd been a professor of education at Washington State University. Here in Pines, she waited tables four nights a week at the Biergarten. With the exception of a brutal integration that almost didn't take, she had been a model resident.

Stop.

He didn't want to think about work, about the private details of his neighbors' lives.

What must they think of him under the surface?

He shuddered at his life.

They hit him occasionally, these moments of despair. There was no way out, no other man he could be—not if he wanted to keep his family safe.

That had been made abundantly clear.

Ethan knew he should probably read the report on McCall, but instead he opened the drawer in the accent table beside him and took out the book of poetry.

Robert Frost.

A short collection of his nature poems.

Whereas Hemingway had crushed him this morning, in Frost, Ethan always found solace.

He read for an hour.

Of mending walls and snowy woods and roads not taken.

The sky darkened.

He heard his wife's footsteps on the porch.

Ethan met her at the door.

"How was your day?" he asked.

Theresa's eyes seemed to whisper, *I sat behind a desk for eight hours at a meaningless job and didn't speak to another soul*, but she forced a smile and said, "It was great. And yours?"

I met with the man responsible for this prison we call home and picked up a secret file on one of our neighbors.

"Mine was great too."

She ran her hand down his chest. "I'm glad you didn't change yet. I love you in uniform."

Ethan embraced his wife.

Breathed in her smell.

Fingers gliding through her long blond hair.

"I was thinking," she said.

"Yeah?"

"Ben won't be home from Matthew's for another hour."

"Is that right?"

She took Ethan by the hand and pulled him toward the staircase.

"You sure?" he asked. They'd only been together twice in the two weeks since their reunion, both times in Ethan's favorite chair in the study, Theresa sitting in his lap, his hands on her hips—an awkward entanglement.

"I want you," she said.

"Let's go in the study."

"No," she said. "Our bed."

He followed her up the steps and down the second-floor hallway, the hardwood groaning under their footfalls.

They stumbled kissing into the bedroom, their hands all over each other, Ethan trying to ground himself in the moment, but he couldn't push the cameras out of his mind.

One behind the thermostat on the wall beside the bathroom door.

One in the light fixture in the ceiling looking straight down on their bed.

He was hesitating, conflicted, and Theresa sensed it.

"What's wrong, baby?" she asked.

"Nothing."

They were standing beside the bed.

Out the window, the lights of Pines were coming on—streetlamps, porch lights, houselights.

A cricket started up, its chirping sliding through the open window.

Quintessential sound of a peaceful night.

Only it wasn't real. There were no crickets anymore. The sound came from a tiny speaker hidden in a bush. He wondered if his wife knew that. Wondered how much of the truth she suspected.

"Do you want me?" Theresa asked in that no-bullshit tone he'd fallen for the first time they'd met.

"Of course I do."

"So do something about it."

He took his time unbuttoning the back of her white summer dress. Badly out of practice, but there was something wonderfully terrifying because of the rust. Not like high school, but close. A lack of control that had him hard before they'd even made it into the room.

He tried to pull the covers over them but she wouldn't have it. Told him she wanted to feel the cool breeze coming through the window across the surface of her skin.

It was a good old-fashioned bed and, like the rest of the house, creaky as hell.

The bedsprings squeaked and as Theresa moaned Ethan tried to put the knowledge of the camera above them out of his mind. Pilcher had assured him that watching couples in their private moments was strictly forbidden. That camera feeds were always killed when the clothes came off.

But Ethan wondered if that was true.

Or if some surveillance tech was watching as he fucked his wife. Studying Ethan's bare ass. The bend of Theresa's legs as they wrapped around his body.

Their first two times together, Ethan had come before Theresa. Now the thought of the camera above him cut into the pleasure. He used the anger to make himself last.

Theresa came with a vengeance that reminded Ethan of how good they could be together.

He let himself finish and then they were still. Breathless and he could feel her heart jackhammering against his ribs. The evening air almost cold where it grazed his sweaty skin. It might've been a perfect moment but the knowledge of everything elbowed in. Would he reach the point one day when he could shut that off? Just take these unexpected respites of peace for their surface beauty and forget the underlying horror? Was that how people managed to live here for years without losing their minds?

"So we *can* still do that," he said, and they laughed.

"Next time we'll take off the training wheels," she said.

"I like the sound of that."

He rolled over and Theresa curled into him.

Ethan made sure her eyes were closed.

Then he smiled straight up at the ceiling and raised his middle finger.

* * *

Ethan and Theresa worked on dinner together, chopping side by side on the butcher-block counter.

It was harvest time in the community gardens, the end of the season, and the Burkes' fridge was loaded down with their share of fresh veggies and fruit. These were, without a doubt, the prime eating months of the year in Wayward Pines. Once the leaves had been burnt with frost and the snowline had begun its rapid descent to the valley floor, the food took a disastrous turn for the freeze-dried. October through March, they could look forward to six months of prepackaged, dehydrated shit. Theresa had already warned Ethan that walking through the town grocery in December was like shopping for a space mission—nothing but shelf after shelf of chrome-colored packaging labeled with the most outrageous dares: crème brûlée; grilled-cheese sandwich; filet mignon; lobster tail. She'd already threatened to serve him freeze-dried steak and lobster for their Christmas dinner.

They had just finished preparing the hearty salad—onions, radishes, and raspberries over a bed of spinach and red lettuce—

when Ben crashed through the front door, rouge-cheeked, smelling of boy-sweat and the outdoors.

Still caught in that delicate blink of time between boy and man.

Theresa went to her son and kissed him and asked about his day.

Ethan turned on the vintage Philips—a tube radio from the 1950s in immaculate condition. Pilcher had inexplicably put one in every inhabited house.

Surfing was easy with one station to choose from. Most of the time, it just blared static, but there were one or two talk shows, and always, between seven and eight o'clock, "Dinner with Hecter."

Hecter Gaither had been a moderately famous concert pianist in his past life.

In Pines, he taught lessons to anyone who wanted to learn, and every night of the week, played music for the town.

Ethan turned up the volume, heard Hecter's voice as he joined his family.

"Good evening, Wayward Pines. Hecter Gaither here."

At the head of the table, Ethan dished out servings of their salad.

"I'm sitting at my Steinway, a gorgeous Boston Baby Grand."

First to his wife.

"Tonight, I'll be playing the Goldberg Variations, *a work originally composed for harpsichord by Johann Sebastian Bach."*

Then to his son.

"The construction of this piece is an aria followed by thirty variations. Please enjoy."

As Ethan served himself and took a seat, he heard the creak of the piano bench come crackling through the speaker.

* * *

After dinner, the Burkes took bowls of homemade ice cream out onto the porch.

Sat in rocking chairs.

Eating and listening.

Through the open windows of the neighboring houses, Ethan could hear Hecter's music.

It filled the valley.

Precise and radiant notes bubbling up between the mountain walls that had become ruddy with alpenglow.

They stayed out late.

A millennium without air or light pollution made for pitch-black skies.

The stars didn't just appear anymore.

They exploded.

Diamonds on black velvet.

You couldn't tear your eyes away.

Ethan reached over and held Theresa's hand.

Bach and galaxies.

The night grew cool.

When Hecter finished, people clapped inside their homes.

Across the street, a man shouted, "Bravo! Bravo!"

Ethan looked over at Theresa.

Her eyes were wet.

He said, "You okay?"

She nodded, wiping her face. "I'm just so glad to have you home."

* * *

Ethan finished the dishes, headed upstairs. Ben's room was at the far end of the hall and the door was closed—just a razor line of light visible underneath.

Ethan knocked.

"Come in."

Ben was sitting up in bed sketching—charcoal on butcher paper.

Ethan eased down on the comforter, asked, "Can I take a look?"

Ben lifted his arms.

The sketch was the boy's current vantage point from the bed—the wall, the desk, the window frame, the points of light outside which were visible through the glass.

"That's amazing," Ethan said.

"It's not exactly like I want it. The night through the window doesn't really look like night."

"I'm sure it'll get there. Hey, I picked up a book from the coffee shop today."

Ben perked up. "What is it?"

"It's called *The Hobbit*."

"I never heard of it."

"It was one of my favorite books when I was your age. I thought maybe I could read it to you."

"I know how to read, Dad."

"I know. But I haven't read this in years. Might be fun to read it together."

"Is it scary?"

"It has some scary parts. Go brush your teeth and hurry back."

* * *

Ethan sat against the headboard, reading by the light of a bedside table lamp.

Ben was asleep before the end of the first chapter, dreaming, Ethan hoped, of dungeons deep and caverns old. Of something other than Wayward Pines.

Ethan set the paperback aside and cut the lamp.

Pulled the blanket up to his son's shoulders.

He laid his hand down against Ben's back.

Nothing better in the world than feeling the rise and fall of his child's sleeping respirations.

Ethan had still not recovered from his son growing up in Wayward Pines. Doubted it was something he would ever accept. There were small things which he tried to tell himself were better. Tonight for instance. Had Ben grown up in the old world, Ethan would probably have entered his son's bedroom to find him glued to an iPhone.

Texting friends.

Watching television.

Playing video games.

Twitter and Facebook.

Ethan didn't miss those things. Didn't wish that his son was growing up in a world where people stared at screens all day. Where communication had devolved into the tapping of tiny letters and humanity lived by and large for the endorphin kick from the ping of a received text or a new e-mail.

Instead, he'd found his almost-teenage son passing his time before bed by sketching.

Hard to feel bad about that.

But it was the years to come that weighed down on Ethan's heart with the black pressure of depression.

What did Ben have to look forward to?

There would be no higher learning. No real career.

Gone were the days of—

You can be whatever you want to be.

Whatever you set your mind to.

Just follow your heart and your dreams.

Golden-age platitudes of an extinct species.

When people failed to pair up on their own, marriages in Pines were often *suggested*. And even when they weren't, the pool of potential mates wasn't exactly deep.

Ben would never see Paris.

Or Yellowstone.

Might never fall in love.

He would never have the experience of going away to college.

Or on a honeymoon.

Or driving across the country nonstop, spur-of-the-moment, just because he was twenty-two and could.

Ethan hated the surveillance and the abbies and Pines's culture of illusion.

But what kept him up with his mind racing late into the night were thoughts of his son. Ben had lived in Pines for five years, almost as long as he'd lived in the world before. Whereas Ethan suspected that the adult residents of Pines struggled every day with the memory of their past lives, Ben was very much a product of this town, of this strange, new time. Not even Ethan was privy to the things his son was being taught in school. Pilcher kept a pair of his men in plainclothes on school property at all times, and parents weren't allowed inside.

* * *

3:30 a.m.

Ethan lay awake in his bed, his wife in his arms.

Miles from sleep.

He could feel Theresa's eyelashes scraping against his chest with each blink.

What are you thinking?

The question had haunted their marriage before, but in Pines it had assumed an entirely new gravity. In the fourteen days they'd been together, Theresa had never broken the surface illusion. Of course, she had welcomed Ethan back home. There'd been a tearful reunion, but five years as a resident of Pines had made her a stone-cold pro. There was no talk of where Ethan had been or of his tumultuous integration. No mention or discussion of the strange events surrounding his becoming sheriff. Or what he might now know. Sometimes, he thought he caught a glint of something in Theresa's eyes—an acknowledgment of their circumstance, a suppressed desire to communicate on a forbidden level. But like a good actor, she never broke character.

More and more, he was coming to realize that living in Pines was like living in an elaborate play whose curtain never closed.

Everyone had their parts.

Shakespeare could have been writing about Pines: *All the world's a stage, and all the men and women merely players. They have their exits and their entrances; and one man in his time plays many parts.*

Ethan had already played a few of his own.

Downstairs, the telephone was ringing.

Theresa sat straight up as if she'd been spring-loaded, no sign of bleariness, snapped instantly to attention, her face gone tight with fear.

"Is it everyone's phone?" she asked, her voice filled with dread.

Ethan climbed out of bed.

"No, honey. Go back to sleep. It's just ours. It's just for me."

* * *

Ethan caught it on the sixth ring, standing in his boxers in the living room, the rotary phone clutched between his shoulder and his ear.

"For a moment, I wondered if you were going to answer."

Pilcher's voice. He'd never called Ethan at home before.

"Do you know what time it is?" Ethan said.

"Terribly sorry to have woken you. Did you get a chance to read the surveillance report on Peter McCall?"

"Yeah," Ethan lied.

"But you didn't go and talk with him like I suggested, did you?"

"I was planning to first thing tomorrow."

"Don't bother. He's decided to take his leave of us tonight."

"He's outside?"

"Yeah."

"So maybe he went for a walk."

"Thirty seconds ago, his signal reached the curve in the road at the end of town and kept right on heading south."

"What do you want me to do?"

There was a beat of silence on the other end of the line. Somehow, Ethan could feel the frustration coming through like a heat lamp.

Pilcher said evenly, "Stop him. Talk some sense into him."

"But I don't know exactly what you want me to say."

"I realize this is your first runner. Don't worry about what to say. Just trust your gut. I'll be listening."

Listening?

A dial tone blared in Ethan's ear.

* * *

He crept upstairs and dressed in the darkness. Theresa was still awake, sitting up in bed and watching as he threaded his belt through the loops.

"Everything okay, honey?" she asked.

"Fine," Ethan said. "Work stuff."

Yeah, just have to stop one of our neighbors from trying to leave our little slice of paradise in the middle of the night. No big deal. Nothing weird here.

Ethan walked over and kissed his wife on the forehead.

"I'll be back as soon as I can. Hopefully before morning."

She didn't say anything, only grabbed his hand and squeezed hard enough to move the bones.

* * *

Nighttime in Wayward Pines.

A wonderland of stillness.

The crickets turned off.

So quiet Ethan could hear the streetlamps humming.

The pounding of his own biologic engine.

He walked down to the curb and climbed into the black Ford Bronco with a light bar across the roof and, on the doors, the exact WP emblem that was engraved on his sheriff's star.

The engine gargled.

Ethan shifted into gear.

Tried to pull gently out into the street, but the 4.9-liter straight six had been bored out and was loud as hell.

The noise would undoubtedly wake people.

Cars were rarely driven in Pines—you could cross town on foot in fifteen minutes.

Cars were *never* driven in Pines at night.

Their purpose was decorative, and anyone whose slumber was disturbed by the roar of Ethan's Bronco would know that something had come off the rails.

He turned onto Main and headed south.

After the hospital, he hit the high beams and pushed the gas pedal into the floor, accelerating into a narrow corridor of tall pines.

With the window down, the cold forest air streamed in.

He drove down the middle of the road, tires straddling the double yellow.

Imagining there was no turn coming, that soon the road would begin to climb.

Out of this valley, away from this town.

He would reach down and turn on the radio, surf the airwaves until he found a station that played the oldies. It would be a three-hour trip back to Boise. Nothing like driving on an open road at night with the windows down and good music blasting. It was only for a split second, but he caught the feeling of living in a world full of others like him. A nightscape light-ridden with the glow of great cities. The distant roar of interstate traffic and jets thundering through the stratosphere.

The sense of not being so goddamn alone.

The endlings of their species, of humanity.

The speedometer needle edged toward seventy, the engine screaming.

He'd already blown past the *sharp curve ahead* sign.

Ethan stomped on the brake and lurched forward as the Bronco skidded to a stop in the vertex of the curve. He pulled over onto the shoulder, killed the engine, climbed out.

Soles of his boots scraping across the pavement.

For a moment, he hesitated with the door open, staring at the Winchester '97 cradled in the gun rack above the seats. He didn't want to take it for the message it might send to McCall. He didn't want to leave it, because these were dark and scary woods and the world they bordered hostile beyond reckoning. There had never been a fence breach to his knowledge, but there was a first time for everything, and being out in these trees in the middle of the night unarmed was just taunting Murphy's Law.

Leaning back in, he opened the center console and jammed his pockets full with shells. Then he reached up and lifted the twelve-gauge off the rack. It was a pump-action tube feed with a walnut stock and fifteen inches of the barrel sawn off.

Ethan fed in five shells, racked one into the chamber, and set the hammer to half-cocked—the closest thing to a safety on this beautiful dinosaur of a weapon.

With the shotgun laid across his shoulder blades and his arms draped over the stock and barrel, Ethan stepped down off the shoulder and started into the woods.

Colder here than in town.

A yard-thick blanket of mist hovered over the floor of the forest.

The moon had yet to clear the wall of cliffs.

It was dark enough under the trees for a flashlight.

Ethan turned on the beam, moved deeper into the woods. Trying to keep on the straightest trajectory possible so he could find his way back to the road.

Ethan heard the electrified hum before he saw it—cutting through the mist like a sustained bass note.

The profile of the fence appeared in the distance.

A rampart running through the forest.

As he drew near, details emerged.

Twenty-five-foot steel pylons spaced seventy-five feet apart. Bundles of conductors stretched between them, separated every ten feet with spacers. The cables an inch thick, studded with spikes and enwrapped with razor wire.

There was ongoing debate within Pilcher's inner circle regarding whether the fence would remain viable in a loss-of-power situation—whether or not the height and the razor wire alone could keep the abbies out. Ethan figured there wasn't much of anything that could stop several thousand starving abbies from tearing through if they wanted—with or without electricity.

Ethan stopped five feet from the wire.

He broke off two low-hanging limbs and marked the spot with an X.

Then he headed east, walking parallel to the fence.

After a quarter mile, he stopped to listen.

There was the constant hum.

His own breathing.

The sound of something moving through the forest on the other side of the fence.

Footfalls in pine needles.

The occasional snap of a branch.

A deer?

An abby?

"Sheriff?"

The voice straightened Ethan's spine like an electrical current had ripped through it and he swung the shotgun off his shoulders and leveled the barrel on Peter McCall.

The man stood ten feet away beside the trunk of a giant pine, dressed in dark clothes and a black baseball cap. He had a small backpack slung over his shoulder. To the pack, he'd lashed two plastic milk jugs filled with water, which sloshed as he stepped forward.

He carried no weapon that Ethan could see beyond a walking stick with more curve than an old man's backbone.

"Jesus, Peter. What the hell are you doing out here?"

The man smiled but Ethan saw fear in it. "If I said I was just out for a late walk, would you believe me?"

Ethan lowered the shotgun.

"You shouldn't be out here."

"I'd heard rumors there was a fence in these woods. Always wanted to see it."

"Well, there it is. Now you've seen it. Let's walk back to town."

Peter said, "'Before I built a wall I'd ask to know what I was walling in, or walling out.' Robert Frost wrote that."

Ethan wanted to say he knew that. That he'd been reading Frost, that very poem in fact, just several hours ago.

"So, lawman," McCall said, pointing at the fence. "Are you walling us in? Or walling something out?"

"It's time to go home, Peter."

"Is it now."

"Yeah."

"And by that, do you mean my house in Wayward Pines? Or my real home in Missoula?"

Ethan edged forward. "You've been here eight years, Peter. You're an important member of this community. You provide an essential service."

"The *Wayward Light*? Come on. That paper's a joke."

"Your family is here."

"Where is *here*? What does that even mean? I know there are people who've found happiness and peace in this valley. I tried to convince myself I had, but it was a lie. I should've done this years ago. I sold myself out."

"I get that it's hard."

"Do you? Because from my perspective, you've been in Pines all of five minutes. And before they made you sheriff you couldn't get out fast enough. So what changed? Did you actually make it?"

Ethan set his jaw.

"You made it past the fence, didn't you? What did you see? What turned you into a true believer? I hear there are demons on the other side, but that's just a fairytale, right?"

Ethan set the butt of the Winchester on the ground, leaned the barrel against a tree.

"Tell me what's out there," McCall said.

"Do you love your family?" Ethan asked.

"I need to know. You of all people should—"

"Do you love your family?"

The question finally seemed to register.

"I used to. When we were real people. When we could talk about the things in our hearts. You know this is the first real conversation I've had in years?"

Ethan said, "Peter, this is your last chance. Are you going to come back with me?"

"My last chance, huh?"

"Yeah."

"Or what? All the phones will start to ring? You'll disappear me yourself?"

"There's nothing for you out there," Ethan said.

"At least there'd be answers."

"What's it worth to you to know? Your life? Your freedom?"

McCall laughed bitterly. "You call that"—he gestured behind him in the general direction of town—"*freedom?*"

"I call it your only option, Peter."

The man stared at the ground for a moment and then shook his head.

"You're wrong."

"How's that?"

"Tell my wife and daughter I love them."

"How am I wrong, Peter?"

"There's never only one option."

His face hardened.

Sudden onset of resolve.

He shot past Ethan like he'd exploded out of the starting blocks, still accelerating when he struck the fence.

Sparks.

Arcs stabbing into McCall from the wire like blue daggers.

The force of the voltage blasted Peter ten feet back from the fence into a tree.

"Peter!"

Ethan knelt at the man's side, but Peter was gone.

Lesioned with electrical burns.

Crumpled and drawn.

Motionless.

Sizzling.

Smoking.

The air reeked of charred hair and skin, his clothes polka-dotted with smoldering, fire-rimmed holes.

"For the best really."

Ethan spun.

Pam stood leaning against the tree behind him, smiling in the darkness.

Her clothes as black as the shadows under the pines, only her eyes and her teeth visible.

And the moon of her pretty face.

Pilcher's beautiful pit bull.

She pushed off the tree and moved toward Ethan like the natural fighter that she was. Slinking. Graceful. Catlike. Complete body control and economy of movement. He hated to admit it, but she scared him.

In his past-life work with the Secret Service he'd only encountered three pure psychopaths. He felt confident Pam was one.

She squatted down beside him.

"It's like yuck, but also makes me hungry for barbecue. Is that weird? Don't worry. You don't have to clean this up. They'll send a team."

"I wasn't worrying about that at all."

"Oh?"

"I was thinking about this poor man's family."

"Well, at least they didn't have to watch him get beat to death in the street. And let's face it—that's where this was heading."

"I thought I could convince him."

"If he'd been a new arrival, maybe. But Peter snapped. Perfect resident for eight years. Not so much as a negative surveillance report until this week. Then suddenly, he's off in the middle of the night with provisions? He'd been holding this inside for a while." Pam looked at Ethan. "I heard what you said to him. There was nothing else you could've done. He'd made up his mind."

"I could've let him go. I could've given him the answers he wanted."

Pam smirked. "But you're smarter than that, Ethan. As you just proved."

"You believe we have the right to keep people in this town against their will?"

"There are no rights anymore. No laws. Just force and fear."

"You don't believe rights exist inherently?"

She smiled. "Didn't I just say that?"

Pam stood and started off into the woods.

Ethan called after her, "Who will talk to his family?"

"Not your problem. Pilcher will handle."

"And tell them what?"

Pam stopped, turned.

She was twenty feet away and barely visible in the trees.

"I'm guessing whatever the fuck he feels like telling them. Was there anything else?"

Ethan glanced at his shotgun leaning against the tree.

A mad thought.

When he looked back at Pam, she was gone.

* * *

Ethan stayed with Peter for a long time. Until it occurred to him that he didn't want to be here when Pilcher's men finally came for the body. He struggled to his feet.

It felt good to walk away from the fence, the noise of its current steadily fading.

Soon, he moved through silent woods and mist.

Thinking, *That was so fucked up and you have no one to tell. Not your wife. No real friend to speak of. The only people you can share this with include a megalomaniac and a psychopath. And that's never going to change.*

After a half mile, he climbed a small rise and stumbled out onto the road. He hadn't returned the way he'd intended, but still he'd only missed his Bronco by a few hundred feet. Exhaustion hit him. No idea what time it was, but it had been a long, long day, a long, long night, and the dawn of a brand-new one loomed.

He reached the Bronco, emptied the shotgun, stowed it on the rack.

So tired he could've lain across the console and slept.

The stench of the electrocution was just as potent—would probably take days to leave.

At some point tomorrow, Theresa would ask him if everything was okay, and he would smile and say, "Yeah, honey. I'm fine. And how are you?"

And she would answer with those intense eyes that seemed completely disconnected from her words, "Just great."

He cranked the engine.

The rage came out of nowhere.

He pinned the gas pedal to the floorboard.

The tires squealed, bit blacktop, launched him.

He tore around the curve and down the straightaway toward the outskirts of town.

The billboard disgusted him more every time he saw it—a family with bright white smiles waving like something out of a 1950s sitcom.

WELCOME TO WAYWARD PINES
WHERE PARADISE IS HOME

Ethan sped alongside a split-rail fence.

Through the passenger window, he could see the herd of cattle congregated in the pasture.

A row of white barns at the edge of the trees glowing in the starlight.

He looked back through the windshield.

The Bronco bounced over something large enough to jar the steering wheel out of his hands.

The vehicle lurched toward the shoulder, beelining for the fence at sixty-five miles per hour.

He grabbed the wheel, cranked it back, felt the suspension lift up on two tires. For a horrifying second, the wheels screeched across pavement and his right side dug into the shoulder strap.

He felt the g-force in his chest, his face.

Through the windshield caught a glimpse of the constellations spinning.

His foot had slipped off the gas pedal and he could no longer hear the engine revving—just three seconds of silence save for the wind screaming over the windshield as the Bronco flipped.

When the roof finally met the road, the collision was deafening.

Metal caving.

Glass crunching.

Tires exploding.

Sparks where the metal dragged across pavement.

And then the Bronco was motionless, upright on four wheels, two of them still holding air. Steam hissing up through the cracks along the hood.

Ethan smelled gasoline. Scorched rubber. Coolant. Blood.

He clutched the steering wheel so hard it took him a moment to pry his hands open.

He was still strapped into the seat. His shirt covered in safety glass. He reached down, unbuckled the seat belt, relieved to feel his arms working without pain. Shifting his legs, they seemed okay. His door wouldn't open, but the glass had been completely busted out of the window. Up onto his knees, he dragged himself through the opening and fell to the road. Now he felt the pain. Nothing stabbing—just a slowly building ache that seemed to flood out of his head and down into the rest of his body.

He made it onto his feet.

Swaying.

Tottering.

Bent over, thought he might be sick, but the nausea passed.

Ethan brushed the glass off his face, the left side stinging from a gash that had already streamed blood over his jawline, down his neck, and under his shirt.

He glanced back at the Bronco. It stood perpendicular across the double yellow, right-side tires robbed of air, the SUV slouched away from him. Most of the glass was gone and there were long scores across the paint job like the claws of a predator had raked it.

He staggered away from the Bronco, following gas and oil and other fluids like a blood trail up the road.

Stepped over the light bar that had been ripped off.

A side mirror lay on its side on the shoulder like a plucked eye, wires dangling from the housing.

Cows groaned in the distance, heads raised, faces turned toward the commotion.

Ethan stopped just shy of the billboard and stared ahead at the object lying in the road, the object that had nearly killed him.

It looked like a ghost. Pale. Still.

He limped on until he stood over her. Didn't immediately recall her name, but he'd seen this woman around town. She'd held some position of authority at the community gardens. Midtwenties he suspected. Black hair to her shoulders. Bangs. Now she was naked and her skin a serene, dead blue like sea ice. It seemed to glow in the dark. Except for the holes. So many of them. Something clinical, not desperate, in the pattern. He started to count but stopped himself. Didn't want that number rattling around in his head. Only her face had been left untouched. Her lips had lost all color, and the largest, darkest slit in the center of her chest looked like a small, black mouth, open in surprise. Maybe that was the one that had killed her. Several others could have easily done the job. But she was clean of any blood. In fact, the only other mark on her skin was the tire track where his Bronco had rolled across her abdomen, the tread clearly visible.

His first thought was that he needed to get the police.

And then: *You* are *the police.*

There'd been talk of him hiring a deputy or two, but it hadn't happened yet.

Ethan sat down in the road.

The shock of the wreck had begun to fade, and he was growing cold.

After a while, he got up. Couldn't just leave her here, not even for a couple of hours. He lifted the woman in his arms and carried her off the road into the woods. She wasn't as cold as he would've thought. Still warm even. Bloodless and warm—an eerie combination. Twenty feet in, he found a grove of scrub oak. He ducked under the branches and set her down gently on a bed of dead leaves. There was nowhere to take her now, but it felt wrong just leaving her here. He folded her hands across her stomach. When he reached for the top button on his shirt, he discovered that his hands were still trembling. He tore it open, took it off, covered her with it.

Said, "I'll be back for you, I promise."

Ethan walked out to the road. For a moment, he considered putting the Bronco into neutral, rolling it off onto the shoulder. But it wasn't like anyone would be driving out here in the next few hours. The dairy wouldn't be making its milk deliveries until late tomorrow afternoon. He'd have time to clean this up before then.

Ethan started back toward town, the lights of the houses of Pines twinkling in the valley ahead.

So peaceful.

So perfectly deceptively peaceful.

* * *

Dawn was on the verge as Ethan walked into his house.

He drew the hottest bath he could stand in the clawfoot tub downstairs. Cleaned up his face. Scrubbed off the blood. The heat dimmed the body ache and the throbbing behind his eyes.

* * *

There was light in the sky when Ethan climbed into bed.

The sheets were cold and his wife was warm.

He should've called Pilcher already. Should've called him the moment he walked inside, but he was too tired to think. He needed sleep, if only for several hours.

"You're back," Theresa whispered.

He wrapped an arm around her, drew her in close.

His ribs on his left side ached when he breathed in deeply.

"Everything okay?" she asked. He thought of Peter, smoking and sizzling after the shock. The dead, naked woman lying in the middle of the road. Of almost dying, and not the first clue as to what any of it meant.

"Yeah, honey," he said, snuggling closer. "I'm fine."

3

Ethan opened his eyes and nearly leapt off the mattress.

Pilcher sat in a chair at the foot of his bed, watching Ethan over the top of a leather-bound book.

"Where's Theresa?" Ethan asked. "Where's my son?"

"Do you have any idea what time it is?"

"Where's my family?"

"Your wife's at work just like she's supposed to be. Ben's in school."

"What the hell are you doing in my bedroom?" Ethan asked.

"It's early afternoon. You never showed up for work."

Ethan shut his eyes against a crushing pressure at the base of his skull.

"You had a big night, huh?" Pilcher said.

Ethan reached for the glass of water on the bedside table, his entire body stiff and brittle. Like he'd been broken into a thousand pieces and haphazardly patched back together.

He drained the glass.

"You found my car?" Ethan asked.

Pilcher nodded. "As you can imagine, we were deeply concerned. There are no cameras near the billboard. We didn't see what happened. Only the aftermath."

The light coming through the window was sharp.

Ethan squinted against it.

He stared at Pilcher—couldn't tell what book he held. The man was dressed in jeans, a white oxford, gray sweater-vest. The same gentle, unassuming style Pilcher always sported around town where people believed he was a resident psychologist. He and Pam were probably seeing patients today.

Ethan said, "I was driving back to Pines after Peter McCall. Assume you heard what happened there?"

"Pam briefed me. So tragic."

"I glanced into the pasture for a split second, and when I looked back, there was something in the middle of the road. I hit it, swerved, overcorrected, flipped my Bronco."

"The damage was severe. You're lucky to be alive."

"Yeah."

"What was in the road, Ethan? My men didn't find anything except debris from the Bronco."

Ethan wondered if Pilcher really didn't know. Was it possible that the woman in the road had been a Wanderer? There was rumored to be a group of residents who had discovered their microchips and cut them out. Who had knowledge of the camera placements and blind spots. People who kept their chips with them during the day, but on occasion, would extract them and leave them in bed to wander undetected in the night. Word was they always wore hooded jackets or sweatshirts to hide their faces from the cameras.

"It makes me nervous," Pilcher said, rising to his feet, "when I see you wrestling with a simple question that should require no thought at all to answer. Or perhaps your head is still cloudy from the wreck. Does that explain the delay? Why, when I look in your eyes, I see the wheels turning?"

He knows. He's testing me. Or maybe he only knows that she was there, but not where I put her.

"Ethan?"

"There was a woman lying in the road."

Pilcher reached into his pocket, pulled out a wallet-sized photo.

Held it up to Ethan's face.

It was her. A candid shot. Smiling or laughing at something off-camera. Vibrant. The backdrop was blurred, but from the color, Ethan guessed that the photo had been taken in the community gardens.

He said, "That's her."

Pilcher's face went dark. He returned the photograph to his pocket.

"She's dead?" He asked it like all the air had gone out of him.

"She'd been stabbed."

"Where?"

"Everywhere."

"She was tortured?"

"Looked that way."

"Where is she?"

"I moved her out of the road," Ethan said.

"Why?"

"Because it didn't seem right to leave her naked out in the open for anyone to see."

"Where is her body right now?"

"Across the road from the billboard in a grove of scrub oak."

Pilcher sat down on the bed.

"So you tucked her away, came home, went to bed."

"I took a hot bath first."

"Interesting choice."

"As opposed to?"

"Calling me immediately."

"I'd been up for twenty-four hours. I was in agony. I just wanted several hours of sleep first. I was going to call you first thing."

"Of course, of course. Sorry to doubt you. The thing is, Ethan, this is kind of a big deal. We've never had a murder in Wayward Pines."

"You mean an unsanctioned murder."

"Did you know this woman?" Pilcher asked.

"I'd seen her around. I don't think I'd ever spoken to her though."

"Read her file?"

"Actually, no."

"That's because she doesn't have a file. At least not one that you have access to. She worked for me. She was due back in the mountain late last night from a mission. Never showed."

"She worked for you as what? A spy?"

"I have a number of my people living in town among the residents. It's the only way to keep a finger on the true pulse of Wayward Pines."

"How many?"

"It's not important." Pilcher patted Ethan's leg. "Don't look so offended, boy. You're one of them. Get dressed, come downstairs, we'll continue this over coffee."

* * *

Ethan walked downstairs in a clean, newly starched sheriff's uniform into the smell of brewing coffee. He took a seat on a stool at the kitchen island as Pilcher pulled the carafe out of the coffeemaker and poured into a pair of ceramic mugs.

"You take it black, right?"

"Yeah."

Pilcher carried the mugs over and set them on the butcher block.

He said, "A surveillance report came across my desk this morning."

"Who was the subject?"

"You."

"Me?"

"Your little temper tantrum upstairs yesterday caught the attention of one of my analysts."

Pilcher raised his middle finger.

"You got a report on *that*?"

"I get a report anytime anyone does anything strange."

"You think it's strange it pisses me off when your peeping toms watch me with my wife?"

"Watching intimate moments is strictly forbidden. You know this."

"The only way an analyst would know that it was no *longer* an intimate moment was if he had been watching *during* the intimate moment. Right?"

"You acknowledged the camera."

"Theresa didn't see."

"But what if she had?"

"You think there's anyone in town who's been here longer than fifteen minutes who *doesn't* know they're under constant surveillance?"

"Whether they know or suspect, I don't care. As long as they keep it to themselves. As long as they walk the line. That includes not ever acknowledging the cameras."

"Do you know how difficult it is to fuck your wife with a camera over your bed?"

"I don't care."

"David—"

"It's against the rules and you know it." For the first time, anger laced his words.

"Fine."

"Say it won't happen again, Ethan."

"It won't happen again. But don't ever let me find out that your analysts are watching. I'll leave them where I find them."

Ethan took a big, hot swallow that burned his throat.

"How you feeling, Ethan? You seem cranky."

"I feel rough."

"First thing, we're taking you to the hospital."

"Last time I was in your hospital, everyone tried to kill me. I think I'll just tough this one out."

"Suit yourself." Pilcher took a sip and made a face. "It's not terrible, but sometimes I could kill to sit outside a café in a European city and drink a proper shot of espresso."

"Oh, come on, you love this."

"Love what, Ethan?"

"What you've created here."

"Sure, it's my life's work. Doesn't mean there aren't parts of the old world I still miss."

They drank coffee and the mood lightened just a touch.

Pilcher finally said, "She was a good woman. A great woman."

"What was her name?"

"Alyssa."

"You didn't know where she was until I told you. Does that mean she wasn't chipped?"

"We allowed her to take it out."

"You must've trusted her."

"Implicitly. Remember the group I told you about?"

"The Wanderers?"

"I'd sent her to infiltrate. These people—they've all managed to remove their chips. They meet at night. We don't know where. We don't know how many. We don't know how they communicate. I couldn't send her in with a microchip. They'd have killed her outright."

"So she got in?"

"Last night was supposed to be her first meeting. She'd have seen all the players."

"They have meetings? How's that possible?"

"We don't know how, but they understand the weaknesses in our surveillance. They've gamed the system."

"And you're saying these people are responsible for her death?"

"That's what I want you to find out."

"You want me to investigate this group?"

"I want you to pick up where Alyssa left off."

"I'm sheriff. They'd never let me get within a thousand miles."

"After your tumultuous integration, I'm thinking the jury is still out on where your loyalties lie. You sell yourself right, they might consider you a prized asset."

"You actually think they'd trust me?"

"I think your old partner will."

It became very quiet in the kitchen.

Just the hum of the refrigerator.

Distant, ebullient noise coming through an open window—children playing somewhere.

Shouts of *You're it!*

Ethan said, "Kate is a Wanderer?"

"Kate was Alyssa's point of contact. Kate showed her how to remove her microchip."

"What do you want me to do?"

"Reach out to your old flame. Discreetly. Tell her you're not really with me."

"What do these people know and what do they want?"

"I believe they know everything. That they've gone beyond the fence and seen what's out there. That they want to rule. They're actively recruiting. Last sheriff, they made three attempts on his life. They're probably already making the same plans for you. This is what I want you to investigate. Top priority. I'll give you every tool you need. Unlimited access to surveillance."

"Why aren't you and your people handling this from the inside?"

"Alyssa's death has been a big blow to all of us. There are a lot of people in the mountain not thinking very clearly right now. So I have to lay this on your shoulders. You alone. I hope you understand the stakes here. Whatever your personal feelings about the way I run this town—and you've shared them with me—it works. This can never be a democracy. There's too much to lose if everything goes to shit. You're with me on that, right?"

"I am. You run a mostly benevolent dictatorship with occasional slaughter."

Ethan thought Pilcher would laugh, but he just stared across the island, the steam coiling off the surface of the coffee into his face.

"That was a joke," Ethan said.

"You with me or not?"

"Yes. But I worked with Kate for years. She's not a murderer."

"No offense, but you worked with her in another time. She's a different person now, Ethan. She's a product of Pines, and you have no idea what she's capable of."

4

Theresa watched the second hand pass the 12.

3:20 p.m.

She tidied up the items on her smooth, clean desk and gathered her purse.

The brick walls of the office were papered with real estate brochures that few people had ever studied. She had rarely used the typewriter or received a phone call. For the most part, she read books all day, thought about her family, and occasionally her life before.

Since her arrival in Pines, she had wondered if this was her afterlife. At the very least, it was her *life after.*

After Seattle.

After her job as a paralegal.

After almost all of her relationships.

After living in a free world, that for all its complexities and tragedies still made sense.

But in her five years here, she had aged, and so had others. People had died, disappeared, been murdered. Babies had been born. That didn't align with any concept of an afterlife she had heard of, but then again, by definition, how could you ever know what to expect outside the realm of the living, breathing human experience?

Over the years of her residency, it had steadily dawned on her that Pines felt much closer to a prison than any afterlife, although perhaps there was no meaningful distinction.

A mysterious and beautiful lifelong sentence.

It wasn't just a physical confinement, but a mental one as well, and it was the mental aspect that made it feel like a stint in solitary. The inability to outwardly acknowledge one's past or thoughts or fears. The inability to truly connect with a single human being. There were moments of course. Few and far between. Sustained eye contact, even with a stranger, when the intensity seemed to suggest the inner turmoil.

Fear.

Despair.

Confusion.

Those times, Theresa at least felt the warmth of humanity, of not being so utterly and helplessly alone. It was the fakeness that killed her. The forced conversations about the weather. About the latest crop from the gardens. Why the milk was late. About everything surface and nothing real. In Pines, it was only ever small talk, and getting accustomed to that level of interaction had been one of the toughest hurdles to her integration.

But every fourth Thursday, she got to leave work early, and for a brief window, the rules let up.

* * *

Theresa locked the door behind her and set off down the sidewalk.

It was a quiet afternoon, but that was nothing new.

There were never loud ones.

She walked south along Main Street. The sky was a staggering, cloudless blue. There was no wind. No cars. She didn't know what month it was—only time and days of the week were counted—but it felt like late August or early September. A transitional quality to the light that hinted at the death of a season.

The air mild with summer, the light gold with fall.

And the aspen on the cusp of turning.

* * *

The lobby of the hospital was empty.

Theresa took the elevator to the third floor, stepped out into the hallway, checked the time.

3:29.

The corridor was long.

Fluorescent lights hummed above the checkerboard floor. Theresa walked halfway down until she reached the chair sitting outside a closed, unmarked door.

She took a seat.

The noise of the lights seemed to get louder the longer she waited.

The door beside her opened.

A woman emerged and smiled down at her. She had perfect white teeth and a face that struck Theresa as both beautiful and remote. Unknowable. Her eyes were greener than Theresa's, and she'd pulled her hair back into a ponytail.

Theresa said, "Hi, Pam."

"Hello, Theresa. Why don't you come on in?"

* * *

The room was bland and sterile.

White walls absent any painting or photograph.

Just a chair, a desk, a leather divan.

"Please," Pam said in a soothing voice that sounded vaguely robotic, gesturing for Theresa to lie down.

Theresa stretched out on the divan.

Pam took a seat in the chair and crossed her legs. She wore a white lab coat over a gray skirt and black-rimmed glasses.

She said, "It's good to see you again, Theresa."

"You too."

"How have you been?"

"Okay, I guess."

"I believe this is the first time you've come to see me since your husband's return."

"That's true."

"Must be so good to have him back."

"It's amazing."

Pam slid the pen out of her lapel pocket and clicked out the tip. She turned her swivel chair toward the desk, put the pen to a legal pad with Theresa's name scrawled across the top, and said, "Do I hear a *but* coming?"

"No, it's just that it's been five years. A lot has happened."

"And now it feels like you're married to a stranger?"

"We're rusty. Awkward. And of course, it's not like we can just sit down and talk about Pines. About this insane situation we're in. He's thrown back into my life and we're expected to function like a perfect family unit."

Pam scribbled on the pad.

"How would you say Ethan is adapting?"

"To me?"

"To you. Ben. His new job. Everything."

"I don't know. Like I said, it's not like we can communicate. You're the only person I'm allowed to really talk to."

"Fair enough."

Pam faced Theresa again. "Do you find yourself wondering what he knows?"

"What do you mean?"

"You know exactly what I mean. Ethan was the subject of a fête, and the only person in the history of Pines to escape one. Do you wonder if he made it out of town? What he saw? Why he returned?"

"But I would never ask him."

"But you wonder."

"Of course I do. It's like he died and came back to life. He has answers to questions that haunt me. But I would never ask him."

"Have you and Ethan been intimate yet?"

Theresa felt a deep blush flooding through her face as she stared up at the ceiling.

"Yes."

"How many times?"

"Three."

"How was it?"

None of your fucking business.

But she said, "The first two times were a little clunky. Yesterday was far and away the best."

"Did you come?"

"Excuse me?"

"There's nothing to be ashamed of, Theresa. Your ability or lack thereof to have an orgasm is a reflection on your state of mind." Pam smirked. "And possibly Ethan's skills. As your psychiatrist, I need to know."

"Yes."

"Yes, you had one?"

"Yesterday, I did."

Theresa watched Pam draw an O with a smiley face beside it.

"I worry about him," Theresa said.

"Your husband?"

"He went out in the middle of the night last night. Didn't come back until dawn. I don't know where he went. I can't ask. I get that. I assume he was chasing someone trying to leave."

"Do you ever have thoughts about leaving?"

"Not in several years."

"Why is that?"

"At first, I wanted to. I felt like I was still living in the old world. Like this was a prison or an experiment. But it's strange—the longer I stayed here, the more it became normal."

"What did?"

"Not knowing why I was here. What this town really was. What was beyond."

"And why do you think it became more normal to you?"

"Maybe this is just me adapting or giving in, but I realized that as strange as this town was, it wasn't all that different from my life before. Not when I really held them up against each other. Most interaction in the old world was shallow and superficial. My job in Seattle was as a paralegal working for an insurance defense firm. Helping insurance companies fuck people out of their coverage. Here, I sit in an office all day long and hardly talk to anyone. Equally useless jobs, but at least this one isn't actively hurting people. The old world was filled with mysteries beyond my understanding—the universe, God, what happens when we die. And there are plenty of mysteries here. Same dynamics. Same human frailties. It just all happens to exist in this little valley."

"So you're saying it's all relative."

"Maybe."

"Do you believe this is the afterlife, Theresa?"

"I don't even know what that means. Do you?"

Pam just smiled. It was a facade, no comfort in it. Pure mask. The thought crossed Theresa's mind, and not for the first time—*who is this woman I'm spilling all my secrets to?* To some extent, the exposure was terrifying. But the compulsion to actually connect with another human being tipped the scales.

Theresa said, "I guess I just see Pines as a new phase of my life."

"What's the hardest thing about it?"

"About what? Living here?"

"Yeah."

"Hope."

"What do you mean by that?"

"Why am I continuing to breathe in and out? I would think that's the hardest question for everyone stuck in this place to answer."

"And how do you answer it, Theresa?"

"My son. Ethan. Finding a great book. Snowstorms. But it's not like my old life. There's no dream house to live for. No lottery. I used to fantasize about going to law school and starting my own practice. Becoming fulfilled and rich. Retiring with Ethan somewhere warm with a clear blue sea and white sand. Where it never rains."

"And your son?"

Theresa hadn't seen it coming. Those three little words hit her with the sneaky power of a surprise right.

The ceiling she'd been staring at disappeared behind a sheet of tears.

"Ben's future was your biggest hope, right?" Pam asked.

Theresa nodded, and when she blinked, two lines of saltwater ran out of the corners of her eyes and down her face.

"His wedding?" Pam asked.

"Yeah."

"An illustrious career that made him happy and you proud?"

"It's more than that."

"What?"

"It's what I was just talking about. Hope. I want it so badly for him, but he'll never know it. What can the children of Pines aspire to be? What foreign lands do they dream of visiting?"

"Have you considered that maybe this idea of hope, at least the way that you conceive of it, is a holdover from your past life, that serves no purpose?"

"You're saying abandon hope all ye who enter here?"

"No, I'm saying live in the moment. That maybe in Pines there's joy to be had in just surviving. That you continue to breathe in and out because you *can* breathe in and out. Love the simple things you experience every day. All this natural beauty. The sound of your son's voice. Ben will grow up to live a happy life here."

"How?"

"Has it occurred to you that your son may no longer share your old-world concept of happiness? That he's growing up in a town that cultivates exactly the sort of in-the-moment living I just described?"

"It's just so insular."

"So take him and leave."

"Are you serious?"

"Yes."

"We'd be killed."

"But you might escape. Some have left, though they've never returned. Do you secretly fear that, as bad as you think it is in Pines, it could be a million times worse on the outside?"

Theresa wiped her eyes. "Yes."

"One last thing," Pam said. "Have you opened up to Ethan about what happened prior to his arrival? Your, um . . . living situation . . . I mean."

"Of course not. It's only been two weeks."

"Why haven't you?"

"What's the point?"

"You don't think your husband deserves to know?"

"It would only cause hurt."

"Your son might tell him."

"Ben won't. We already talked about it."

"Last time you were here, you rated your depression on a scale of one to ten as a seven. How about today? Are you feeling better, worse, or the same?"

"The same."

Pam opened a drawer and took out a small white bottle that rattled with pills.

"You've been taking your medication?"

"Yes," Theresa lied.

Pam set the bottle on the desktop. "One a day, at bedtime, just like before. It'll last you until our next appointment."

Theresa sat up.

She felt like she always did after these things finished—emotionally ragged.

"Can I ask you something?" Theresa said.

"Sure."

"I assume you talk to a lot of people. Hear everyone's private fears. Will this place ever feel like home?"

"I don't know," Pam said as she stood. "That's entirely up to you."

5

The morgue was in the basement of the hospital through a pair of windowless doors.

Far end of the east wing.

Pilcher's men had arrived ahead of Ethan with the body, and they stood in jeans and flannel shirts outside the entrance. The taller of the two, a man with Nordic features and head of Pilcher's security team, looked visibly upset.

"Thanks for bringing her down," Ethan said as he moved past and shouldered through one of the doors. "You don't have to wait."

"We were told to wait," the blond said.

Ethan shoved the door closed after him.

The morgue smelled like a morgue. Antiseptic not quite masking the embedded musk of death.

The flooring was white tile, badly stained, and slightly concave with a large drain in the center.

Alyssa lay naked on the stainless-steel autopsy table.

The sink behind the table was leaking, the sound of dripping water echoing off the walls.

Ethan had only been inside the morgue once before. He hadn't liked it then, and he found it infinitely less charming with a corpse in situ.

There were no windows, no other source of light but the examination lamp.

Standing next to the autopsy table, everything beyond was lost to darkness.

Over the *drip-drip-drip* came the hum of the refrigerated morgue drawers—a stack of six stationed against the wall beside the sink.

The truth was he didn't know what he was doing. He wasn't a coroner by a long shot. But Pilcher had insisted he examine the body and produce a report.

Ethan set his Stetson on the organ scale above the sink.

Reaching up, he took hold of the lamp.

In the hard light, the wounds looked clean. Neat. Impeccable. No ragged skin. Just dozens and dozens of black windows into devastation.

The woman's skin was the color of primer under the burn.

He went appendage by appendage studying the punctures.

It grew harder with her lying dead on a table under this cruel clinical light to think of her as Alyssa.

He raised her left arm into the light and studied her hand. There was dirt under her fingernails. Or blood. He imagined her hands desperately pushing into the fresh wounds, fighting to stanch the blood that must have been pouring out of her.

So why, aside from the oak leaf fragments in her hair, was she otherwise clean? Without a trace of blood or bloodstain on her skin? He hadn't seen any blood where he'd found her in the road. She'd obviously been killed elsewhere and moved to that place. Why had they drained her blood? To transport her without leaving a trail? Or something more sinister?

Ethan studied her other arm.

Her legs.

He didn't want to, but he shined the light briefly between her thighs.

No bruising or damage evident to his untrained eye that might suggest sexual assault.

Because he couldn't help but handle her body gently, it took him three tries to roll her over.

Her arms clanged against the metal table.

He brushed the bits of gravel and dirt off her back.

There was a recent wound on the back of her left leg.

A scarred-over incision.

The cut made—he guessed—to extract her microchip.

He pushed the light away and eased down onto the steel, adjustable stool. The way she lay draped across the cold table—exposed, degraded—ignited something inside of him.

Ethan sat in the dark wondering if Kate could really have done this.

After a while, he got up and walked to the door.

Pilcher's men stopped talking when he stepped out. He looked at the tall blond and said, "Could I speak with you for a minute?"

"In there?"

"Yeah."

Ethan held the door and the man walked into the morgue.

"What's your name?" Ethan asked.

"Alan."

Ethan pointed to the stool. "Have a seat."

"What is this?"

"I'm asking you a few questions."

Alan looked dubious. "I was told to bring her here and put her into cold storage when you were finished."

"Well I'm not finished."

"Nobody said anything about answering questions."

"Quit flexing and sit down."

The man didn't move. He had a good four inches on Ethan. His shoulders were miles apart. Ethan could feel his body priming for a fight, heart rate ramping, battle trance coming on. He didn't want to throw first, but if he didn't have surprise, if he didn't bring Alan down in the first few seconds, the likelihood of beating this man who was built like a Norse god seemed a bit of a stretch.

Ethan dropped his chin an inch.

A half second before he exploded off the balls of his feet and drove his forehead into the man's face, Alan turned and took a seat as instructed.

"This isn't what I was told," Alan said.

"David Pilcher, your boss, has given me unlimited access, unlimited resources, to find out who did this. You want me to find out, don't you?"

"Of course I do."

"Did you know Alyssa?"

"Yeah. There are only a hundred and sixty of us in the mountain."

"So it's a tight-knit group?"

"Very."

"Were you aware of Alyssa's activities in Pines?"

"Yep."

"So you two were close?"

Alan stared at her body on the table. The muscles in his jaw fluttered—rage, sadness.

"Had you been intimate with her before, Alan?"

"Do you know what happens when a hundred and sixty people live in close quarters, knowing they're all that's left of mankind?"

"Everybody fucks everybody?"

"You got it. We're a family in that mountain. We've lost some of our own before. Mostly nomads who never returned. Got themselves eaten. But never anything like this."

"Everybody's shaken up?"

"Big time. You know that's the only reason Pilcher's letting you do this, right? He banned everyone from investigating her death."

"Because of retaliation."

A subtle, raging smile tugged at the corner of Alan's mouth.

"Do you have any concept of the slaughter I could rain down on this town with a team of ten armed men?"

"You understand not everyone in Wayward Pines is responsible for her death."

"Like I said, there's a reason Pilcher's letting you run this show."

"Tell me about Alyssa's assignment."

"I knew she was living with the townies. But no details really."

"When's the last time you saw her?"

"Two nights ago. Sometimes, Alyssa would come back to the mountain to stay the night. It was strange. You ever seen our barracks?"

"I think so."

"There are no windows. We're talking small, cramped, impersonal spaces. In Pines, she got to live in a house all to herself, but she missed sleeping in her room in the mountain. Go figure. Considering who she was, she could've lived anywhere. Done whatever she wanted. But she pulled her weight. She was one of us."

"What do you mean by 'considering who she was'?"

"You don't know?"

"Know what?"

"Fuck. Look, it's not my place to talk about this."

"What am I missing?"

"Forget it, okay?"

Okay. For now.

"So where'd you see her last?" Ethan asked.

"Mess hall. I was finishing up my meal when she walked in. She got her tray and came over."

"What'd you talk about?"

Alan stared off into the dark beyond the light.

He looked briefly at peace, as if the memory of it pleased him.

"Nothing profound. Nothing memorable. Just about our day. We'd both been working our way through the same book and we talked about our impressions so far. Other stuff, too, but that's all that sticks out. She was my always friend and my sometimes lover. We were at ease with each other, and I didn't know it was the last time I would ever see her alive."

"You didn't discuss her work in town?"

"I think I asked how her mission was coming along. And she said something like, 'It'll all be over soon.'"

"What do you think she meant by that?"

"I don't know."

"And that was it?"

"That was it."

"Why would Pilcher ask you to transport her body? Kind of insensitive considering—"

"I requested the assignment."

"Oh."

Ethan was annoyed to discover that he was beginning to like Alan. He'd been to war with men like him. Recognized that hard decency. Fearlessness and loyalty backed by awesome physical strength.

"Was there anything else, Ethan?"

"No."

"Find who did this."

"I will."

"And hurt them."

"You want a hand putting her in the drawer?"

"No, I'll take care of it. But first, I'd like to sit with her for a little while."

"Sure."

Ethan reached over and grabbed his hat off the organ scale. At the doors, he stopped and glanced back. Alan had scooted the stool within range of the autopsy table, and he was reaching out for Alyssa's hand.

6

Theresa sat on the front porch waiting for her husband.

The leaves of the aspen tree in the front yard were fluttering and making shushing noises, and the light passing through the branches smeared quivering shadows across the greener-than-AstroTurf grass.

She spotted Ethan walking down Sixth Street, moving slower than his usual pace. His gait was off, and he favored his right leg.

He turned off the sidewalk and came up the stone path. She could see that it was hurting him to walk, but the tension in his face vanished behind a wide smile when he saw her.

"You're hurting," she said.

"It's nothing."

Theresa got up and moved down the steps into the grass that was already cool against her sandaled feet.

She reached up and touched a lavender-colored bruise on the left side of his face.

He winced.

"Did someone hit you?"

"No, it's fine."

"What happened?"

"I wrecked the cruiser."

"When?"

"Last night. It's not a big deal."

"Did you go to the hospital?"

"I'm fine."

"You didn't get checked out?"

"Theresa—"

"What happened?"

"A rabbit or something ran out in front of the car. I swerved to miss it. Flipped."

"You *flipped*?"

"I'm okay."

"We're going to the hospital right now."

He leaned down, kissed her forehead. "I'm not going to the hospital. Drop it. You look beautiful. What's the story?"

"There has to be a story if I look beautiful?"

"You know what I mean."

"You forgot."

"Entirely possible. It's been a crazy couple of days. What'd I forget?"

"We have dinner at the Fishers'."

"That's tonight?"

"Fifteen minutes."

For a moment, she thought he might say they weren't going. That they would just cancel. Could he do that? Did he have that power?

"All right. Let me get out of these nasty clothes, and I'll be back down in five."

* * *

Theresa had spoken to Mrs. Fisher two weeks ago at the Saturday morning farmers' market—a friendly exchange after they'd both reached for the same cucumber.

Then one evening last week, the Burkes' phone had rung. The voice on the other end introduced herself as Megan Fisher. She wanted to invite Ethan and Theresa over for dinner on Thursday the week following. Could they join?

Of course, Theresa knew that Megan hadn't woken up that morning with a burning desire to make new friends. Megan had gotten a letter in the mail *suggesting* that she reach out to the Burkes. Theresa had received her share of similar letters, and she figured that on some level, it made sense. Considering the prohibition on real human contact, she would never take it upon herself to initiate get-togethers with her neighbors. It was all too strained and strange.

So much easier to just disappear into your own private world.

* * *

Theresa and Ethan walked down the middle of the street holding hands, Theresa clutching a loaf of bread in her right arm that was still warm from the oven.

With Ben at home, it felt like she and Ethan had snuck out for a date night.

The lush coolness of evening had settled into the valley. They were running a little late. Already a few minutes past seven. *Dinner with Hecter* had begun, the velvet beauty of his piano creeping through every open window.

"Do you remember what Mr. Fisher does?" Theresa asked.

"He's a lawyer. His wife's a teacher. Ben's teacher."

Of course Theresa knew she was Ben's teacher, but she wished Ethan hadn't mentioned it. The school was a strange place. Education in Pines was compulsory from age four to fifteen, and the curriculum was a mystery. She had no idea what her son was learning there. Kids never had homework and were forbidden from discussing what they learned with anyone, including their parents. Ben never shared, and she knew better than to pry. The only time they were allowed a window into that world was the end-of-year play. It happened in June, and around Wayward Pines, the celebration rivaled Christmas and Thanksgiving. Three years ago, a fête had been called on a parent who forced his way into the school. She wondered how much Ethan knew.

"What kind of law does Mr. Fisher practice?" Theresa knew it was a stupid question. All likelihood, Mr. Fisher sat in a silent, rarely visited, rarely called office all day just like she did.

"Not sure," Ethan said. "We'll have to put that on our list of things to talk about." He squeezed her hand. It was sarcasm in her husband's voice. No one else would have picked it up, but to her it was biting. She looked up at him, smiled. Something shared and knowing in his eyes. The intimacy of an inside joke.

It was the closest she'd felt to him since his return.

She could envision a lifetime spent trying to create such flashes of connection.

* * *

The Fishers lived in a cozy house at the northern edge of town.

Megan Fisher opened the door before Ethan even had a chance to knock. She was midtwenties and very pretty in a white dress with lacing along the bottom. The brown headband that kept her hair back was the same color as her tanned, freckled shoulders.

Her smile reminded Theresa of a movie star smile—toothy and wide, and if you stared too hard at it, not quite real.

"Welcome to our home, Theresa and Ethan! We're so thrilled you could make it!"

"Thanks for having us," Ethan said.

Theresa presented the bread wrapped in cloth.

Megan cocked her head disapprovingly. "Now, I told you not to bring a thing." She accepted it nonetheless. "Oh, it's still warm!"

"Fresh out of the oven."

"Please come in."

Theresa reached up and swiped Ethan's cowboy hat.

"I can take that," Megan said.

The house smelled like supper, and supper smelled good. The heat coming out of the kitchen brought with it chicken roasting with garlic and potatoes.

Brad Fisher was in the dining room, arranging the last of four place settings at an elaborately candled table.

He walked into the foyer with a smile and a hand outstretched. Two or three years older than his wife and still wearing—Theresa guessed—his work clothes. Black wingtips, gray slacks, a tieless white oxford with the sleeves rolled halfway up his forearms. He looked like a young lawyer, exuding a streak of hard, scrappy intelligence.

Ethan shook his hand.

"Sheriff, great to have you in our home."

"Great to be here."

"Hello, Mrs. Burke."

"Please. Theresa."

Megan said, "I've got a couple things to finish up before we sit down. Theresa, want to help me in the kitchen? Perhaps the guys can enjoy a beverage on the back porch."

* * *

Theresa washed a bag of salad greens. Through the window over the sink, she could see Ethan and Brad standing out in the grass with glasses of whiskey. She couldn't tell if they were actually talking. The yard was fenced. It backed right up against a cliff that soared over a thousand feet in a series of dwindling, pine-studded ledges.

"Megan, you have a beautiful home," Theresa said.

"Thank you. You're too kind."

"I believe you're teaching my son this year." She didn't mean to say it. The words just came. It could've been an awkward moment, but Megan recovered graciously.

"I sure am. Ben's a lovely boy. One of my best."

And offered nothing else.

Their conversation moved in fits and starts.

Theresa sliced a warm beet into livid-purple medallions.

"Where do you want these?" she asked.

"Right here would be great."

Megan held out a wooden bowl and Theresa scooped in two handfuls. She thought beets smelled like dirt in a weirdly pleasing way.

"You work in real estate, right?" Megan asked.

"I do."

"I've seen you through the storefront window, sitting behind that desk." She leaned in confidentially. "Brad and I are *trying*, if you know what I mean."

"Really?"

"If we're successful and Mr. Stork brings us a special delivery, we'll be in the market for a bigger place. Maybe we'll come see you. Let you be our agent. Show us some of the best properties Pines has to offer."

"I'd love to help out," Theresa said.

She still couldn't get over the strangeness of standing in Megan's kitchen like everything was normal. Megan had only come to town a couple of years ago, and her integration had been disastrous. She'd made two escape attempts. Tried to claw the former sheriff's eyes out. Theresa could still remember sitting at her desk one afternoon and staring through the window as Megan broke down in the middle of Main Street in broad daylight, screaming at the top of her voice, "What the fuck is wrong with this place? What the fuck is *wrong* with this place? None of you are real!" Theresa had expected a fête that night, but the phones had never rung. Megan vanished. Three months later, Theresa saw her back in town—Megan walking down the sidewalk with a look of total peace. Soon she was teaching at the school. Then married to Brad. Megan had played important roles in subsequent fêtes. Had even wandered into the circle with a tire iron and dealt a blow to a dying runner.

Now they were cooking together while their husbands drank whiskey outside.

A question repeated in the back of Theresa's mind as she washed the purple stains from her hands.

How did they finally break you?

* * *

Ethan stared up at the cliff and sipped his whiskey.

It was excellent—a Highland single malt. Aside from the awful-tasting beer on tap at the Biergarten, you couldn't buy booze in town on a regular basis. Ethan supposed he understood Pilcher's thinking—life in Wayward Pines was struggle enough. The presence of a liquor store might very well turn it into a town of drunks in short order. But every now and then, Pilcher released a few bottles of good stuff into circulation. They'd turn up at the grocery store, as expensive pours in the restaurants. And when the town was in a dry spell, people made their own.

"Scotch okay, Ethan?"

"It's great. Thank you."

Brad Fisher.

Ethan had read his file for the second time just last week.

Born in Sacramento.

Harvard law grad.

General counsel for a start-up in Palo Alto.

Brad had been traveling through Idaho on a two-week summer road trip with his new bride when they'd stopped in Wayward Pines for a night. The report had been unspecific regarding whether Pilcher had orchestrated the same type of collision he'd used on Ethan and many others.

Like everyone else in Pines, the Fishers had woken up eighteen hundred years later in this beautiful prison of a town.

Two months after their arrival, the first Mrs. Fisher climbed one of the cliffs on the northern end of town and leapt five hundred feet to her death.

It had torn Brad up, but otherwise, his integration had gone smoothly. No escape attempts. No erratic behavior. There was only one surveillance report in the man's file. A couple of exterior cameras had caught him on a later-than-approved walk one night following a fight with Megan. The report had ultimately received an NSA (No Suspicious Activity) rating, and Brad had never raised suspicion again.

"How's the new job treating you?" Brad asked.

"No complaints. Finally starting to get my sea legs. Tell me about your law firm."

"Oh, it's nothing special. Just my secretary and me. I call it a 'door practice.' I handle whatever walks in the door."

Like anyone has ever walked in your door.

They stood in the semi-dark in the shadow of the cliff and drank.

After a while, Brad said, "Sometimes, I see mountain sheep up on those cliff ledges."

"Oh yeah? Never seen one."

Two minutes of silence elapsed and then Ethan commented on their garden.

The punctuations of silence weren't completely uncomfortable. Ethan was beginning to understand that in Wayward Pines these periods of shared quiet were normal, expected, inevitable. Some people, by nature, were better at surface conversation than others. Better at walking the line, steering clear of forbidden topics. There was much more thinking before speaking. Like living in a novel of manners. Ethan had encountered one or two residents who could engage with seemingly effortless speed on a deep well of approved subject matter. But as a whole, conversations in Pines unfurled at a measured, almost plodding pace, with a rhythm distinctly alien to the world before.

It had been some time since Ethan had had liquor, and he already felt lightheaded. A sudden distance from the moment that troubled him. He set the glass of scotch on the fence and hoped it wouldn't be too much longer before their wives called them in to the table.

* * *

Dinner was almost nice.

They kept the small talk going and the conversation only stalled a handful of times.

Even then, between the clink of silverware and Hecter Gaither's piano playing on the tube radio, the silence was not unpleasant.

Ethan was fairly certain he had seen this room before on one of Pilcher's monitors. If he wasn't mistaken, there was a camera embedded in the drywall in the corner of the ceiling above the china hutch.

He knew for a fact that gatherings of three or more received monitoring priority from Pilcher's surveillance techs.

They were being watched at this very moment.

* * *

After dessert, they played Monopoly. Board games were hugely popular at dinner parties. With clearly defined rules, they allowed people to laugh, joke, and interact with more spontaneity and with a shared sense of purpose and competition.

Men versus women.

Theresa and Megan snagged Park Place and Boardwalk early on.

Ethan and Brad focused on infrastructure—railroads, utilities, waterworks.

A little before nine thirty, Ethan landed their tiny metal shoe on Boardwalk.

Bankruptcy ensued.

* * *

The Burkes waved back at the Fishers from the driveway—the young couple standing arm in arm in the illumination of the porch light. They yelled back and forth how much fun was had. Made promises to get together again soon.

Theresa and Ethan walked home.

There was no one out but the two of them.

A cricket chirped from a hidden speaker in a bush they passed, and Ethan caught himself pretending that it was real. That all of this was real.

Theresa rubbed her arms.

"Want my jacket?" Ethan asked.

"I'm fine."

"Nice couple," Ethan said.

"Please don't ever do that with me, darling."

"Do what?"

She glanced up at Ethan in the dark. "You know."

"I don't."

"Surface conversation. Filling the silence with bullshit. I do it every day of my life, and I will continue to do as I'm told. But I can't stand it with you."

Ethan flinched internally.

Wondered if any microphone in the vicinity was capturing their conversation. From his limited experience in the mountain and studying surveillance reports, he knew it was hit or miss whether conversations were legible outside. Even if they were being recorded, it wasn't like Theresa was openly violating any rule. But she was straying dangerously close into gray territory. She was acknowledging the strangeness and voicing dissatisfaction with the way of things. At the very least, their last exchange would generate a report.

"Be careful." Ethan said it at just above a whisper.

She let go of his hand and stopped in the middle of the street, stared up at him through eyes beginning to sheet over with tears.

"Around who?" she asked. "You?"

* * *

In the middle of the night, Ethan's phone rang.

He went downstairs, answered.

"I'm sorry about the late call," Pilcher said.

"It's all right. Everything okay?"

"I had a word with Alan this evening. He said you two spoke in the morgue today."

"Yeah, he was helpful."

"This is hard," Pilcher said, his voice turning hoarse as if he'd begun to cry. "Ethan, I need you to know something."

7

Cahn Auditorium
Northwestern University
Chicago, 2006

The thousand-seat auditorium was at capacity and the lights shining up from the orchestra pit burned his eyes. Twenty years ago, lecturing to a full house would've given him a rush to last for days, but he was long over the thrill. This lecture tour, beyond generating much-needed funds, wasn't pushing him any closer to completing his work. Lately, all he wanted was to be in his lab. With only seven years left in this world, he needed to make every second count.

As the applause died down, he forced a smile, looked up from his notes, and rested his hands on the lectern.

He could do the opening by memory. Hell, he could do it *all* by memory, this being his tenth and last talk on the circuit.

He began, "Suspended animation is not a concept of twentieth-century science. We didn't invent it. It belongs, like all the great mysteries of the universe, to nature. Consider the seed of a lotus plant. It can still germinate after thirteen hundred years. Bacterial spores have been discovered in bee amber, perfectly preserved and viable after tens of millions of years. And recently, scientists from West Chester University successfully revived bacteria that had been trapped for 250 million years inside salt crystals, deep underground.

"Quantum physics seems to hint at the possibility of time travel, and while intriguing, those are theories that only apply to particles on the subatomic level. Real time travel doesn't need wormholes or flux capacitors."

Chuckles rippled through the auditorium. That line always sparked a laugh.

He smiled out at all those faces he couldn't see.

Like they weren't even there.

Nothing but the crowd energy and the lights and the heat of the lights.

He said, "Real time travel is already here, has been for eons, occurring in nature, and that's where we, as scientists, must look."

It was a forty-minute presentation, and for the duration, his mind was elsewhere—in the tiny town of Wayward Pines, Idaho, that was more and more feeling like home.

With his collector, Javier, who had promised to deliver ten new "recruits" by year's end.

With the last phase of his research and the pending sale to the military that would fully fund everything to come.

When he'd finished, he took questions, people lining up behind a microphone positioned at the front of the center aisle.

The fourth question came from a biology student with long black hair. It was the inevitable question that had come at some point during every one of his lectures.

She said, "Thanks so much for coming, Dr. Pilcher. It's been a real privilege to have you on campus these last few days."

"Pleasure's all mine."

"You've talked a lot about medical applications for suspended animation—using it to keep trauma patients in stasis until proper care can be administered. But what about what you alluded to at the beginning of your talk?"

"You mean time travel?" David said. "The fun stuff?"

"Exactly."

"Well, I was just trying to get your attention."

Everyone laughed.

"It worked," the student said.

"You're asking if I think it's possible."

"Yes."

He took off his glasses, set them down on his leather notepad.

"Well, it's certainly fun to dream about, isn't it?" he said. "Look, there have been successful tests on mice—de-animating them by initiating hypothermia—but as you can imagine, getting human test subjects to sign up for such an experiment is a whole other matter. Especially long-term dormancy. Is it possible? Yes. I think so. But we're still decades away. For now, I'm afraid, suspended animation as a time travel application for humanity is the stuff of bad science fiction."

* * *

They were still clapping as he walked offstage.

The young, overachieving escort who'd been at his side during his entire stay on campus was waiting in the wings with a blinding smile.

"That was so amazing, Dr. Pilcher, oh my God, I'm so inspired."

"Thank you, Amber. I'm glad you enjoyed it. Would you mind showing me to the nearest exit?"

"What about your book signing?"

"I need a breath of fresh air first."

She led him through the backstage corridors, past dressing rooms, to a pair of doors in the back of the building next to a loading bay.

"Is everything okay, Dr. Pilcher?" she asked.

"Of course."

"And you'll be right back? They're already lining up at your signing table. I have a book for you to sign too."

"Wouldn't miss it."

David pushed through the double doors and stepped out into the alley.

The darkness and the quiet and the cold so welcome.

The nearby Dumpsters reeked and he could hear the central heating units on top of the auditorium rumbling away.

It was that period between Thanksgiving and Christmas, the fall semester drawing to a close, the smell of dead leaves in the air, and the quiet that befalls a campus in advance of exam week.

His ride—a black Suburban—was parked in the alley.

Arnold Pope, bundled up in a North Face jacket, sat on the hood, reading a book in the light of a streetlamp.

David walked over.

"How'd it go?" Arnold asked.

"It's over, this tour's over, and that's a good thing."

"You're already done signing?"

"I'm skipping out. Small present to myself."

"Congratulations. Let's get you back downtown." Arnold closed the paperback.

"Not just yet. I want to take a little walk across campus first. If they come asking for me . . ."

"Never saw you."

"Good man."

David patted his arm and headed off down the alleyway. Pope had been with him now for four years, initially on the payroll as a driver, but with his law enforcement background David had let him branch out into PI work.

The man was talented, capable, and scary.

David had come to value not only Pope's investigative acumen, but also his counsel. Pope was fast becoming his right-hand man.

Crossing Sheridan, he soon found himself walking into an open field.

Despite the late hour, the stained-glass windows of the library glowed.

The sky was clear, the moon climbing over the spires of a large, Gothic hall in the distance.

He'd left his coat in the Suburban, and the cold wind cut through his wool jacket, coming off the lake that was less than a quarter of a mile away.

But it felt good.

He felt good.

Alive.

Halfway across Deering Meadow, he caught the scent of cigarette smoke riding on the breeze.

Two steps later, he nearly tripped over her.

Caught himself, staggered back.

Saw the tobacco ember first, and then, as his eyes adjusted in the growing moonlight, the girl behind it.

"Sorry," he said. "I didn't see you there."

She looked up at him, her knees drawn into her chest.

Dragging deeply on the cigarette, the ember flaring and fading, flaring and fading.

Even in the poor light, he could see she wasn't a student here.

David knelt down.

She cut her eyes up at him.

She was shivering.

The backpack in the grass beside her was packed to the gills.

"Are you okay?" he asked.

"Yeah."

"What are you doing out here?"

"How the fuck is that any of your business?" She smoked. "Are you like a professor here?"

"No."

"Well, what are *you* doing out here in the dark and the cold?"

"I don't know. Just needed to get away from people for a minute. Clear my head."

"I know the feeling," she said.

As the moon cleared the spires of the hall behind them, its light brightened the girl's face.

Her left eye was black, swollen, half-closed.

"Someone hit you," he said. He looked at her backpack again. "You on your own?"

"Of course not."

"I won't turn you in."

She'd smoked her cigarette down to her fingers. Flicking it into the grass, she pulled another one out of her pocket, fired it up.

"That's really bad for you, you know," David said.

She shrugged. "What's the worst that'll happen?"

"You could die."

"Yeah, that'd be so tragic."

"How old are you?"

"How old are *you*?"

"Fifty-seven."

David reached into his pocket, found his wallet, took out all the cash he had.

"This is a little over two hundred dollars—"

"I'm not going to blow you."

"No, I'm not . . . I just want you to have this."

"Seriously?"

"Yeah."

Her hands were shaking with cold as she took the wad of cash.

"You'll get yourself a warm bed tonight?" David asked.

"Yeah, because hotels rent out rooms to fourteen-year-olds all the damn time."

"It's freezing out here."

She smirked, a glint of spirit in her eyes. "I have my methods. I won't die tonight, don't worry. But I will get a hot meal. Thank you."

David stood.

"How long have you been on your own?" he asked.

"Four months."

"Winter's coming."

"I would rather freeze to death than go back to another foster home. You wouldn't understand—"

"I grew up in this beautiful neighborhood in Greenwich, Connecticut. Cute little town just a forty-minute train ride from Grand Central Station. Picket fences. Kids playing in the streets. It was the 1950s. You probably don't know who Norman Rockwell is, but it's the kind of place he would've painted. When I was seven years old, my parents left me with the sitter one Friday evening. They were going to drive into the city to have dinner and see a show. They never came back."

"They left you?"

"They were killed in a car wreck."

"Oh."

"Never assume you know where someone else is coming from."

He walked away, pant legs swishing through the grass.

She called out after him, "I'll be gone by the time you tell the cops you saw me."

"I'm not telling the cops," David said.

After ten more steps, he stopped.

He glanced back.

Then he walked back.

Knelt down in front of her again.

"I knew you were a fucking pervert," she said.

"No, I'm a scientist. Listen, I could give you real work. A warm place to stay. Safety from the streets, the cops, your parents, child services, whatever it is you're running from."

"Fuck off."

"I'm staying downtown at the Drake Hotel. My last name is Pilcher. I'll already have your very own room waiting for you if you change your mind."

"I wouldn't wait up."

He stood.

"Take care of yourself. I'm David by the way."

"Have a nice life, David."

"What's your name?"

"What do you care?"

"I honestly don't know."

She rolled her eyes, blew out a stream of smoke.

"Pamela," she said. "Pam."

* * *

David slipped quietly into his suite and hung his coat on the rack beside the door.

Elisabeth was sitting in the parlor, reading in the soft light of a floor lamp that overhung the leather chair beside the window.

She was forty-two years old. Her short blond hair had begun to lose its vibrancy—yellow considering silver.

A stunning winter beauty.

"How'd it go?" she asked.

He leaned down and kissed her. "It went great."

"So this means you're done?"

"*We're* done. We're going home."

"You mean to the mountain."

"That is home now, my love."

David walked over to the window and swept aside the heavy drapes. There was no view of the city. Just the lights of late traffic on Lake Shore Drive and the black chasm of the lake beyond, yawning out into darkness.

He crossed the suite and carefully opened the door to the bedroom.

Crept inside.

His footfalls soundless on the thick carpeting.

It took a moment for his eyes to adjust to the darkness. Then he saw her. Curled up in a ball on the immense bed. She had kicked away the blankets and rolled over to the edge. He moved her back into the center of the mattress and covered her again and eased her head gently onto a pillow.

His little girl took a deep breath, but didn't wake.

Leaning over, he kissed her on the cheek and whispered, "Sweet dreams, my sweet Alyssa."

When he opened the bedroom door, his wife was standing there.

"What's wrong, Elisabeth?"

"We just had a knock at the door."

"Who was it?"

"A teenage girl. She said her name is Pam. That you told her to come here. She's waiting out in the hallway for you."

II

8

Tobias finished tying off his bivy sack and descended the pine tree. In the failing light, he huddled over the circle of rocks and kindling with his flint and steel, building the nerve. It was a risk, always a risk. But it had been weeks since he'd felt the glow of a fire. Since he'd steeped pine needles in a pot of boiling water and let something warm run down his throat. He had thoroughly scouted the area. No footprints. No scat. Nothing to indicate it was frequented by anything other than a doe and two fawns. He'd seen a tuft of coarse white hair caught in the thorns of a raspberry bush.

He struck a spark onto the char cloth. A yellow flame licked up and impaled a bundle of Old Man's Beard that was laced with a dismembered branch of dead fir. The spikes of dried-out, russet-colored needles ignited. Smoke coiled out of the tinder.

His heart swelled with primal joy.

Tobias built up a cone of sticks over the growing flames and held his hands to the heat. He hadn't bathed since his last river crossing. That had been at least a month ago. He still remembered catching his reflection in the glass-smooth current—beard down to his sternum, skin embedded with dirt. He looked like a caveman.

Tobias added a single log to the blaze and leaned back against the tree. He felt reasonably safe in this little grove of pines, but there was no sense in pushing the luck he'd already pushed so many times to the breaking point.

At the bottom of his Kelty backpack, he pulled out the one-liter titanium camp kettle and filled it halfway with water from his last remaining bottle.

Dropped in a handful of sharp-smelling pine needles, fresh off the branch.

Kicked back waiting for his tea to boil was as close to human as he'd felt in ages.

* * *

He drank the pot of tea and let the fire die. Before he lost its light completely, he took inventory of the contents of his pack.

Six one-liter water bottles, only half of one still full.

Flint and steel.

A first aid kit down to a single pill of Advil.

A dry bag filled with buffalo jerky.

Pipe, book of matches, and the last of his tobacco, which he was holding on to for his final night—if it ever came—in the wilderness.

His last box of .30-30 Winchester cartridges.

A .357 Smith & Wesson revolver for which he'd run out of ammo over a year ago.

Pack fly.

A leather-bound journal sealed in plastic.

He pulled out a stick of jerky and scraped off the carpeting of mold. Allowed himself five small bites before returning it to the bag. He finished off the pine tea and packed everything back. Shouldering the pack, he climbed twenty feet up to his perch in the tree and fastened the Kelty to a branch.

He untied his hiking boots—the soles long since worn through the tread and the leather beginning to disintegrate—and laced them to the tree. He slid his arms out of his Barbour duster. The coat was months overdue for a thorough waxing but so far it still kept him dry.

He maneuvered into the bivy sack and zipped himself in.

Wow, he stunk. It was almost like he'd developed his own musk.

His mind wouldn't stop running.

The chances of a swarm stumbling through this grove of pines were admittedly slim. A small group or a loner—better.

Tree bivouacking was a good news/bad news proposition.

The good news—it kept him out of the obvious lines of sight. Countless times, he'd heard a branch snap in the middle of the night and rolled quietly over to stare down twenty or thirty feet at an abby creeping past underneath him.

The bad news—if one ever looked up, he was treed.

He reached down and touched the smooth, leathered handle of his Bowie.

It was the only real weapon in his arsenal. The Winchester would get him killed in close combat, and he only used it anymore to hunt *his* food.

He slept always with his hand on the knife, sometimes waking in the dark, other-side of midnight to find himself clutching it like a talisman. Strange to think that an object of such violence had assumed a place as comforting in his mind as the memory of his mother's voice.

* * *

Then he was awake.

He could see the sky through the branches above him.

His breath steamed in the cold.

It was absolutely quiet save for the slow *bump bump bump* of his heart beating in the predawn.

He craned his neck, stared down at the remains of his campfire.

White smoke trickled up out of the embers.

* * *

Tobias wiped the dew off the long barrel of his high-powered rifle and shouldered his Kelty. He walked to the edge of the grove and crouched down between a pair of saplings.

It was damn cold.

First freeze of the season couldn't be more than a night or two away.

He took a compass out of his pocket. He was facing east. A series of meadows and forests gradually climbed toward a range of mountains in the far distance. Fifty, possibly sixty miles away. He didn't know with any certainty, but he held out hope that they were what had once been called the Sawtooth.

If they were, he was almost home.

Raising his rifle to his shoulder, he stared through the telescopic sight and glassed the terrain ahead.

There was no breeze.

The weeds in the open fields stood motionless.

Two miles out, he spotted bison—a cow and her calf grazing.

The next stretch of forest looked to be three or four miles away. Long time to be in the open. He slung the rifle over his shoulder and walked away from the protection of the trees.

Two hundred yards out, he glanced back at the grove of pines dwindling behind him.

It had been a good night there.

Fire and tea and the closest thing to a restful night's sleep as he could ever hope to experience in the wild.

He walked into the sun, stronger than he'd felt in days.

Between his black beard, black cowboy hat, and black duster that fell to his ankles, he looked like a vagabond prophet sent to roam the world.

And in some ways, perhaps he was.

He hadn't made the notation in his journal yet, but this was day 1,287 of his trek.

He'd made it as far west as the Pacific and as far north as where the great port city of Seattle had once stood.

He'd nearly been killed a dozen times.

Had killed forty-four abbies. Thirty-nine with a revolver. Three with his Bowie knife. Two in hand-to-hand combat that he had come very close to losing.

And now, he just needed to get home.

Not only for the warm bed that awaited him and the promise of sleep without the ever-present threat of death. Not just for the food and the long-dreamt-of-sex with the woman he loved.

But because he had some news to report.

My God did he have some news.

9

Ethan followed Marcus down the Level 2 corridor past a series of doors labeled *Lab A*, *Lab B*, *Lab C*.

Near the far end, within spitting distance of the stairwell, Ethan's escort stopped at a door inset with a circle of glass.

Marcus pulled out his keycard.

"I don't know how long I'm going to be," Ethan said, "but I'll have them notify you when I'm ready to go back to town."

"It's not a problem. I'll be by your side the whole time."

"No, you won't."

"Sheriff, my orders—"

"Go cry to your boss. You may be my driver, but you aren't my shadow. Not anymore. And while you're at it, wrangle up Alyssa's reports on her mission."

Ethan snatched the young man's keycard, swiped it through the reader, and shoved it back into his chest. Stepping across the threshold, he turned and stared the escort down as he shut the door in his face.

The room wasn't dark, but it was dim—like a theater five minutes before the movie starts. A five-by-five stack of monitors glowed on the wall straight ahead. There was another door to the right of the screens that was accessed by a keycard entry. Ethan had never been granted access to surveillance.

A man wearing a headset turned in his swivel chair.

"I was told you could help me," Ethan said.

The man stood. Short-sleeved button-down adorned with a clip-on tie. Balding. Mustached. What appeared to be a coffee stain on his lapel. He looked like he belonged in mission control, and the room certainly emanated a nerve-center vibe.

Ethan closed the distance between them, but he didn't offer his hand.

Said, "I'm sure you know plenty about me, but I'm afraid I don't even know your name."

"I'm Ted. I head up the surveillance group."

Ethan had tried to prepare himself for this moment. For meeting Pilcher's number three, the man tasked with spying on the people of Wayward Pines in their most private moments. The urge to break his nose was even stronger than Ethan had anticipated.

Have you watched Theresa and me together?

"You're investigating Alyssa's murder?" Ted asked.

"That's right."

"She was a great woman. I want to do whatever I can to help."

"Glad to hear that."

"Please, have a seat."

Ethan followed Ted over to the monitors. They sat down in swivel chairs on wheels. The control panel looked ready-made to fly an alien spacecraft. Multiple keyboards and touchscreen technology that looked more advanced than anything Ethan remembered from his world.

"Before we start," Ethan said, "I want to ask you something."

"Sure."

"All you do is sit in here and eavesdrop on private lives. Correct?"

Ted's eyes seemed to cloud—was that shame?

"That is my life."

"Were you aware of Alyssa's mission in town?"

"I was."

"Okay. So here's my question. You're in command of the most sophisticated surveillance system I've ever seen. How did you miss her murder?"

"We don't catch everything here, Mr. Burke. There are thousands of cameras in town, but most of them are indoors. We had a far more extensive exterior network when Pines began fourteen years ago, but the elements have exacted considerable damage. They've killed cameras. Drastically limited our eyesight."

"So whatever happened to Alyssa . . ."

"Occurred in a blind spot, yes."

"These blind spots—do you know where they are?"

Ted turned his attention to the controls, his fingers moving at light speed across an array of touchscreens.

The camera feeds vanished.

Twenty-five monitors now merged into a single image—an aerial photograph of Wayward Pines.

Ted said, "So we're looking at the town and the valley. Pretty much every square foot of real estate inside the boundary of the electrified fence. We can push in anywhere we want." The image zoomed down onto the school—the playground equipment crystallizing into sharp focus.

"Is this real time?" Ethan asked.

"No. This photo was taken years ago. But it's the grid upon which all of our tracking relies."

Ted tapped the screen at his fingertips.

A DayGlo overlay appeared.

Most of the town was covered.

Ted pointed at the screens.

"Everywhere you see this overlay, we have a current, real-time, microchip-triggered camera feed. But you'll notice black spots, even within the coverage." He tapped his controls and a single house filled the screen. The overhead perspective changed to a three-dimensional street-level view. With a swipe of his finger, the Victorian's windows and wood siding stripped away and the image became an interactive blueprint.

"You'll note there are three blind spots in this residence. However . . ." The DayGlo overlay was replaced with solid red. "There are no what we call 'deaf spots.' This house, like every other residence in town, is sufficiently miked to capture anything above thirty decibels."

"How loud is thirty decibels?"

Ted whispered, "A library conversation." He returned the screens to the aerial image of Pines with the DayGlo overlay. "So aside from a few blind spots in each house, most of indoor Pines is thoroughly wired. But once you get outside, even in town, the system begins to show cracks in its veneer. Look at all the black areas. There's a backyard with no visual surveillance whatsoever. The cemetery is a disaster—just a few cameras here and there. And as you move away from the center of Pines and toward the cliffs, it only gets worse. Look at these blind spots on the south side. Twenty-acre stretches of completely unmonitored terrain. Now, in theory, we have a way to handle that."

Ted punched in something on a keyboard.

A new overlay meshed with the DayGlo.

Hundreds of red blips appeared.

The vast majority clustered in a six-block radius near the center of town.

Some were moving.

"Recognize those?" Ted asked.

"The microchips."

"We're reading four hundred sixty signals. One short."

"That's because I'm sitting here with you?"

"Correct."

Ted moved the cursor over a stationary blip in a building on Main Street. He tapped the touchscreen. A text bubble blossomed.

Ethan read, "Brad Fisher."

"I believe you had dinner with Brad and his wife last night. It's 10:11 a.m., and Mr. Fisher is in his law office. Right where he's supposed to be. Of course, all this data can be massaged any number of ways."

Every blip disappeared except for Fisher's.

The time stamp at the bottom of the screen began to run backward.

His blip moved out of the building, north up Main Street, and into his house.

"How far back can you go?" Ethan asked.

"All the way to Mr. Fisher's integration."

The red dot raced all over town.

Months rewinding.

Years.

"And I can give him a trail," Ted said.

A trail appeared and scribbled everywhere, like someone pushing a stylus across the screen.

"Impressive," Ethan said.

"Of course, you understand our problem."

"System works until people cut out their microchips."

"It's not an easy or painless procedure. Of course, you know that."

"So what exactly do you do all day?" Ethan asked.

"You mean how does one go about monitoring an entire town?"

"Yeah."

"Put on that headset."

Ethan grabbed it off the console.

"Can you hear me?" Ted's voice came loud and clear through the speakers.

"Yep."

Ted's fingers worked the touchscreens and the image of Wayward Pines and Brad Fisher's lifelong trajectory switched back to twenty-five separate images.

"I'm one of three real-time surveillance techs," Ted said. "Through that door over there, we have four more surveillance techs reviewing flagged footage and audio round-the-clock. Tracking persons of interest. Generating reports. Communicating with our in-town team. With you. Do you understand how the system gathers and sorts data?"

"No."

"I'm not saying video isn't crucial, but it's really the audio that we lean most heavily on. Our system runs state-of-the-art voice recognition software, which pings off certain words, tones of voice. We're not looking as closely at the actual words as the emotion behind them. We also have body-language recognition, but it's less effective."

"Care to demonstrate?"

"Sure. Bear with me. It'll be disorienting at first."

The screens began to change.

Ethan saw—

—a woman washing dishes—

—a schoolroom, with Megan Fisher pointing at a blackboard—

—the riverside park, empty—

—a man sitting in a chair in a house staring into nothing—

—a man and woman fucking in a shower—

It went on like this.

Images coming faster and faster.

Snippets of audio.

Pieces of conversation meaningless and out of context, like a child turning through stations on a radio dial.

"You catch that?" Ted asked.

"No, what?"

The images froze. One of them filled the screens.

The view looked down from a ceiling at a woman leaning against a refrigerator, her crossed arms outlined in DayGlo.

"There," Ted said. "That's a defensive posture. See the recognition overlay?"

A man stood in front of her, his face out of view.

"Let's see if we can't capture a better angle."

Three different camera views of the kitchen streamed past too quickly for Ethan to process any of it.

"Nope, that's as good as it gets."

Ethan watched Ted's right hand raise a digital volume bar.

The eavesdropped-upon conversation became prominent in his headset.

The woman said, "But I saw you with her."

The man said, "When?"

"Yesterday. You guys were sitting at the same table in the library."

"We're friends, Donna. That's all."

"How do I know it's not more than that?"

"Because you trust me? Because I love you and would never do anything to hurt you?"

Ted killed the volume. "Okay. I remember this couple. He is actually cheating on her. He's done it with at least four women I can think of. Real scumbag."

"So you won't continue to monitor this?"

"No, we will." He typed as he talked. "I'm flagging this camera feed right now. Later today, one of my techs will scan Mr. Cheater's footage from the last week or so. Confirm none of his trysts are getting out of control. Mr. Pilcher and Pam will have surveillance reports on their desks first thing tomorrow."

"And then?"

"They'll take whatever action they deem necessary."

"You mean they'll stop him from doing this?"

"If his behavior is seen as a threat to the general peace? Absolutely."

"What will they do to him?"

Ted looked up from the controls and smiled. "You mean what will *you* do. All likelihood, you'll be the one to handle it, Sheriff Burke."

Ted reset the screens to the single aerial view of Wayward Pines.

"Now that you have a basic understanding of how our system works and its capabilities, I'm at your disposal. What do you want to see?"

Ethan leaned back in his chair.

"Can you pull up Alyssa's tracking chip?"

A red blip appeared in a house at the east end of town.

Ted said, "Obviously, that's not her. The night of her death, Alyssa removed her microchip and left it in her bedside table drawer."

"I didn't even know Pilcher had a daughter. How's he holding up?"

"To be honest, I don't know. David's a complicated man. Values, above all, control of his emotions. He's grieving privately, I'm sure."

"Where's Alyssa's mother?"

"Not here," Ted said in a tone that discouraged further inquiry.

"All right, let me see her movement around town going back one week."

Ted worked at the controls.

The blip went from the house, to the community gardens, and back.

Then it moved out of the house and off the map.

"Was that when she was last inside the mountain?" Ethan asked.

"Yes."

Alyssa's microchip moved back into town.

Up and down Main Street.

The community gardens.

Then home again.

Ethan stood up from his chair and stretched his arms over his head.

"Can you pull another microchip?" Ethan asked.

"Sure. Whose?"

"Kate Hewson's."

"You mean Kate Ballinger."

Ted keyed in her name and tapped a panel with his right hand.

A second blip materialized in another part of town.

Ethan asked, "Is it possible for you to isolate all instances where these two dots were in the same place at the same time?"

"Now you're talking. How far back?"

"Same date range. Starting one week ago."

Ethan watched Ted input the parameters into a data field.

When he looked back at the screens, there were four paired blips on the aerial map.

"Can you—"

"Pull video and audio feed from each encounter? Thought you'd never ask." Ted exploded the first of two pairs of dots in the community gardens. "This was the first encounter," he said. "Happened six days ago. Give me a second. Let me find the best angle." He cruised through a number of vantage points—far too fast for Ethan to comprehend anything. "Okay, here's our winner."

Kate filled the screens. She wore a summer dress, sunglasses, a straw hat. She strolled toward the camera between rows of raised flowerbeds. A woven basket dangled from one arm, bulging with vegetables and fruit.

The back of someone's head filled the lower part of the screens.

"Is that Alyssa?" Ethan asked.

"Yes."

Ted upped the volume.

Kate: "No more apples?"

Alyssa: "No, they went fast."

Kate reached into her basket and handed something to Alyssa.

"Freeze it," Ethan said.

The image held—Kate's arm outstretched.

"What is that?" Ethan asked.

"A green apple?"

Ted rolled video.

Kate: "You're always bringing the loveliest fruits and veggies to us. I thought I'd bring you something from *my* garden."

Alyssa: "What a gorgeous pepper."

Kate: "Thank you."

Alyssa: "I'll have this tonight."

Kate moved out of frame.

"Wanna see it again?" Ted asked.

"No, play the next one."

They watched Kate and Alyssa rendezvous three more times.

Next day, on Main Street, the women passed each other and Alyssa shook her head.

The day after, at the riverside park, their paths crossed again.

This time, Alyssa nodded.

"Wonder what that was all about?" Ted said. He glanced at Ethan. "Any ideas?"

"Not yet."

Ted played Alyssa and Kate's last encounter.

It happened the day of Alyssa's death at the community gardens, and the interaction was identical to their first.

Kate stopped at Alyssa's vegetable stand.

They exchanged a few words.

Then Kate handed her another bell pepper.

Ted paused the video.

Ethan said, "There's probably a note in that pepper."

"That says what?"

"I don't know. Meeting place and time? Instructions for Alyssa to remove her microchip? Explain something to me. I understand that when these Wanderers remove their chips you can't track them. But don't the cameras still pick up their movement?"

"No."

"No?"

"Our cameras only key off microchip proximity and motion."

"What does that mean exactly?"

"Look, there's no way to monitor this town using the thousands of cameras all running at once. Most of the time, we'd just be scrolling through empty space. So our cameras key off the microchips. In other words, until a chip moves within range of a sensor, the camera is in sleep mode. It only transmits a video feed when a microchip pings it. And even then, when a chip is motionless for fifteen seconds, the camera reverts to sleep mode."

"So what you're saying is—"

"The cameras don't run all the time. When a resident removes their microchip, for all intents and purposes, they become a ghost. Somehow, these Wanderers have figured out a way to game the system."

"Show me."

Ted brought up a new image, said, "Here's the last thirty seconds we have of Kate on the night Alyssa was murdered."

On the screens, a bedroom appeared.

Kate entered the room wearing a nightgown that fell to her knees.

Her husband followed.

They climbed into bed together, killed the lights.

The overhead camera switched to night vision.

The Ballingers lay absolutely still in bed.

After fifteen seconds, the feed went dark.

Next time it picked up, morning light filled the room, and both Kate and her husband were sitting up in bed.

"Reinserting their chips," Ethan said.

"Yes. But all night, from approximately ten fifteen until seven thirty the next morning, they were ghosts. And in that period of time, Alyssa Pilcher lost her life."

"This is why Pilcher really runs the fêtes, isn't it?" Ethan looked at Ted. "Am I right? It's not only because he wants the town to police itself. It's because when someone removes their chip, he actually needs our help to find them."

* * *

Ethan called for Marcus.

When his escort arrived, Ethan said, "I want to see Alyssa's quarters."

They climbed the stairwell two flights to Level 4.

Five steps into the corridor, Ethan knew which doorway opened into Alyssa's room by the bunches of fresh flowers scattered across the floor. He wondered if Pilcher had sent someone into town for them. All around the doorframe the wall had been papered with notes, cards, photographs, banners.

Whoever and whatever else Alyssa had been, at least inside this mountain, she was a loved woman.

"Sir," the escort said, "I got those reports you asked for."

Marcus handed Ethan a manila folder.

"I'd like to go inside," Ethan said.

"Of course."

Marcus took out his keycard and swiped it through the scanner.

Ethan turned the doorknob, walked inside.

It was a tight living space.

Windowless.

No more than a hundred square feet.

A single bed had been positioned against the far wall. There was a desk. A chest of drawers. A wall of bookshelves, half of which held books, the other half framed photographs.

Ethan studied them, the photos all of the same woman at varying ages—young girl to fifty-year-old woman.

Alyssa's mother?

Ethan sat down on Alyssa's bed.

The wall across from the bookshelves was a masterful mural of a beach—palm trees, green water over dark reefs, white sand, a sky that went on forever.

Ethan leaned back into the pillows, kicked his boots up on the bed.

Smiled.

From this angle, when you stared at the mural it felt like you were there, reclining in the sand, staring off into that false line on the horizon where the sea touched the sky.

The folder was entitled "Mission #1055 Contact Log."

He opened it.

Five pages.

Five reports.

Day #5293
From: Alyssa Pilcher
To: David Pilcher
Mission #1055
Contact Report #1
Subject: Resident 308, a/k/a Kate Ballinger

First contact made at approximately 1125 at the corner of Main and Ninth. Note slipped to Kate Ballinger that read, "Sick of being watched." Brief eye contact made. No words spoken. No further contact was made on this date.

Day #5311
From: Alyssa Pilcher
To: David Pilcher
Mission #1055
Contact Report #2
Subject: Resident 308, a/k/a Kate Ballinger

Eighteen days post-initial contact, Ballinger approached me at the gardens and gave me a bell pepper. The pepper had been sliced open and there was a note inside that read: "Tracking chip on hamstring in your left leg. Cut it out in a closet, but keep with you until further notice." Two potential rendezvous times were given for me to confirm I had removed the chip. The first at 1400 on Day 5312. The next at 1500 on Day 5313. If I failed to remove the chip by Day 5313, we would have no further interaction. No further contact was made on this date.

Day #5312
From: Alyssa Pilcher
To: David Pilcher
Mission #1055
Contact Report #3
Subject: Resident 308, a/k/a Kate Ballinger

At 1400, I passed Ballinger walking south on Main Street near the intersection of Sixth. I shook my head. No further contact was made on this date.

Day #5313
From: Alyssa Pilcher
To: David Pilcher
Mission #1055
Contact Report #4
Subject: Resident 308, a/k/a Kate Ballinger

At 1500, I passed Ballinger walking south on the riverside trail. I nodded to her. She smiled. No further contact was made on this date.

Day #5314
From: Alyssa Pilcher
To: David Pilcher
Mission #1055
Contact Report #5
Subject: Resident 308, a/k/a Kate Ballinger

Ballinger returned to my stand at the gardens with a second bell pepper. The note inside read: "Tonight. 1:00 a.m. The cemetery mausoleum. Leave your chip in your bedside table. Wear a jacket with a hood." Will follow up with a new report tomorrow.

* * *

Ethan moved through the Level 3 corridor with his escort in tow.

Halfway down, he stopped at a pair of double doors. Through the glass, he saw a full-court basketball game in progress. Shirts versus skins. The impact of the ball on the hardwood. The squeak of shoes. For a millisecond, he had the mad thought of joining in the game.

They walked on.

"Mind if I ask you something, Marcus?"

"Shoot."

"How old are you?"

"Twenty-seven."

"And how long have you lived here in the superstructure?"

"Mr. Pilcher brought me out of suspension two years ago to replace a guard who was killed on a mission out beyond the fence."

"Everyone in the mountain knew what they were getting themselves into when they signed on with Pilcher, correct?"

"That's right."

"So why'd you do it?"

"Do what?"

Ethan stopped outside the doors to a cafeteria.

He faced Marcus.

"Why'd you throw your old life away for this?"

"I didn't throw anything away, Mr. Burke. In my life before, you know what I was?"

"What?"

"A tweaker and a drunk."

"And what? Pilcher found you? Gave you a chance to be all you could be?"

"I met him just out of prison—a three-year stint for vehicular manslaughter. I was high and drunk and killed a family on New Year's Eve. He saw something in me I never knew was there."

"Didn't you have a family? Friends? A life that was at least your own? What made you trust him in the first place?"

"I don't know, but he was right, wasn't he? We're a part of something here, Mr. Burke. Something that matters. All of us."

"Here's the thing, Marcus, and I don't want you to ever forget it. Nobody fucking asked me or anyone in that valley if we wanted to be a part of this."

Ethan walked on.

At the bottom of the stairwell leading out into Level 1, a noise stopped him.

Marcus was already swiping his card at the glass-door entrance to the cavern.

Ethan started down the corridor.

"Mr. Burke, where are you going?"

The noise was something screaming.

Banshee-like.

Tortured.

Inhuman.

He'd heard it before and it chilled him to his core.

"Mr. Burke!"

Ethan was jogging down the corridor now, the screams getting louder.

"Mr. Burke!"

He stopped at a wide window.

Stared through the plate glass into a laboratory.

There were two men in white coats and David Pilcher.

They surrounded an aberration.

The creature had been strapped to a steel gurney.

Stout leather restraints buckled down across its legs, below its knees and above.

One across its torso.

Another across its shoulders.

A fifth securing its head.

Its thick wrists and ankles had been clamped down to the sides of the gurney with heavy-gauge steel bracelets, and the thing convulsed against the leather straps as if in the throes of electrocution.

"You shouldn't be here," Marcus said, sidling up to Ethan.

"What are they doing to it?"

"Come on, let's go. Mr. Pilcher won't be happy if he sees—"

Ethan pounded on the glass.

Marcus said, "Oh geez."

The men turned.

The two scientists scowling.

Pilcher said something to them and then walked over to the lab entrance. When the door opened, the abby's screams amplified, echoing up and down the corridor like something calling out from hell.

The doors whisked closed.

"Ethan, how can I help you?"

"I was on my way out. I heard screams."

Pilcher turned toward the plate glass. The abby had calmed down or worn itself out. Only its head swiveled under the strap, its screams reduced to croaks. Ethan could see its massive heart beating furiously through its translucent skin. There was no detail. Only color and form and motion, all obscured as if behind frosted glass.

"Quite a specimen, no?" Pilcher said. "He's a three-hundred-seventeen-pound bull. One of the largest males we've ever seen. You'd think he'd be alpha male of a sizeable swarm, but my sniper spotted him coming down the canyon this morning, all by his lonesome. Took four hundred milligrams of Telazol to bring him down. That's the full-grown adult male jaguar dosage. And he was still only *sluggish* by the time we reached him."

"How long did that keep him sedated?"

"These tranqs only work for about three hours. After that, you better have them locked up, because boy do they come back angry."

"He's a big boy."

"Bigger than the one you tangled with for sure. I think it's fair to say if you'd met this bull in the canyon, we wouldn't be speaking right now."

"What are you doing with it?"

"Getting ready to remove a gland at the base of its neck."

"Why?"

"Abbies communicate through pheromones. These are airborne signals that give information and trigger responses."

"Don't humans do the same thing?"

"Yeah, but it's at a much more instinctual, broader level for us. Sexual attraction. Mother-infant recognition. Abbies use pheromones like we use words."

"So why are you effectively cutting out that thing's tongue?"

"Because the last thing we want is for him to tell all his friends he's in trouble. Don't get me wrong. I love the fence. I trust the fence. But several hundred abbies on the other side trying to figure out how to save their brother makes me a little uncomfortable." Pilcher glanced down at Ethan's waist. "You still aren't wearing your revolver."

"I'm here. In the mountain. What does it matter?"

"It matters, Ethan, because I asked you to do it. It's a simple thing, isn't it? Wear a gun at all times. Look the goddamn part."

Ethan stared back through the glass.

One of the scientists was leaning over the abby's face, shining a penlight into its left eye as it hissed.

It looked to be between six and seven feet tall.

Arms and legs like cords of intertwined steel fiber.

Ethan couldn't take his eyes off the beast.

Its black talons as long as his fingers.

"Are they intelligent?" Ethan asked.

"Oh my, yes."

"As smart as chimpanzees?"

"Their brains are larger than ours. Because of obvious communication barriers, testing their intelligence—on our terms—becomes problematic. I've attempted a battery of social and physical tests, and it's not that they can't do them. They just refuse. It would be like me trying to test you and you telling me to stick it up my ass sideways. That sort of a response. We did capture a somewhat compliant specimen several months ago. She's down in cage nine. Low hostility rating. We call her Margaret."

"How low?"

"I gave her recall tests sitting across a table from her in her cage. Now I did have two guards behind me pointing shotguns loaded with twelve-gauge slugs at her chest. But still—she displayed no signs of aggression."

"How'd you test her?"

"With a simple child's memory game. Walk with me."

Pilcher knocked on the glass and held up one finger to the scientists.

They moved down the corridor toward the glass doors at the far end, Marcus trailing ten feet behind.

"I use small cardboard tiles. One side is blank. The other has a photograph—a frog, a bicycle, a glass of milk. I arrange them all picture-side up on the table and then let Margaret see them. We start easy. Five tiles. Then ten. She gets two minutes to study them. Then I turn them over so she can't see the picture. I reach into a bag containing duplicates of the tiles. I show her, for instance, the one with the glass of milk. She touches her talon to the corresponding tile on the table, and I turn it over to see if she got it right."

"How'd she do?"

"Ethan, we worked our way up to one hundred and twenty tiles, with Margaret only getting thirty seconds to memorize their positions."

"And she got them all right?"

Pilcher nodded, pride in his voice. "Total recall." He stopped and pointed at a small window in a door whose only point of access appeared to be a keycard entry. "I keep her in here. Would you like to meet Margaret?"

"Not even a little bit."

There was a glare off the glass from the overhead fluorescent lights.

Ethan cupped his hands around his face and stared into the cage.

"I know what you're thinking," Pilcher said. "But I don't believe she's an anomaly. Her intelligence I mean. She's only different in temperament. Which is not to say that she wouldn't tear my throat out if she thought she could get away with it."

The cage was only floor, walls, ceiling, monster.

The thing called "Margaret" sat in the corner with its legs curled into its chest. It watched the window in the door through small, opaque eyes that never blinked.

"I've already taught her fifty-two signs. She's a natural learner. Wants to communicate. Unfortunately, her larynx is structured differently than ours to the point of making speech, at least in the sense which we understand it, impossible."

The aberration looked almost meditative.

It struck Ethan as infinitely more unsettling to see one sitting still and docile.

Pilcher said, "I don't know if you saw my report this morning."

"No, I came straight here."

"We're bringing a prospective resident out of suspension. Wayne Johnson. It's his first day. He's probably waking up in the hospital as we speak. Pam's handling orientation. We'll see how it goes, but you may be called upon to assist in the coming days."

"Okay."

"I hope Ted in surveillance was helpful."

"He was."

"So you'll be reaching out to your old partner soon?"

"Tonight or tomorrow."

"Excellent. You have a game plan?"

"Working on it."

"You will report to me every day on your progress."

Ethan said, "David, about your phone call last night."

"Forget it. I just thought you should know."

"I wanted to tell you again how sorry I am for your loss. If you need anything . . ."

Pilcher stared at Ethan, his eyes raging but his voice cool. "Find who did this to my little girl. That's all I need from you. Nothing more."

10

Pam was sitting on the end of the bed in her classic nurse's uniform when Wayne Johnson woke up.

For a long time, he lay motionless under the comforter, blinking at the ceiling.

Finally, he sat up and looked at her.

He was shirtless, balding.

Forty-two years old.

Never married.

No children.

Wayne had come to Wayward Pines, Idaho, on August 8, 1992, as a traveling encyclopedia salesman. He'd arrived late and knocked on five doors. In the evening, after one sale, he'd checked into the Wayward Pines Hotel and then walked to a family-style restaurant. En route, he was struck by a motorcycle in the crosswalk, a perfect hit and run—enough head trauma to render him unconscious, but not enough to kill or permanently damage his brain.

In light of the death of Peter McCall two nights ago at the fence, the town was primed for the introduction of a new resident.

Wayne Johnson's skin still looked gray. He was only ten hours post-suspension blood transfusion, but his color would be back by day's end.

Pam smiled and said, "Hello there."

He squinted at her, his vision probably still blurred as his system rebooted.

His eyes darted around the room.

They were on the fourth floor of the hospital. The window was cracked and the white linen curtains pushed in and out as the breeze ebbed and flowed, the rhythm as steady as if the room itself was breathing.

Wayne Johnson said, "Where am I?"

"Wayward Pines."

He pulled the covers up around his neck, but it wasn't modesty that drove him.

"I'm . . . freezing."

"Totally normal. You'll feel better by the end of the day, I promise."

"Something happened," the man said.

"Yes. Something happened. Do you remember what?"

His eyes narrowed.

"Do you know your name?" Pam asked.

Total amnesia, especially during the first forty-eight hours, occurred thirty-nine percent of the time.

"Wayne Johnson."

"Very good. Do you remember what brought you here?"

"I came to sell encyclopedias?"

"Yes. Good. Did you make any sales?"

"I don't re . . . one. I think. Yes. One sale."

"And then what happened?"

"I was walking to dinner and . . ." She could see the memory of the trauma wash over him, the fear and the shadow of the fear passing across his face. "Something hit me. I don't know what. I don't remember anything after. Is this a hospital?"

"Yes. And this is your town now."

"*My* town?"

"That's right."

"I don't live here. I live in Scottsbluff, Nebraska."

"You did live in Scottsbluff, but now you live here."

Wayne sat up a little straighter.

This was far and away Pam's favorite part of integration. Watching a new resident begin to comprehend that their life—or whatever this new existence was—had irrevocably changed. Nothing beat the fêtes, but these moments of quiet, devastating revelation were, at least for her, a close second.

"What does that mean exactly?" Wayne Johnson asked.

"It means that you live here now."

Sometimes they connected the dots on their own.

Sometimes she had to nudge them over the line.

She waited a minute, watching the wheels turn frantically behind Mr. Johnson's eyes.

He finally said, "In the accident . . . was I hurt?"

Pam reached across the bed and patted the lump that was his leg under the blankets.

"I'm afraid you were."

"Hurt bad?"

She nodded.

"Was I . . . ?"

He looked around the hospital room.

He looked at his hands.

She could feel the question coming.

Willed it to come.

He was tiptoeing right up to the edge of it.

"Was I . . . ?"

Pam thinking, *Ask it. Just ask it.* The data was conclusive—almost every time a resident arrived at the question on their own and found the courage to give voice to it, their integration progressed without incident. Failing to ask the question was a frighteningly accurate predictor for unbelievers, fighters, runners.

Wayne closed his mouth.

Swallowed the question down like a bitter pill.

Pam didn't push it. No point in that.

It was still early.

Still plenty of time to make Mr. Johnson think that he was dead.

11

Ethan sat at a window table in the Steaming Bean, sipping a cappuccino and watching the toy store across the street. It was called Wooden Treasures, and it adjoined a workshop where a man named Harold Ballinger spent his weekdays building toys. His wife, Kate Ballinger, formerly Kate Hewson, formerly Ethan's partner in the Secret Service, worked in the toy store.

Ethan had only spoken to her once since coming to Wayward Pines, in the midst of his horrifying integration. But since becoming sheriff, they hadn't said two words to each other, and he'd managed to avoid her entirely.

Now he studied her through the glass.

She sat at the cash register in the empty toy store, engrossed in a book. It was late afternoon and the light angling through the storefront glass fired her prematurely white hair into a shock of almost blinding brilliance.

Like a cumulous cloud backlit by sunlight.

He'd read her resident file. Read it several times.

Kate had lived in Wayward Pines for almost nine years. When he'd come looking for her, she'd been thirty-six. She would turn forty-five in three weeks. In their life before, he'd been a year older. Now she had him by eight.

Her file told of a brutal integration.

She'd fought, tried to escape, pushed Pilcher's patience right up to the brink of ordering a fête.

Then—she'd simply relented.

Settled into her assigned house.

Settled into her assigned job.

And two years later when the word came down from Pilcher's sheriff at the time, she'd married Harold Ballinger and moved in with him without the slightest protestation.

For five years, they were model residents.

The first surveillance report was triggered off an audio strike from the microphone over their bed.

A whispered phrase that just squeaked into the detectible decibel range.

Kate's voice: *The Englers and the Goldens are in.*

Then nothing for a month until Kate's microchip popped one night at two in the morning in the cemetery.

Sheriff Pope had tracked her down. Found her out wandering alone. He'd questioned her, but she played dumb. Made her apologies. Lied and said she'd had a fight with Harold, needed to get some fresh air.

There had been one last incident two days later—Harold and Kate disappearing for an hour inside their bedroom closet, which incidentally happened to be one of the few blind spots in the house.

The footage was flagged, a report generated, but nothing came of it.

There were no further reports for a year and a half until Ted from surveillance sent a memo to Pilcher and Pam.

Ethan read it as he sipped his cappuccino.

> **Day #5129**
> **From: Ted Upshaw**
> **To: David Pilcher**
> **Subjects: Residents 308 and 294; a/k/a Kate and Harold Ballinger**
>
> I've harbored a mounting suspicion over the last few months, which I feel compelled to share with you now. After midnight, once every couple of weeks, in eleven households that we know of (Ballinger, Engler, Kirby, Turiel, Smith, Golden, O'Brien, Nighswander, Greene, Brandenburg, and Shaw), the interior cameras produce no video feed for extended periods of time—roughly between four and seven hours. A typical night feed is two hours of tossing and turning with all the motionless activity missing. The only thing that could cause such extended video blackouts would be a complete absence of microchip movement. In other words, no motion to ping the cameras.

But this is impossible.

For a camera to shut off at night for hours at a time, the subjects would have to sleep perfectly still. Or be dead. The cameras are highly sensitive and programmed to wake at the slightest movement, even the rise and fall of someone's chest associated with heavy breathing.

The cameras have not been disabled. If this was one instance in one household, I might write it off as an anomaly. But the sheer number of extended blackout occurrences, their repetition, and the fact that they're happening concurrently across multiple households leads me to the conclusion that something bigger, covert, and coordinated is taking place behind our backs.

I believe the above-named residents and possibly more have not only discovered their microchips, but also found a way to remove them at any time in plain view of the cameras. Obviously, without their microchips embedded, residents could move unseen and undetected, in their homes, through town, even beyond the fence.

The possibility of a growing contingent of residents meeting together in secret is a disturbing development, which I believe requires immediate action.

Ethan polished off the rest of his cup and walked out of the coffee shop into the street.

Chimes jingled over the door as he pulled it open and stepped into the toy store.

He had breathed deeply crossing Main, but still his heart was beating like crazy.

Kate looked up from the book—a tattered Lee Child paperback, the last Reacher novel.

It was her shock of white hair that made her look older from a distance. Close up, she was youthful. A few laugh lines, but still so goddamn pretty. Not long ago, at least from his perspective, he'd been in love with this woman.

Their affair had been three of the most intense, reckless, terrifying, happy, alive months of his life. Like how he imagined being on heroin felt if the high never ended, if every syringe didn't also contain the possibility of death.

They'd been partners at the time, and there had been one week when they'd been on the road together in northern California.

Every night, they rented two rooms. Every night, for five days, he stayed with her. They barely slept that week. Couldn't keep their hands off each other. Couldn't stop talking when they weren't making love, and the daylight hours when they had to pretend to be professionals made it all the more beautifully excruciating. He had never felt such a complete lack of self-consciousness around anyone. Even Theresa. Unconditional acceptance. Not just of his body and mind, but also of something more, of something indefinably him. Ethan had never connected with anyone on this level. The most generous blessing and life-destroying curse all wrapped up in the same woman, and despite the pain of the guilt and the knowledge of how it would crush his wife, whom he still loved, the idea of turning away from Kate seemed like a betrayal of his soul.

So she had done it for him.

On a cold and rainy night in Capitol Hill.

In a booth over glasses of Belgian beer in a loud dark bar called the Stumbling Monk.

He was ready to leave Theresa. To throw everything away. He had asked Kate there to tell her that and instead she had reached across the scuffed wood of a table worn smooth by ten thousand pint glasses and broken his heart.

Kate wasn't married, had no children.

She wasn't ready to jump off the cliff with him when he had so much pulling him back from the ledge.

Two weeks later, she was in Boise, pursuant to her own transfer request.

One year later, she was missing in a town in Idaho in the middle of nowhere called Wayward Pines, with Ethan off to find her.

Eighteen hundred years later, after almost everything they had known had turned to dust or eroded out of existence, here they stood, facing each other in a toy shop in the last town on earth.

For a moment, staring into her face at close range blanked Ethan's mind.

Kate spoke first.

"I was wondering if you'd ever drop in."

"I was wondering that myself."

"Congratulations."

"For?"

She reached over the counter and tapped his shiny brass star.

"Your promotion. Nice to see a familiar face running the show. How are you adjusting to the new job?"

She was good. In this short exchange, it was obvious that Kate had mastered the superficial conversational flow that the best of Wayward Pines could achieve without straining.

"It's going well," he said.

"Good to have something steady and challenging, I bet." Kate smiled, and Ethan couldn't help hearing the subtext, wondered if everyone did. If it ever went silent.

As opposed to running half naked through town while we all try to kill you.

"The job's a good fit," he said.

"That's great. Really happy for you. So, to what do I owe the pleasure?"

"I just wanted to pop in and say hi."

"Well, that was nice of you. How's your son?"

"Ben's great," Ethan said.

"He's sure growing up fast."

"That's the truth."

God, it felt so stilted talking to her. Like bad dialogue in a novel or actors reading lines.

Hammering started up next door—Harold building something.

"How's your husband?" Ethan asked.

He didn't like the word—not when it applied to the man who'd been fucking Kate for the last seven years. Or was it possible their marriage was a sham? That she secretly hated him, but kept up appearances? Had never let him touch her.

"He's wonderful," she said, and the authenticity of her smile contradicted everything that had come before, called it all out for the lie it was. She loved Harold. She'd lit up saying his name. In this moment, and only for a flicker of time, Ethan had glimpsed the real Kate.

"He's next door?" Ethan asked.

"Yes. That's him hammering away at something. We like to say he's the brawn, and I'm the brains of this operation."

Ethan forced a laugh. Said, "I've never met him. Well, not *really* met him."

He thought she might read his intent. Offer to make an introduction.

But she only said, "You will. He's a little under the gun this afternoon filling an order for the school. Why don't you pick out something for Ben? Anything in the store. On the house."

"I couldn't."

"I insist."

"You're too kind."

Ethan moved away from the cash register. It wasn't a large store, but shelves brimmed—floor to ceiling—with handmade toys. He lifted a wooden car. It had wheels that spun. Doors, hood, and a trunk that opened and closed.

"This is really good," he said.

"Harold's work is amazing."

Ethan put the car back on the shelf.

Kate moved out from behind the counter. She wore a yellow dress the color of turning aspen leaves. Her figure almost unchanged.

"How old is Ben now?" she asked.

"He's twelve."

"Hmm. Tough age when traditional toys begin to lose their appeal." She walked to the back of the store. Bare feet on hardwood that almost glowed under the late-afternoon light slanting through the storefront windows. "But I might have just the thing."

She stood on the balls of her feet and reached up to a slingshot on the highest shelf.

The craftsmanship was simple but exact.

Carved, raw wood, sanded smooth.

A thick rubber band attached to the forks of the Y and a brown leather pocket.

"This is perfect," Ethan said.

"It's my pleasure."

As he grasped the slingshot, his other hand reached down and touched Kate's hand. The hammering had stopped next door, but the commotion of Ethan's heart sounded deafening in the quiet of the store.

He stared down into her eyes, which seemed somehow bluer than he remembered, and unfurled the fingers of her left hand.

Fighting to ignore the electricity as their skin touched.

She didn't pull away.

Her eyes flicked down at their hands.

She took the scrap of paper from him, clutched it in her fist.

Ethan said, "It's really good to see you again."

And walked out of the store.

* * *

The bells jingled on the inner doorknob of Wayward Pines Realty Associates.

Theresa looked up from her desk as a man she'd never laid eyes on before walked into her office.

She could tell immediately that he was new in town, whatever that meant.

He looked sheet-pale and bewildered.

Stopping at the edge of her desk, he asked, "Are you Theresa Burke?"

"I am."

"They said I should talk to you about a house, but I don't really know what—"

"Yes, of course, I can help you with that. What's your name?"

"Um, Wayne. Wayne Johnson."

She reached over and shook his hand. "Pleasure to meet you, Wayne. Please have a seat."

She pulled out her binder of available listings and slid it across the desk to him.

He hesitated.

For a moment, she wondered if he was on the verge of storming out.

But he flipped it open, started turning through the pages.

She hated this. It was one thing to help someone who'd been in Wayward Pines for several years upgrade to a new house. They knew the deal, knew how to bullshit. But this poor man had just arrived. He had no idea what was happening to him. Why he was here. Why he couldn't leave. She wondered if they'd threatened him yet.

After a minute, he leaned forward.

"See something you like?" Theresa asked.

He whispered under his breath, "What's going on here?"

Theresa said, "What do you mean? We're just looking at real estate. Look, I know buying a new house can be overwhelming, but I'm here to help."

And she said it like she almost believed it.

Through the storefront window, something caught her eye—across the street, Ethan was emerging from Wooden Treasures with a slingshot in his hand.

* * *

Through the window behind the kitchen sink, Ethan watched the sky fading toward dusk. Houses began to glow. The valley filled with piano, courtesy of Hecter Gaither.

A winter's-coming chill sharpened the breeze pushing through the screen. Ethan had been noticing it more and more—when the sun went behind the mountains, the cold sank almost instantly into town. An aggressiveness to the onset, which he found disturbing. He'd heard talk that the winters here were long and legendary.

Ethan let his hands linger in the warm dishwater.

Suddenly Theresa was beside him.

She set a plate down hard on the butcher block.

"Everything okay?" Ethan asked.

She'd been weird during dinner. Weird even for Wayward Pines. Hadn't spoken a word. Hadn't taken her eyes off her plate.

She looked up at him.

"Aren't you forgetting something?" she asked.

"No."

She was angry. Her green eyes smoldering.

"Didn't you have something for Ben?"

Shit.

She'd seen him. Somehow, she'd seen him in the toy shop. But he hadn't brought the slingshot home. He'd gone to his office instead, checked in with Belinda, stashed Kate's gift in the bottom drawer of his desk.

Hoping to avoid this exact conversation.

"What'd you do with it?" she asked. "I think our son would love to own a slingshot."

"Theresa—"

"Oh my God, are you actually going to try and deny it?"

He pulled his hands out of the water, dried them on the towel hanging from the stove door handle.

Felt an awful metal burn in the back of his throat that reminded him of the night he'd told Theresa about Kate. His ex-partner was already in Boise when he'd sat Theresa down and spilled everything. He couldn't live with the lie between them. Respected her too much. Loved her too much. It had *never* been about him not loving his wife.

Theresa didn't understand.

That hadn't been a surprise.

But she didn't throw him out either.

And that had been.

She had cried and been devastated, but in the end, loved him all the same.

Still.

Despite.

And the strangest thing happened—her response made him love her more. Showed him his wife in a light he'd never seen. Or rather, had missed.

Theresa took a step toward him.

"I saw you there," she said. "In her shop. I *saw* you."

"I was there," Ethan said. "She gave me the slingshot for Ben, and I didn't bring it home—"

"Because you wanted to hide it from me."

"Why would she give me something clearly from her if we were doing something behind your back?"

"But you did hide it from me."

"Yes."

Theresa shut her eyes, and for a moment, Ethan thought she might be on the brink of going to pieces.

She opened them again, said, "Then why did you go to see her?"

Ethan put his hands on the stovetop and leaned back.

"It's work, Theresa, and that's all I can say."

"Work."

"I would never have gone to her otherwise."

"And I'm just supposed to take your word for that?"

"I love you, and I wish I'd never met her. You have no idea."

"What am I supposed to do with that?"

Theresa ran the tap and filled a glass.

Drank it down.

Set it down.

Staring through the window screen, she said, "Look, you got something from her that you couldn't get from me. Some kind of experience beyond ours. I don't hate you for it. I never did." She turned from the sink and faced him, steam rising off the surface of the soapy water. Gaither was playing one of Mozart's piano concertos. "But that doesn't mean you didn't hurt me," she said.

"I know that."

"I wonder if she makes you feel the way you make *me* feel. You don't have to try and answer that. So it's for work, huh?"

"Yeah."

"So I guess that means . . ."

"I can't talk about it."

She nodded. "I'm gonna draw a bath."

"I'm over her, Theresa. Completely."

He watched his wife walk out of the kitchen, listened to the hardwood floor creaking under her footfalls as she moved down the hall toward the bathroom.

A door closed.

After a minute, he heard the muffled sound of water splashing into the clawfoot tub.

* * *

Ethan crawled into bed under the covers.

He lay on his side with his head propped up with one arm, watching his wife sleep.

The warmth of her body heated the space between the sheet and the comforter.

She'd left the window cracked open an inch off the sill and the air creeping in was cold enough to make him wish he'd pulled another blanket out of the oak chest at the foot of their bed.

He thought he might drift off for a half hour or so, and he tried to shut his eyes, but it just wasn't happening.

So rarely did his mind ever stop.

Kate had undoubtedly read his note.

But what had she made of it?

Sitting in the coffee shop seven hours ago, he'd finally decided on a course of action.

Ripped a strip of blank newsprint off the latest edition of the *Wayward Light* and written:

> *They know about you. They're watching you. They sent me to investigate you. Mausoleum. 2:00 a.m. Tonight.*

12

1:55 a.m.

No moon and a billion stars in a black, black sky.

Frigid.

The small, duckless pond in the city park beginning to rim with ice.

In the afternoon, one of Pilcher's men had delivered a new Bronco to the curb in front of Ethan's house, the SUV identical to its predecessor, if not a trace shinier.

But Ethan had chosen to walk.

He thrust his hands deep into the pockets of his parka, fingertips tingling in the cold.

Soon he was moving alongside the river, the ruckus of water passing over rocks and the clean, sweet smell of it in the night air.

Had it only been two weeks since he'd crossed this river in the dead of night, the entire town in pursuit, and fled upcanyon?

He didn't feel anything like that man anymore.

Ethan climbed over a disintegrating stone wall that looked straight out of a Frost poem, the rocks cold as blocks of ice to the touch.

The gravestones glowed like ancient faces under the starlight and the sound of the river fell away.

Ethan passed through waist-high weeds, through groves of scrub oak.

Here among the dead at the south end of town, the lights of Wayward Pines were all but invisible.

The mausoleum appeared in the distance.

Had she come?

The old Kate would have. No question.

But what about the new one? The Kate who'd lived in Wayward Pines for nine years. The Kate he no longer knew.

Something loitered in the back of his mind. Something ugly and off-balance.

Fear.

What if Kate and her group *had* tortured and murdered Alyssa Pilcher?

You have no idea what she's capable of.

He couldn't rid himself of what Pilcher had said yesterday morning, and as he approached the crypt, it occurred to him—*I should've brought my gun.*

The mausoleum stood in a stand of mature aspen trees that had already dropped their leaves—gold coins scattered in the dying weeds. The stone planters that framed the iron door had long since crumbled, but the columns retained their form.

There was no wind.

The river nothing more than a whisper.

He said, "Kate?"

No answer.

Dug a flashlight out of his pocket, swept the beam through the aspen, called her name again.

Ethan forced the heavy door open, its bottom dragging across the stone with a teeth-aching groan.

He put his light inside.

It fired the stone walls.

The stained-glass window in the back.

She wasn't here.

He walked slowly around the perimeter of the crypt, shining his light into the surrounding weeds, which were already bending under the weight of a fragile glaze of frost.

Ice crystals glittering in the beam.

He arrived back at the entrance and sat down on the steps between the columns as the realization slowly dawned that she hadn't come. He'd made a risky play, tipped his hand, and scared her off.

What would she do now? Run?

He killed the light.

The walk over from his house and the anticipation of seeing her had bolstered him against the cold, but now it came screaming in.

He struggled onto his feet.

Drew in a sudden breath.

Kate stood five feet away, a ghost in the dark, dressed completely in black with a hoodie pulled over her head.

As she moved forward, the blade of the butcher knife in her hand threw a glint of starlight.

Ethan said, "A knife? Really?"

"Thought I might be coming to a fight."

"Did you now?"

"Never know these days."

"Will you put it the fuck down? I didn't even bring a gun." She just stared at him. He couldn't read her eyes in the low light, but her mouth was a thin, tight line. "What? You don't believe me? Wanna pat me down, Agent Hewson?"

"Open your jacket."

Kate slipped her knife into a makeshift sheath that had been constructed out of duct tape.

Her hands slid around his waist.

Then up and down his thighs.

Fast, thorough.

"You still got it," Ethan said.

"Got what?"

"Still frisk like a pro."

Kate stepped back. She looked at him with a hardness he'd not seen in her eyes before. At least not aimed at him.

"Are you fucking with me?" she said.

"No. Are you here alone?"

"Yes."

"Where's Harold?"

"You think we're dumb enough to let you take both of us?"

"No one's trying to take you, Kate. At least not tonight."

"I don't even know if I believe you."

"But you came."

"I had a choice?"

"How about we talk inside."

"Fine."

Ethan followed her up the stone steps into the crypt.

When they were both inside, she put her shoulder into the door and forced it shut.

Turned around.

Faced Ethan in the dark.

"Are you chipped?" she asked.

"Yeah."

"So they know you're here."

"Probably."

Kate spun and grabbed for the door handle, but Ethan dragged her back.

"Let go!"

"Relax, Kate. It doesn't matter."

"The hell it doesn't. They know you're here."

"Only my location. The mausoleum isn't miked. I'm not miked."

"But they know you're talking to me tonight?"

"They sent me."

She shoved him back toward the stained-glass window with a surprising burst of force and smoothed her clothes.

Ethan fished his flashlight out of his pocket, turned it on, set it on the floor between them. The light streaming up lit their faces grotesquely.

Their breath steaming in the cold.

"I need you to trust me, Kate."

She leaned back against the wall, said, "I need you to prove that I can."

"How do I do that?"

"What do they know about me?"

"They know that you and others remove your microchips. That sometimes you go out at night."

"And they sent you to investigate me?" she asked.

"That's right."

"For what?"

"You really want to play it that way?"

"I don't know what you're talking about. Two weeks ago you're turning this town upside down, desperate to leave. Now you're sheriff. Clearly working for *them*."

"So you know there's a 'them.'"

"What idiot doesn't?"

"What else do you know, Kate?"

She eased down onto the floor.

Ethan sat too.

"I know there's a fence around the outskirts of town. I know we're all under surveillance. All the time. I know that two weeks ago you wanted the truth."

"Have you gone beyond the fence?"

Kate hesitated, then shook her head. "Have you?" She must have read it in his face, said before he even had a chance to lie, "Oh my God, you have."

"Tell me about Alyssa."

Kate didn't flinch exactly, but he read the surprise in her eyes.

"What about her?"

"You know she was killed two nights ago?"

"Are you serious?"

"She was found naked in the middle of the road, stabbed to death. Tortured."

"Oh Jesus." She let out a long, trembling breath. "Who found her?"

"I did."

"Why are you asking me about this?"

"Kate."

"What?"

"You think they didn't know you were talking to Alyssa?"

Her eyes darted, a flicker of panic setting in.

"She came to me," Kate whispered.

"I know. I saw the footage. You were supposed to meet with her the night she died."

"How do you know that?" He didn't answer, just let the realization come. Kate's face fell. "Oh. I see. She was with them."

"Yeah."

"A spy."

"What happened that night, Kate? You were supposed to meet her here at one in the morning. She documented everything. What happened?"

Kate stared at the floor.

He said, "Maybe you'll believe this. Maybe you won't. But I am here as your friend."

"I don't believe it."

"Why?"

"Because I can't take the risk of being wrong."

"Tell me what happened. I can help you."

"Do I need your help?"

"In the worst way."

"What's on the other side of the fence?"

"Don't ask me that."

"I need to know."

"What happened to Alyssa?"

"I don't know."

"Did you kill her?"

"You tell me. Am I a murderer?"

"I don't know you anymore."

Kate stood. "That hurts more than you know."

"Did you kill her?"

"No."

Ethan grabbed his flashlight, struggled up onto his feet. "Tell me what you're into."

"Goodbye, Ethan."

"I need to know."

"For you? Or for the people who hold your leash?"

"They will kill you, Kate. You and Harold. They will disappear you."

"I know the risk."

"And?"

"And I live my life on my terms. If my terms lead me down that road, so be it."

"I just want to help you."

"Whose side are you on, Ethan? Really?"

"I don't know yet."

She smiled. "First honest thing you've said to me. Thank you for that." She reached out and took hold of his hand. Her fingers were ice, but the shape of the hand was familiar. The last time he'd held it was two thousand years ago on a beach in northern California.

Kate said, "You're scared."

Her face was inches from his. Her attention like a heat lamp.

"Aren't we all?"

"I've been here nine years. I don't know where I am. Or why. Sometimes I think we're all dead, but in the quiet, dark hours of the night, I know that isn't true."

"What are you doing when you leave your house at night?"

"What's beyond the fence?"

"I can protect you, Kate, but you have to—"

"I don't want your protection."

She tugged the door open, stepped back out into the night.

Five steps from the crypt, she stopped, turned, stared back at Ethan.

"The last time I saw Alyssa alive was two nights ago."

"Where did you see her last?"

"We parted ways on Main Street. We didn't kill her, Ethan."

"But she was with you the night she died."

"Yes."

"Where?"

Kate shook her head.

"Where do you go at night, Kate? And why?"

"What's beyond the fence?" When he didn't answer, she smiled. "Thought so."

"Do you love him?"

"Excuse me?"

"Your husband. Do you love him? Is it real?"

The smile vanished.

"See you later, Sheriff."

* * *

He walked home not knowing.

Not knowing if Kate had lied to him.

Not knowing if she had been on the other side of the fence.

Not knowing if she had killed Alyssa.

Not knowing a goddamn thing.

She'd had that effect in their relationship too. He'd spend a day with her that felt like bliss in the moment, then come out on the other side unsure of where he stood. Second-guessing everything. He'd never understood if it was a conscious play on her part, or his own failing in letting this woman get so deep and tangled in his head.

He pulled off his boots just inside the front door and crept across the hardwood to the staircase. It was cold in the house, the floor cracking and popping under the weight of his footsteps.

Down the upstairs hallway to his son's bedroom.

The door was open.

He moved to the bed.

Couldn't have been warmer than forty-five degrees in the room.

Ben slept buried under five blankets, but Ethan pulled them up a little closer around his neck, touched the back of his hand to the boy's cheek.

Soft and warm.

Truckloads of firewood were due to arrive any day now. Word was the town burned copious amounts of pine for heat through the winter, with each household receiving six cords. Pilcher had a small army of men making daily trips beyond the fence under heavily armed protection. Cutting trees and splitting wood for the entire town.

Ethan headed for his bedroom.

Stripped off his pants and shirt, left them in a pile in the doorway.

The floor was freezing.

He hustled to the bed.

Crawling under the covers, he turned over onto his side and pulled Theresa in close.

She radiated heat.

He kissed the back of her neck.

Sleep seemed like a long shot. Almost impossible lately to turn down the noise in the back of his mind.

He shut his eyes.

Maybe it would come anyway.

"Ethan."

"Hey baby," he whispered. She rolled over, faced him. Her breath in his face a familiar, gentle heat.

"Get your feet off of mine. They're ice."

"Sorry. I wake you?" he asked.

"When you left. Where'd you go?"

"Work."

"To see her?"

"I can't—"

"Ethan."

"What?"

"Where?"

"It doesn't matter, Theresa. It really doesn't—"

"I can't keep doing this."

"Doing what? Us?"

"This town. And us in it. You. Her. Your job." She leaned in close, pressed her lips against his ear, whispered, "Can I keep talking like this or will they hear us?"

He hesitated.

"I'm going to do it anyway, Ethan."

"Then just be still."

"What?"

"Be completely still."

"Why?"

"Will you just do it? In particular, don't move your left leg."

They lay still.

He could feel his wife's heart beating against his chest.

Ethan counted to fifteen in his head, then whispered, "Speak no louder than this."

"I used to think that if I could only be with you again, have you here with us, that I could do this. Buy into the lie."

"And?"

"I can't."

"You don't have a choice, Theresa. Do you know the danger you're putting our family in just having this conversation?"

Her mouth pushed hard into his ear.

A chill shot down his spine.

"I want to leave this place. I'm done, Ethan. I don't care what *could* happen to us. I just want out."

"Do you care what happens to our son?" Ethan whispered.

"This isn't a life. I don't care if we all die."

"Good. Because we will."

"You know that for sure?"

"A hundred percent."

"Because you know."

"Yes."

"What's out there, Ethan?"

"We can't have this conversation."

"I am your wife."

Their bodies were pushed against each other.

Her legs were cool and smooth against his skin and the heat coming off her was driving him mad. He wanted to shake her. Wanted to fuck her.

"Why the hell are you getting hard?"

"I don't know."

"What's out there, Ethan?"

"You really want to know."

And then her hand was on his cock.

"Are you thinking about her?"

"No."

"Swear to me."

"I swear."

She slid away, down under the covers, and took him in her mouth. Brought him right to the edge. Then she came up and pulled off her nightie. She was sitting on top of him and her breath clouding. She leaned over and kissed him. Her nipples hard against his chest in the cold.

Theresa rolled over onto her back and pulled Ethan with her, pulled him inside.

She was loud and she sounded so beautiful.

As she started to come, she brought Ethan's head down, her lips to his ear, his lips to hers. She moaned and said, "Tell me."

"What?" He was breathless.

"Tell me . . . *ooohhhhgodEthan* . . . where we really are."

Ethan buried his face into her ear. "We're all that's left, baby." They were coming together, loud and hard, as in sync as they'd ever been. "This is the last town on earth."

Theresa shouting *yesyesyesohgoddontstop*. Loud enough to cover his words.

"And we're surrounded by monsters."

* * *

They lay entwined and sweaty and perfectly still.

Ethan whispering into her ear.

He told her everything.

When they were. Where they were. About Pilcher. About the abbies.

Then he lay with his head propped up on one elbow, stroking her face.

Theresa stared at the ceiling.

She'd been here five years, a helluva lot longer than he had, but it had been a state of limbo. Of not really knowing. Now she did. Perhaps she had suspected before, but all uncertainty had just been burned away: aside from Ethan and Ben, she would never again see all of the people she had loved in her life before. They had been dead two millennia. And if she'd ever held out hope for leaving Wayward Pines, Ethan had just destroyed it.

There was no end date for her sentence in this place.

She was a lifer.

Ethan wondered which emotion was dominant—figured a full cocktail was flailing away inside her head: anger, despair, heartbreak, fear.

By the light of a distant streetlamp coming through the window, he watched tears form in her eyes.

Felt her hand begin to tremble in his.

13

Water Tower
Volunteer Park
Seattle, 2013

As Hassler approached the entrance to the water tower, a woman stepped out of the shadows beside the door.

She said, "You're late."

"By five minutes. Relax. He up there?"

"Yeah."

She couldn't have been much older than twenty. A thin, muscular build, crazy gorgeous, but with dead eyes. An interesting choice for Pilcher's muscle. She certainly put out the confidence of someone who could handle herself.

She stood between Hassler and the door, blocking his way.

He said, "Do you mind?"

For a beat, it seemed like she might, but she finally stepped aside.

As Hassler moved past, he said, "Don't let anyone come up."

"Thanks for telling me how to do my job, g-man."

The metal clanged under Hassler's wing tips.

He trudged up the stairs.

The observation level was low lit, a circular brick wall punctuated with arched windows that had been covered in heavy-gauge screens to stop anyone from going through. More floor-to-ceiling fencing guarded the seventy-five-foot drop into the open spiral staircase.

Wearing a long black coat and a bowler hat, David Pilcher sat on a bench on the other side of the observation deck.

Hassler circled around and took a seat beside him.

For a moment, nothing but the sound of rain hammering on the roof above them.

Pilcher looked over with the faintest smile.

"Agent Hassler."

"David."

Out the window, the skyline of Seattle looked like a neon blur through the low cloud deck.

Pilcher reached into his coat and took out a fat envelope.

Set it in Hassler's lap.

Hassler carefully opened it, peeked inside, thumbed through the hundred-dollar bills.

"Looks like thirty thousand to me," he said, resealing the envelope.

"You have news?" Pilcher asked.

"It's been fifteen months since Agent Burke's disappearance and Agent Stallings's death. There have been no leads. No new evidence. Now don't misunderstand me. I'm not saying anyone at the Treasury Department is ever going to forget that we had one agent killed and three go MIA in Wayward Pines, Idaho. But with no new information, they're just spinning in their tracks and they know it. Two days ago, the internal investigation into my missing agents was officially deprioritized."

"What do your people think happened?"

"The theories?"

"Yeah."

"It's all over the map, but nothing remotely close to a bull's-eye. They had Ethan Burke's 'hope service' today."

"What's a hope service?"

"Fuck if I know."

"You went?"

"I went to the after-party at Theresa's house."

"I'm going to pay her a visit after you and I are finished."

"Really."

"It's time."

"Theresa and Ben?"

"I have a theory that if I can keep families together when possible, the transition will be smoother on the other side."

Hassler stood.

Walked over to the window.

Stared out past the glass conservatory, which was illuminated with holiday lights.

He could hear traffic and live music down in Capitol Hill, but up here at the top of the water tower, he felt removed from everything.

Hassler said, "Have you given any thought to what we talked about last time?"

"I have. And you?"

"It's all I think about." Hassler turned, stared at Pilcher. "What will it be like?"

"What will what be like?"

"Wayward Pines. When you come out of whatever it is you call—"

"Suspended animation." Pilcher's face grew dark. He said, "You already know far more about my project than I'm comfortable with."

"If I wanted to bring you down, David, I could've done that months ago."

"If I wanted you dead, Agent Hassler—you and everyone you love—there is nothing in the world stopping me from making that happen. Not from prison. Not from the grave."

"So we've established trust," Hassler said.

"Perhaps. Or at the very least, assured mutual destruction."

"No difference in my book." Freezing spits of rain blew in the window. Hassler felt them misting the back of his neck with an unpleasant chill. "So, back to my question, David. What will it be like when you all wake up?"

"At first, work. Lots and lots of work. The town will have to be rebuilt. That'll take some time. But then? I don't know. We're talking two thousand years from now. This tower we're standing in will be in ruin. That skyline? Gone. All the people in this city and their children and grandchildren and great grandchildren disintegrated into nothing. Even their bones."

Hassler clutched the fencing over the window.

"I want to be a part of it."

"It's no guarantee, Adam."

"I understand that."

"This is Columbus in search of the East Indies. Man flying to the moon. A million things could go wrong and we never wake up. An asteroid could hit. An earthquake. We could wake to a toxic atmosphere or a hostile world we never imagined."

"Do you really think that'll happen?"

"I have no idea what we'll be waking up to. Only an image in my head of this perfect little town where humanity gets a chance to start over. That's all that's ever driven me."

"So you'd let me come along?"

"I'm already fully staffed. What skill set would you bring?"

"Intelligence. Ability to lead. Survival skills. I was a Delta Force operator before I joined the Secret Service, but I'm sure you already know that."

Pilcher just smiled, said, "Well, I guess you're in."

"I have one favor to ask, and if you agree to it, you can have this envelope back."

"What?"

"Ethan Burke never wakes up."

"Why?"

"I want to be there with Theresa."

"Theresa Burke."

"That's right."

"Ethan's wife."

"Yes."

Pilcher said, "Are you in love with her?"

"I am actually."

"And is she in love with you?"

"Not yet. She's never stopped loving him." Hassler felt the ulcer flaring in his stomach. That green flame of envy. "He cheats on her with his ex-partner, Kate Hewson, and still she takes him back. Still she loves him. Have you ever met Theresa Burke?"

"No, but I will shortly."

"He doesn't deserve her."

"And you do."

"I would love that woman like she was meant to be loved. She'll be happier with me in Wayward Pines than she's ever been in her life." It took his breath away to say the words, to give them voice. He'd never shared this with anyone.

Pilcher laughed as he rose to his feet. "So at the end of the day, this is all just about you getting a girl?"

"No, it's—"

"I'm kidding. I'll make it happen."

The men shook hands.

"When do we go under?" Hassler asked.

"It's called de-animation. My superstructure is finished. All that's left is to stock the warehouse and collect the last few recruits. I'm sixty-four years old, not getting any younger, and there's going to be loads to do on the other side."

"So . . ."

"We're having a party on New Year's Eve in Wayward Pines. Me, my family, and a hundred and twenty members of my crew are going to drink the best champagne money can buy and go to sleep for a couple thousand years. You're welcome to join."

"Two weeks?"

"Two weeks."

"Where will people think you've gone?"

"I've made arrangements. It's been seven years since my last public lecture. I've become a recluse. I'm guessing it's fifty-fifty whether the AP even carries my obit. What about you? Considered how you'll make your exit?"

"I'll cash out my 401(k), empty my bank accounts, leave a messy trail to some shady purveyor of fake passports. That isn't the hard part."

"What is?"

Hassler glanced back out the window toward the mist-enshrouded hills of Queen Anne—Theresa Burke's neighborhood.

"Knowing I have to wait two thousand years to be with the woman of my dreams."

III

14

Tobias lay flat on his stomach in the swaying grasses.

He barely breathed.

Five hundred yards away, the abby emerged out of the forest of lodgepole pines.

It entered the field, moving at a comfortable lope in Tobias's general direction.

Fuck.

Tobias had just come out of a forest on the opposite side of the field not five minutes prior. Thirty minutes before that, he'd crossed a stream and lingered half a second on the bank, debating whether or not to stop for a drink. He'd decided to push on. If he hadn't, he'd have spent five or ten minutes drinking his fill and replenishing his one-liter bottles. Upshot being he would've arrived at the edge of this field with the abby already out in the open. Could've tracked its trajectory from the cover and safety of the woods. Made certain to avoid the precise situation of fuckedness he now found himself in: he was going to have to shoot it. A run-in was inevitable. It was midday. The abby was downwind. No other option with him stuck out here and the nearest patch of trees several football fields away. The creature's sense of smell, sight, and hearing was so finely tuned, the moment he stood it would spot him. Considering the wind direction, it was going to smell him any second now.

Tobias had dropped his pack and rifle in the grass at his first glimpse of movement in the distance. Now he reached out, grabbed his Winchester Model 70.

He gripped the forend stock and came up on his right elbow.

Settled in behind the scope.

It hadn't been zeroed out in ages, and as the abby came into focus in the reticle, Tobias thought of all the times the scope had been jostled when he'd leaned the gun against a tree or thrown it down. All the rain and the snow that had beat the shit out of his weapon in his thousand-plus days in the wild.

He gauged its distance at two hundred yards now. Still a long shot, but its center mass loomed large in the crosshairs. He made a slight adjustment for the wind. His heart beating against the ground that was still cold from last night's freeze. It had been weeks, months maybe, since his last encounter. He'd had ammo for his .357 then. God, he missed that gun. If he'd still had his revolver, he'd have stood up, shouted, let that beast come running at him.

Blown its brains out from close range.

He could see its heart pulsing in the crosshairs.

Pushed off the safety.

Touched his finger to the trigger.

He didn't want to pull.

A gunshot out here would announce his presence to everything in a three-mile radius.

Thinking, *Just let it pass, maybe it won't see you.*

And then, *No. You have to put it down.*

The report echoed across the field, deflected off the distant wall of trees, and began to slowly fade away.

Miss.

The abby stood motionless, frozen midstride on two legs that looked as sturdy as oak, its nose tipped up to the wind. There was a beard of dried blood down its face and neck from a recent kill. Tough to judge size through a scope, and truthfully, it didn't matter. Even the smaller ones that clocked in around a hundred twenty pounds were absolutely lethal.

Tobias turned the bolt handle up, jerked it back.

The spent cartridge spit out with a puff of smoke.

He shoved the bolt forward, locked it down, looked back through the scope.

Damn had it covered some ground, the abby hauling ass now across the meadow at a full sprint in that low, scuttling gait reminiscent of a pit bull.

In his life before, Tobias had seen combat all over the world. Mogadishu, Baghdad, Kandahar, the coca fields of Colombia. Hostage rescues, high-value target acquisitions, off-grid assassinations. None of it could hold a candle to the shit-yourself-fear evoked by a charging abby.

A hundred fifty yards and closing and no idea how off his scope was.

He put the crosshairs center mass.

Squeezed.

The rifle bucked hard against his shoulder and a streak of blood appeared across the abby's left side. He'd barely grazed its ribs, the creature still coming, undaunted.

But now he knew the scope's deviation—off a few degrees right and down.

Tobias ejected the spent shell.

Jacked a new cartridge into the chamber, locked down the bolt, made the adjustment to the scope.

He could hear it now—rapid breathing and the sound of talons ripping through grass.

Noted a strange swell of confidence.

He put the crosshairs on its head and fired.

When the wind pushed the gun smoke out of the way, Tobias saw the abby facedown and motionless in the grass, the back of its head blown out.

Kill number forty-five.

He sat up.

Hands sweating through his fingerless gloves.

A scream erupted from the woods.

He raised the rifle, scoped the line of trees a third of a mile away.

A second scream followed.

A third.

He couldn't see anything distinctly in the trees.

Just movement in the shadows.

The realization hit with a sickening burst of fear—there were more of them.

He'd only killed a scout for a larger swarm.

Shouldering his pack, he grabbed the Winchester and took off across the field.

The forest he moved toward stood a quarter mile away. He slid the rifle strap over his shoulder and accelerated to a dead run, arms pumping, glancing left every few strides in the direction of the screams that were growing louder and more frequent over his own breathless gasps.

Hit the trees before they see you. For God's sake. If you reach the woods, you might live. If the swarm spots you, you die in the next ten minutes.

He looked back, saw the dead abby in the grass, the line of woods beyond, but no other movement in the field.

Straight on, the trees that would save him stood fifty yards away.

He hadn't run for his life in more than a year. Staying alive beyond the fence was an art based upon the principle of avoidance. You never charged ahead into unknown territory. You always took your time. Walked softly. Stayed in the trees whenever possible. Ventured out into the open only when necessary. You didn't rush. Left nothing to track. And if you stayed alert every second of every day, you had a chance at staying alive.

He finally reached the trees just as the first of the abbies broke out into the clearing. He didn't know if he'd been seen and he couldn't see them now. Couldn't hear them. There was nothing but the riot inside his own chest, his own gasping.

He plowed between trees, branches grabbing at his arms.

A limb sliced open the right side of his face.

Blood ran over his lip.

He leapt over a downed log and glanced back when he hit the ground on the other side—nothing to see but a blur of joggling green.

His legs burned.

Lungs burned.

He couldn't keep this up much longer.

Out into a clearing studded with boulders and backed by a seventy-foot cliff. The temptation to climb to safety was primal but misguided. Abbies could climb almost as fast as they could run.

A stream meandered through the clearing.

His boots pounded in the water.

Screams tore through the woods behind him.

He was coming to his end. Simply couldn't keep going like this.

He shot into a grove of scrub oak, the leaves crimson.

Done.

He hit the wall within range of a thicket, fell to his knees, dragged himself into the bushes. Dizzy with exhaustion, Tobias set the gun down and ripped his pack open.

Is this, after everything, the place where I die?

The box of .30-30 cartridges was on top.

Always.

Tore it open, started feeding rounds into the receiver just forward of the bolt. He loaded two in the magazine, the last into the chamber, and shoved the bolt home.

Rolled over onto his stomach.

The foliage surrounding him was orange.

The air carried the scent of dying leaves.

His heart still slamming like it was trying to bust out of his chest.

He stared back through the woods into the clearing.

They were coming.

No telling how large of a swarm he was dealing with.

If he was spotted and their number was more than five, buenas fucking noches.

If he was spotted, their number was five or under, and he made every shot count, he had a slim chance.

But if he missed or didn't make kill shots every time—if he was forced to reload—he would die.

No pressure.

He glassed the boulder-strewn clearing through the scope.

It wasn't the first time he was faced with the prospect of not making it back to Wayward Pines. He was already overdue by four months. It was possible they had declared him KIA. Pilcher would wait a little longer. Give him a good six-month past-due window to return before sending someone else beyond the fence deep into hostile country. But what were the chances another nomad would find what he had found? What were the chances they would survive as long as he had?

An abby streaked into the clearing.

Then another.

And another.

A fourth.

Fifth.

No more. Please. No—

A group of five joined the others.

Then ten more.

Soon there were twenty-five of them milling around the boulders in the shadow of that cliff.

His heart fell.

He crawled back deeper into the thicket, dragging his pack and his rifle with him out of sight.

No chance now.

* * *

The light began to fail.

He kept replaying what had happened, trying to pinpoint the lapse in judgment, the misstep, but there wasn't one. He had waited at the edge of that field five minutes before walking out into it. Glassed the surrounding terrain. Listened. He hadn't rushed out into anything.

Sure he could've circumnavigated that piece of open country. Kept to the perimeter of the woods. That would've taken him the entire day.

No. You couldn't second-guess a choice like that. There'd been nothing reckless in it.

By his reckoning, Wayward Pines lay nestled thirty or forty miles east of his position.

Four days of smooth-sailing travel.

Ten in bad weather or with minor injuries.

He was almost there, for Christ's sake.

For the last three days he'd been climbing into high country. Fir and aspen starting to mix in with the pines. Colder mornings. He could even feel the air thinning out in those deep breaths that never quite filled his lungs.

For fuck's sake.

Now this?

Calm down, soldier.

Secure that shit.

He shut his eyes, willed the panic to subside. A small rock lay in the leaves beside his right hand. He picked it up and began to quietly carve the forty-fifth notch into the stock of his Winchester.

* * *

Evening fell.

They hadn't detected him, but they hadn't left either.

It was strange—he'd witnessed abbies following scent trails before. Recalled a night he'd spent forty feet up in a pine tree. In the moonlight, he'd watched an abby pass fifty yards away, its nose to the ground, clearly on the trail of something.

Maybe it was the brook.

He'd crossed in a frenzy, but the water had come to his knees. Perhaps he'd shed his scent trail, or at least enough of it to throw them off. Truth was he didn't know exactly how keen the abbies' olfactory abilities were. Or what exactly they tracked. Dead skin cells? The odor of freshly trampled grass? God forbid they were as gifted as bloodhounds.

The sun dropped.

The abbies settled into the clearing.

Some of them curled into small, fetal balls against the boulders and slept.

Others lounged by the stream and dipped their claws into the current.

After a while, a band of four disappeared into the woods.

He'd never been so close to a swarm.

Hidden in the thicket, he glimpsed abbies no taller than four feet. Forty yards from where he lay, a trio of them splashed in the stream where it hooked back into the forest, their interaction an unsettling amalgamation of wrestling lion cubs and human children playing a game of tag.

He grew cold and his thirst was maddening.

He had a half-filled bottle in his pack, and he could see his thirst driving him to risk discovery and reach for it, but he wasn't that desperate.

Yet.

* * *

At dusk, the four abbies returned from the woods.

They had brought something back, which two of their number carried between them, the creature thrashing and bleating as they emerged into the clearing.

The swarm surrounded them.

The clearing filled with clicks and screeches.

He'd heard this many times—some kind of communication.

As the abbies formed a circle, there was enough noise for Tobias to risk lifting his rifle to watch through the scope.

The hunters had caught an elk—a gangly teenage buck with the start of a rack of antlers just beginning to rise between its ears.

It stood tottering in the circle, its right hind leg badly broken, hoof raised off the ground, a white streak of bone showing through its hock.

One of the large males shoved a young abby out into the circle.

The swarm screeched in unison, talons lifting to the sky.

The young abby stood frozen.

It received another hard shove.

After a moment, it began to stalk its prey, the elk retreating awkwardly on three legs. This went on for a while like some horrifying ballet.

Suddenly, the young abby charged and flung itself at the wounded animal—talons out. The elk swung its head, connected, sent the abby sprawling back across the ground.

The swarm descended into mayhem that sounded disturbingly like laughter.

Another youngster was pushed out into the circle.

Four and a half feet tall, eighty pounds if Tobias had to guess.

It charged the elk and leapt onto its back, talons digging in, its weight bringing the wounded buck to its knees. The elk raised its head and made a helpless bugle as the young abby buried its face into the hide and slashed wildly.

The game went on, the young ones taking turns chasing the elk around the circle. Biting. Scratching. Drawing blood here and there, but none of them coming close to inflicting serious damage.

Finally, a six-foot bull jumped out into the circle, grabbed the young abby by its neck and pried it off the elk's back. Holding the youngster up inches away from its own face, it screeched something that sounded like annoyance.

It dropped the cub and turned to the elk.

As if sensing the escalated threat, the buck struggled to stand but its hind leg was ruined.

The bull approached.

The darkness falling fast.

It leaned in toward the elk.

Raised its right arm.

The elk screamed.

The bull shrieked something and the three young abbies leapt out into the circle and piled onto the elk, eating its guts which lay spilled and steaming in the grass.

As the circle of abbies closed in to watch their young ones feed, Tobias lowered the rifle.

There was enough noise and commotion that he reached for the pack and forced his hand inside. Kept reaching and reaching until his fingers finally touched the bottle. He pulled it out, unscrewed the lid, poured the water down his throat.

* * *

He slept shivering and dreaming of all that he had seen.

The ruins of Seattle—a dense Pacific rainforest interspersed with toppled skyscrapers. The lower hundred feet of the Space Needle still standing, enwrapped in a riot of vines and undergrowth. Nothing remotely recognizable save Mount Rainier. From sixty miles away, and after two thousand years, it stood seemingly unchanged. He'd sat in a tree at the top of what had once been Queen Anne Hill and wept at the sight of that mountain while the rainforest hummed with the chattering of animals that had never seen or smelled a human being.

He dreamed of standing on a beach in Oregon.

Rock formations looming out of the mist like phantom ships.

He'd taken a stick and scrawled *Oregon, United States of America* in the sand. Sat watching the sun go into the sea as the tide came in and smoothed the words out of existence.

He dreamed of walking with no end in sight.

Of sleeping in trees and crossing rivers.

Dreamed of dreaming about his home in Wayward Pines. As many blankets as he wanted. A bellyful of warm food. A door that locked.

Safety behind the fence.

Sleep without fear.

And his woman.

When you come back—and you will come back—I'm gonna fuck you, soldier, like you just came home from war.

She'd scribbled those words on the first page of his journal the night before he left. She didn't know where he was going of course, only that he probably wouldn't make it back.

He felt so tender toward her.

And more so now than ever.

If she only knew the number of cold and rainy nights when he'd read her last words and felt the glow of comfort.

He dreamed of dying.

Of returning.

And last, he dreamed of the most terrifying thing he'd seen in a long chain of terrifying things.

He'd heard it and smelled it from ten miles away, the noise coming from an old-growth redwood forest of four-hundred-foot trees somewhere along the border of what had once been California and Oregon.

As he approached, the noise became tremendous.

Like hundreds of thousands of sustained screeches.

It was the biggest risk he'd taken in his four years beyond the fence, but his curiosity wouldn't let him turn back.

Even days after, his hearing wasn't right. The volume ten times louder than the loudest rock concert. Like a thousand jets taking off in unison. He'd crawled toward it, covered in make-shift forest-floor camo.

At a half mile away, fear overrode his curiosity, and he couldn't bring himself to move another foot closer.

He caught glimpses of it through the giant trees—the size of ten football stadiums, the highest spires rising several hundred feet above the canopies of the redwoods. He'd stared through the scope of his rifle and tried to process what he saw—a structure made of millions of tons of dirt and logs and rock, all cemented together with some sort of resin. From where he'd lain, it had resembled a giant piece of black honeycomb—tens of thousands of individual cells teeming with aberrations and their stores of putrefying kills.

The smell was eye watering.

The noise like a hundred thousand people being simultaneously skinned alive.

It looked utterly alien, and as he crawled away from it, the realization hit him right between the eyes.

That monstrosity was a city.

The abbies were building a civilization.

The planet was theirs.

* * *

He woke.

There was light again—a soft, tentative blue loitering in the clearing.

Everything glazed with frost and his pant legs had frozen stiff below the knee.

The abbies were gone.

He was shivering uncontrollably.

He needed to get up, get moving, take a piss, build a fire, but he didn't dare.

No telling how long since the swarm had moved out.

* * *

The sun climbed above the cliff and sunlight hit the clearing.

Frost steamed off the grass.

He'd been awake now for three or four hours and there hadn't been so much as the sound of a leaf twittering in the surrounding forest.

Tobias sat up.

The soreness from yesterday's sprint fired inside every muscle—like overtightened guitar strings. He looked around, his extremities beginning to burn as the blood reached them.

Struggling to his feet, it dawned on him.

He was still breathing.

Still standing.

Somehow—alive.

Above him, the scarlet leaves in the scrub oaks glowed, backlit by the sun.

He stared past them into a blue unrivaled by any sky in his life before.

15

When Ethan woke, Theresa and Ben had already left for work and school.

He'd barely slept.

He walked naked across the frigid hardwood to the window and scraped the glaze of ice off the inside of the glass.

The light coming through was still weak enough to suggest the sun had yet to clear the eastern wall of mountains that loomed over town.

Theresa had warned him that in the heart of winter there always came a month-long span—the four weeks that framed the solstice—when the sun never made it above the cliffs that encircled Wayward Pines.

He skipped breakfast.

Grabbed a coffee to go at the Steaming Bean.

Walked south out of town.

He'd woken up with regret fermenting, like a morning-after hangover—everything still hazy from the night before and a sinking feeling he'd fucked up badly.

Because he had.

He'd told Theresa.

It was almost inconceivable.

To be fair, he'd already been messed up after seeing Kate, and his wife had used her formidable wiles to get exactly what she wanted. Truth was, he didn't yet know how tragic of a mistake it was. Worst case—Theresa slipped, told others, and slit this town down the middle. Pilcher would call a fête. He'd lose a wife. Ben would lose his mother. It killed him to even imagine it.

On the other hand, he couldn't deny that it had felt so damn good to finally tell *someone*, no less his wife. The woman from whom he was supposed to keep no secrets. If she could keep her mouth shut, if she could handle the information—no slips, no moments of weakness, no lapses, no freak-outs—then at least there was another human being to share the weight of this crushing knowledge. At least Theresa might finally understand the burden he shouldered every day of his life.

Walking down the middle of the road, he glanced up at the Wayward Pines "goodbye" sign—a family of four frozen mid-smile, mid-wave.

WE HOPE YOU ENJOYED YOUR VISIT TO
WAYWARD PINES!
DON'T BE A STRANGER! COME BACK SOON!

Of course, that was only the setup to Pilcher's grand joke.

The road simply curved back around a half mile later to deliver its hysterical punch line.

That same perfect, smiling family on a billboard, greeting everyone with:

WELCOME TO WAYWARD PINES
WHERE PARADISE IS HOME

It wasn't that Ethan didn't appreciate the irony, and on some level, even the humor. But considering last night and the shit-show his life was fast becoming, more than anything he just wished he'd brought his twelve gauge along to pepper those obnoxious, happy faces with buckshot.

Next time.

The proposition certainly held the promise of therapy.

He finished his coffee as he reached the woods and chucked the dregs.

Had started to crumple the Styrofoam cup when he saw something on the inside.

It was Kate's handwriting.

In fine, black Sharpie:

3:00 a.m. Corner of Main and Eighth. Stand by the front doors of the opera house. No chip or don't bother coming.

* * *

The tunnel door was already raised and Pam waited for him, sitting on the front bumper of the Jeep in black spandex shorts and a Lycra tank top. Her brown hair was pulled back into a ponytail but still sweat-darkened from what looked to have been a punishing workout.

Ethan said, "You look like the cover of a bad muscle car magazine."

"I'm freezing my tits off out here."

"You're barely dressed."

"Just finished ninety minutes on the bike. Didn't figure you'd be this late."

"I had a long night."

"Chasing down your old flame?"

Ethan ignored this and climbed into the passenger seat.

Pam cranked the engine, gunned them out into the forest, and spun a one-eighty that would've flung Ethan out of the Jeep if he hadn't grabbed the roll bar at the last second.

She floored it back into the tunnel, and as the camouflaged door closed behind them, they screamed up into the heart of the mountain.

* * *

Riding the elevator to Pilcher's floor, Pam said, "Do me a favor this afternoon."

"What?"

"Check in on Wayne Johnson."

"The new arrival?"

"Yeah."

"How's he doing?"

"Too early to tell. He just woke up yesterday. I'll have a copy of his file sent back to town with you, but I saw a surveillance report that indicated he had walked the road to the edge of town this morning."

"He make it to the fence?"

"No, he didn't leave the road, but he apparently stood there staring into the trees for a long time."

"What do you want me to do exactly?"

"Just talk to him. Make sure he understands the rules. What's expected. The consequences."

"You want me to threaten him."

"If you think that's what's needed. It'd be nice if you could help lead him down the path to believing he's dead."

"How?"

Pam grinned and punched Ethan in the arm hard enough to give him a charley horse.

"Ouch."

"Figure it out, dummy. It can be fun, you know."

"What? Telling a man he's dead?"

The elevator arrived, the doors parted, but when Ethan moved to exit the car, Pam's arm shot out in front of him. She wasn't ripped in the cartoonish female bodybuilder sense of the word, but her muscle tone was damn impressive. Lean and hard.

"If you have to tell Mr. Johnson he's dead," she said, "you've missed the entire point. He needs to arrive at that conclusion under his own steam."

"That's cruel."

"No, it's going to save his life. Because if he honestly believes there's a world still out there, do you know what he's going to do?"

"Try to escape."

"And guess who gets to hunt him down? Give you a hint. Rhymes with Beethan."

She smiled that psychobitch smile and let her arm drop. "After you, Sheriff."

Ethan headed through Pilcher's residence and then down the corridor to his office, where he dragged open the double oak doors and strolled in.

Pilcher was standing by the window in the rock behind his desk, staring down through the glass.

"Come here, Ethan. I want to show you something. Hurry or you'll miss it."

Ethan moved past the wall of flatscreens and around Pilcher's desk.

Pilcher pointed through the glass as Pam arrived on the other side of him, said, "Now just watch."

From this vantage point, the valley of Wayward Pines stood in shadow.

"Here it comes."

The sun broke over the eastern wall.

Sunbeams slanting down into the center of town in a blaze of early light.

"My town," Pilcher whispered. "I try to catch the first light that reaches it every day."

He motioned for Ethan and Pam to take a seat.

"What do you have for me, Ethan?"

"I saw Kate last night."

"Good. What was your play?"

"Total honesty."

"I'm sorry?"

"I told her everything."

"What am I missing?"

"Kate isn't an idiot."

"You told her you were investigating her?" There was heat in Pilcher's words.

"You think she wouldn't have immediately assumed that?"

"We'll never know now, will we?"

"David—"

"*Will* we?"

"I know her. You don't."

Pam said, "So you told her we were onto her, and she said, 'Great, here's what's going on.'"

"I told her that she was under suspicion, and that I could protect her."

"Played up those old feelings, huh?"

"Something like that."

"Okay, might not be the worst approach. So what'd you learn?"

"She says the last time she saw Alyssa was on Main Street the night she died. They parted ways. Alyssa was still alive."

"What else?"

"She has no idea what's beyond the fence. Asked me repeatedly."

"Then why is she running around in the middle of the night?"

"I don't know. She wouldn't tell me. But I have a chance to find out."

"When?"

"Tonight. But I need my chip taken out."

Pilcher looked at Pam, back to Ethan.

"Not possible."

"Her note explicitly said, 'No chip or don't bother coming.'"

"So just tell her you took it out."

"You think they won't check?"

"We can make an incision in the back of your leg. They'll never know the difference."

"What if they have some other way of finding out?"

"Like what?"

"Fuck if I know, but if there's a microchip in my leg tonight, I'm staying home."

"I made that mistake with Alyssa. Let her go dark. If she'd been chipped, we'd already know where she went. Where she was killed. I won't make that mistake again."

"I can handle myself," Ethan said. "You've both seen that. Firsthand."

"Maybe we aren't as concerned," Pam said, "with your safety as we are with your loyalty."

Ethan turned in his chair.

He'd fought this woman once in the basement of the hospital. She'd come at him with a syringe, and he'd crashed into her at full speed, driven her face into a concrete wall. He relived that moment now like the memory of a good meal, wishing he could experience it again.

"She raises a point, Ethan," Pilcher said.

"And what point is that? You don't trust me?"

"You're doing great, but it's still early times. Lots to prove."

"I want the chip out, or I don't go. It's that simple."

Pilcher's voice assumed a harder edge.

"You will be in my office crack of dawn tomorrow with a full report. Is that understood?"

"Yes."

"And now I have to threaten you."

"With what will happen to my family if I should decide to run or otherwise misbehave? Can't I just imagine the worst and assume you'll deliver? What I really need is to have a word with you in private." Ethan glanced at Pam. "You don't mind, do you?"

"Of course I don't mind."

When the door had closed behind her, Ethan said, "I'd like to get a better picture of who your daughter was."

"Why?"

"The more I know her, the better chance I'll have of finding out what happened to her."

"I think we know what happened to her, Ethan."

"I was down in her quarters yesterday. There were flowers and cards all around her door. A real outpouring. But I was wondering—did she have any enemies in the mountain? I mean, she was the boss's daughter."

Ethan thought Pilcher might erupt at this intrusion into his privacy and grief.

But instead, Pilcher leaned back in his chair and said, almost wistfully, "Alyssa was the last person to trade on her status. She could've lived in this suite with me in luxury, done whatever she wanted. But she insisted on keeping spartan living quarters and she took assignments just like everyone else. Never once sought out preferential treatment because of who she was. And everyone knew. And it made everyone love her even more."

"Did you two get along?"

"Yes."

"What did Alyssa think about all this?"

"All what?"

"The town. The surveillance. Everything."

"Early on, after we all came out of suspension, she had her idealistic moments."

"You mean she didn't agree with how you ran Wayward Pines?"

"Right. But by the time she hit twenty, she'd begun to really mature. She understood the reasons behind the cameras and the fêtes. The fence and the secrets."

"How did she become a spy?"

"Her request. The assignment came up. There were a lot of volunteers. We had a big fight about it. I didn't want her to do it. She was just twenty-four. So bright. So many other things she could've contributed to that wouldn't have put her in danger. But she stood here and said to me several months ago, 'I'm the best candidate for this mission, Daddy. You know it. I know it. Everyone knows it.'"

"So you let her go."

"As you'll find with your son soon enough, letting go is the hardest, greatest thing we can do for them."

"Thank you," Ethan said. "I feel like I know her a little bit now."

"I wish you'd really gotten the chance. She was something else."

Halfway to the doors, Ethan stopped, glanced back at Pilcher.

"Mind if I ask one more prying question?"

Pilcher smiled sadly. "Sure. Why stop now?"

"Alyssa's mother. Where is she?"

It was like something broke inside the man's face. He looked suddenly old, as if the underpinnings had been washed away.

Ethan instantly regretted asking.

The air was sucked out of the room.

Pilcher said, "Out of everyone who went into suspension, nine people never woke up on the other side. Elisabeth was one of those nine. Now I've lost my daughter too. Hug your family tonight, Ethan. Hold them tight."

* * *

The OR was down on Level 2, and the surgeon was waiting for them.

He was a roundish man with a bowed back and awkwardness of movement, as if his bones had atrophied after years of living in this mountain, and too little exposure to sunlight. His white coat dropped to his wing tips and he was already wearing a surgical mask.

As Ethan and Pam entered, the doctor looked up from a sink that ran steaming tap water.

He washed his hands furiously.

Didn't introduce himself.

Just said, "Take off your pants and lie on your stomach on the table."

Ethan looked at Pam. "You're staying for this?"

"You honestly think I'd pass up a chance to watch you get cut?"

Ethan sat down on a stool and began to pull off his boots.

Everything had been prepped.

Spread out on blue surgical cloth on a tray beside the operating table: a scalpel, tweezers, forceps, sutures, needle, scissors, needle holder, gauze, iodine, and a small, unlabeled bottle.

Ethan tugged his boots off, unbuckled his belt, and dropped his khaki pants.

The floor was cold through his socks.

With his elbow, the surgeon shut off the tap.

Ethan climbed onto the table and lay on his stomach on the cloth.

There was a mirror on the wall across the room beyond the heart monitors and IV stands. He watched the doctor finish pulling on his surgical gloves and wander over.

"How deep is the microchip?" Ethan asked.

"Not terribly," the doctor said.

He opened the bottle of iodine.

Poured some onto a cloth.

Scrubbed the back of Ethan's left leg.

"We affix them to the biceps femoris." The doctor jabbed the syringe into the smallest bottle. "Few little pinches coming," he said.

"What's in that?"

"Just a local anesthetic."

Once the back of his leg was numb, it went fast.

Ethan couldn't feel a thing, but in the reflection of the mirror, he watched the doctor lift the scalpel.

He felt some pressure.

Soon there were smears of blood on the doctor's latex gloves.

A minute later, he traded the scalpel for the tweezers.

Twenty seconds later, the microchip plunked into the metal tray beside Ethan's head.

It looked like a flake of mica.

"Do me a favor," Ethan said as the doctor pushed a piece of gauze into the wound.

"What's that?"

"Do a sloppy job on the sutures."

"Smart," Pam said. "It'll buy you some Kate cred if she thinks you cut it out yourself. Like maybe you're going rogue."

"That's what I'm thinking."

The doctor lifted the needle holder, a length of dark thread dangling.

* * *

The pain from the incision was beginning to warm in the back of Ethan's leg as he and Pam moved down the Level 1 corridor toward the cavern.

Ethan stopped at the door to Margaret's cell, leaned in toward the glass window, and cupped his hands around his eyes.

"What are you doing?" Pam asked.

"I want to see her again."

"You can't."

He squinted through the glass into darkness.

Couldn't see a thing.

"Have you worked with her?" Ethan asked.

"I have."

"What do you think of her?"

"She should be put in the incinerator with all of our specimens. Come on."

Ethan looked at Pam. "You see no benefit to learning from the abbies? They do outnumber us by a few hundred million."

"Oh, you mean so we can coexist? What kind of let's-hold-hands hippie shit are you suggesting?"

"Survival," Ethan said. "What if they aren't all mindlessly violent? If they actually possess a real intelligence, then communication is possible."

"We have everything we need in Wayward Pines."

"We can't live in this valley forever."

"How do you know that?"

"Because I don't consider the conditions in town 'living.'"

"What would you call it?"
"Imprisonment."
He turned back to the cage.
Margaret's head filled the circular window, inches away.
She stared into Ethan's eyes.
Lucid.
Utterly calm.
"A penny for your thoughts," he said.
Her black talons began to tap against the glass.

16

It was a two-bedroom Victorian on the northeast side of town, freshly painted, with two pine trees in the front yard and Wayne Johnson's last name already stenciled on the black mailbox.

Ethan stepped up onto the front porch and rapped the brass knocker.

After a moment, the door opened.

A rotund, balding, gray-skinned man looked up at Ethan, squinting against the light.

He wore a bathrobe, and what hair he still had looked slept-on and uncombed.

"Mr. Johnson?" Ethan said.

"Yes?"

"Hi, I just wanted to swing by and introduce myself. I'm Ethan Burke, sheriff of Wayward Pines." It felt strangely dirty claiming that position.

The man stared at him, confused.

"Would it be all right if I came in for a minute?"

"Um, sure."

The house still smelled unlived-in and sterile.

They sat at a small kitchen table.

Ethan took off his Stetson and unbuttoned his parka.

Casserole dishes and plates wrapped in tinfoil lined the counters.

Neighbors no doubt had been called and urged to bring lunch and dinner to Mr. Johnson during this first difficult week.

The three plates within eyeshot looked untouched.

"Are you eating?" Ethan asked.

"Haven't really had much of an appetite. People have been bringing food over."

"Good, so you're meeting the neighbors."

Wayne Johnson ignored this.

The Wayward Pines Welcome Manual issued to each resident upon their arrival lay open across the table's faux-wood veneer.

Seventy-five pages of dire threats sugarcoated as "suggestions" for living a happy life in Pines. Ethan's first week as sheriff had been spent memorizing it cover-to-cover. The book was currently open to the page that explained how food was distributed through the winter months when the gardens were in deep freeze.

"They tell me," Wayne said, "that I'm going to be working soon."

"That's right."

The man put his hands in his lap and stared at them.

"What will I be doing?"

"I'm not sure yet."

"Are you one of the people I can actually talk to?" the man asked.

"Yes," Ethan said. "Right now, you can ask me whatever you want, Mr. Johnson."

"Why is this happening to me?"

"I don't know."

"You don't know? Or you won't tell me?"

There was a section toward the beginning of the welcome manual entitled "How to Handle Questions, Fears, and Doubts About Where You Are."

Ethan pulled the manual over and thumbed through to that section.

"This chapter might offer you some guidance," Ethan said.

He felt like he was reading off a very bad script, which he didn't believe in.

"Guidance for what? I don't know where I am. I don't know what happened to me. And no one will tell me anything. I don't need guidance, I need fucking answers."

"I understand your frustration," Ethan said.

"Why doesn't the phone work? I've tried to call my mother five times. It just rings and rings. That isn't right. She's always home, always by the phone."

Ethan had been in Wayne Johnson's shoes not long ago.

Frantic.

Terrified.

Coming unhinged as he ran around town trying to make contact with the outside world.

Pilcher and Pam had set out to make Ethan believe he was losing his mind. That had been their integration plan for him from the start. Wayne Johnson's was different. He was getting what most people got: several weeks to explore town, explore the boundaries, and have several freak-outs before the tough love kicked in.

"I walked the road out of town this morning," Wayne said. "Guess what? It just looped back around into town. That isn't right. Something's off. I just drove here a couple days ago. How is it possible that the road I came in on is no longer there?"

"Look, I understand you have some questions and—"

"*Where am I?*"

His voice filled the house.

"*What the hell is this place?*"

His face was red and he was shaking.

Ethan heard himself say, "It's just a town, Mr. Johnson." And the scary thing was he hadn't even considered his answer. It had just sprung out of him like it had been programmed. He hated himself for it. He'd been told that very thing over and over during his integration.

The man said, "Just a town? Yeah. Just a town where you aren't allowed to leave or have contact with the world outside."

"Understand something," Ethan said. "Every person in Wayward Pines has sat where you sit, including me. It gets better."

Congratulations. Now you're out and out lying to the man.

"I'm telling you that I want to leave, Sheriff. That I don't want to be here any longer. That I want to go home. Back to my life like it was before. What exactly do you say to that?"

"It's not possible."

"Not possible for me to leave?"

"That's right."

"And what authority do you think you have to hold me here against my will?"

Ethan stood.

He was beginning to feel sick.

"What authority?" the man asked.

"The sooner you make your peace with your new life here, the better things will be for you."

Ethan put on his hat.

The back of his leg was beginning to hurt.

"I wish you'd just say what you mean," Mr. Johnson said.

"I'm sorry?"

"If I try to leave, you'll kill me. That's the gist of it, right? The hard bit of truth you've been dancing around?"

Ethan patted the welcome manual. "Everything's here," he said. "All you need to know. Inside the town is life. Outside is death. It's really that simple."

As Ethan walked out of the kitchen and back toward the front door, Wayne Johnson called after him, "Am I dead?"

Ethan's hand was on the doorknob.

"Please, Sheriff, just tell me. I can handle it. Did I die in that accident?"

He didn't need to look back to know the man was crying.

"Is this hell?"

"It's just a town, Mr. Johnson."

As Ethan walked outside, a single thought ran through his head.

Pam would be proud.

And he felt, for the first time in his life, truly evil.

* * *

Ethan timed his walk home from work to stop by the jewelry store and then to pass by Theresa's real estate office just as she was quitting for the day. He rounded the corner onto Main, the back of his leg throbbing at the incision site.

The sky had gone overcast and the streetlamps were on and it was bitterly cold.

There she was, a half block down, locking up for the night.

She wore a gray, woolen trench coat and a knit hat that tied under her chin—just a few sprigs of blond hair poking out. She hadn't seen him yet, and as she fought to tug the key out of the lock, the vacancy in her face broke something inside of him.

She looked shattered.

Threadbare.

He called her name.

She glanced back at him.

She was in a dark place. He could see that instantly. Would've bet money she'd been fighting tears all day. He reached her and put his arm around her.

They walked together down the sidewalk.

There were a handful of people out, locking up shops, walking home from work.

He asked how her day was and she said, "Fine," in a voice that undercut the meaning of the word.

They moved catty-corner across the intersection of Sixth Street.

Theresa said, "I can't do this."

There were tears in her voice now, her throat clogged with emotion.

"We need to talk," he said.

"I know."

"But not here. Not like this."

"Can they hear us now?"

"If we aren't careful. Speak softly and stare at the ground. There's something I didn't tell you last night."

"What?"

Ethan hooked his arm around her waist, pulled her in close, said, "Hang on a second." They went past a streetlamp on the corner that Ethan knew housed a camera and a microphone. When they were fifty feet from the lamp, he said, "Were you aware there's a microchip in the back of your leg?"

"No."

"It's how they track you."

"Do you have one too?"

"I just had mine removed. Temporarily."

"Why?"

"I'll explain later. I want to take yours out. It's the only way we'll be able to really talk."

Their house stood a little ways down the hill.

"Will it hurt?" she asked.

"Yes. I'll have to cut you. We'll do it in the chair in the study."

"Why there?"

"It's a blind spot in our house. The only one. The cameras can't see us there."

Her lips curled into the tiniest smile. "So that's why you always want me in the study."

"Exactly."

"Sure you can do this?"

"I think so. Are you up for it?"

Theresa drew in a deep breath, blew it out.

"I will be."

* * *

Ethan stood under the archway between the kitchen and the dining room, staring at Ben, who sat at the table, swallowed in a big coat with a blanket draped over his shoulders. The only sound in the house was the squiggle of the boy's pencil across a sheet of paper.

"Hey, buddy," Ethan said. "How goes it?"

"Good."

Ben didn't look up from his drawing.

"What are you working on there?"

Ben pointed at the centerpiece of the table—a crystal vase holding a bouquet of flowers that had long since succumbed to the interior cold. Cast-off, colorless petals wilted on the table around the base of the vase.

"How was school today?"

"Good."

"What'd you learn?"

This snapped Ben out of his concentration.

It was an honest slip—a holdover from Ethan's life before.

The boy looked up, confused.

Ethan said, "Never mind."

Even inside the house, it was cold enough for Ethan to see his son's breath.

The rage came out of nowhere.

He turned suddenly and walked down the hallway, jerked open the back door, crossed the deck into the yard.

The grass was yellowed, dying.

The row of aspen trees that separated their property from the neighbor's had dropped their leaves practically overnight.

The floor of the woodshed was still littered with scraps of bark and chips of pine from last year's load. Prying the ax out of the flat-topped splitting stump, Ethan had a vision of Theresa out here, chopping firewood alone in the cold, him still in suspension.

He stormed back into the house, dark energy riding on his shoulders.

Theresa was in the dining room with Ben, watching him sketch.

"Ethan? Everything okay?"

"Fine," he said.

The first strike split the coffee table down the middle, its two sides caving inward.

"Ethan! What the hell?"

Theresa in the kitchen now.

"I can see . . ." Ethan raised the ax. "My son's fucking breath inside our fucking house."

The next strike devastated the left half of the table, fracturing the oak into three pieces.

"Ethan, that's our furniture—"

He looked at his wife. "*Was* our furniture. Now it's heating fuel. There a copy of the paper lying around?"

"In our bedroom."

"Mind getting it?"

By the time Theresa returned with the *Wayward Light*, Ethan had broken the coffee table into small enough pieces to put inside the stove.

They wadded up sheets of newsprint and stuffed them under the kindling.

Ethan opened the damper, lit the paper.

As the fire grew, he called for Ben.

The boy appeared, sketchpad under his arm. "Yes?"

"Come draw by the fire."

Ben looked at the butchered coffee table.

"Come on, son."

The boy took a seat in a rocker beside the woodstove.

Ethan said, "I'll leave the door open for you. When that fire gets going, add another piece."

"Okay."

Ethan looked at Theresa, cut his eyes toward the hall.

He grabbed a plate from the kitchen and followed her back to the study.

Locked them inside.

The light coming through the window was gray, weak, and fading.

Theresa mouthed, "You sure they can't see us in here?"

He leaned in, whispered, "Yeah, but they will be able to hear."

He sat her down in the chair, touched his finger to his lips.

Reaching into his pocket, he pulled out a slip of paper, which he'd folded thirty minutes ago at the station.

Theresa opened it.

I need access to the back of your left leg. Take off your pants and turn over. I'm sorry but this is going to hurt a lot. You have to keep quiet. Please trust me. I love you so much.

She looked up from the note.

Scared.

Reaching down, she began to unbutton her jeans.

He helped her slide them down her thighs, something inescapably erotic as he tugged them off—the impulse to keep going, to keep undressing her. Was after all their fuck chair.

Theresa turned crosswise and extended her legs into the air like she was stretching.

Ethan moved around to the side of the chair.

Ninety percent sure he was out of view of the camera, which, from what he'd seen in Pilcher's office, aimed down at the bookshelf across the room.

He set the plate on the floor and removed his coat.

Kneeling down, he opened one of the large flap pockets and took out everything he'd raided from his office that afternoon.

Bottle of rubbing alcohol.

Handful of cotton balls.

Gauze.

Tube of superglue.

Penlight.

A pair of forceps he'd pocketed from the OR in the superstructure.

A Spyderco Harpy.

He stared at the back of Theresa's left leg as the scent of woodsmoke crept in from the living room under the door. It took him a moment to zero in on the old, white incision scar, which resembled the footprint of a tiny caterpillar. Opening the bottle of rubbing alcohol, he held a cotton ball to the mouth and turned it upside down.

The sharp bright smell of isopropyl filled the room.

He wiped the wet cotton ball across her scar and then scrubbed down the plate. He opened the Spyderco folder. Its blade was an evil-looking piece of cutlery—fully serrated and curving to a point like the claw of a bird of prey. He wet another cotton ball and sterilized the blade and then the forceps.

Theresa watched him, the look in her eyes something akin to horror.

He mouthed, "Don't watch."

She nodded, lips pursing, tension hardening her jawline.

When he touched the knifepoint to the top of the scar, her body went rigid. He didn't have the nerve built up to just start cutting her, but he dove in anyway.

Theresa sucked a hard breath through her teeth as the blade entered.

Ethan's eyes fixed briefly on her hands, balled into sudden fists.

He detached himself.

The blade was psycho-sharp, but this was a small gift. With no resistance—like cutting warm butter—he pulled it easily down the length of his wife's scar. It didn't feel like he was hurting her, but her face was scrunched and turning red while her knuckles blanched and a straight line of blood ran down the back of her leg.

The knifepoint was in a quarter, maybe half an inch, and he wondered if he'd gone deep enough to expose the muscle.

He carefully withdrew the blade and laid it on the plate. Blood coated the end of the Harpy with the consistency of motor oil. The beads and spatters popped on the white porcelain. Theresa's panties were stained red and blood pooled in the crevices of the chair.

Ethan took the forceps.

He turned on the penlight and stuck it between his teeth.

Leaned in close to study the new incision.

With his left hand, he spread the mouth of the cut open.

With his right, he worked the forceps inside the incision.

Tears streamed down Theresa's face, her hair clutched in both hands. He doubted she could stand more cutting in the event he needed to go deeper.

Slowly, he opened the forceps.

Theresa made her loudest noise yet—something deep and guttural in the back of her throat.

Her fingers clawing the upholstered arms of the chair.

The hardest part was not offering her a single word of encouragement or comfort.

He shined the penlight into the wound.

Saw the muscle.

The microchip reflected a mother-of-pearl shimmer from the surface of Theresa's hamstring.

He lifted the Harpy off the plate.

Steady hands.

Sweat burned in his eyes.

Almost there, baby.

He pushed the blade back into the wound as blood poured down her leg. Theresa flinching when the tip of the Harpy touched the muscle, but he didn't hesitate.

Ethan worked the knifepoint between the muscle and the chip and broke it free.

He withdrew the blade, the microchip barely clinging to the end.

He hadn't been breathing.

Drew in a big gulp of air as he set the knife on the plate.

Theresa eyeing him, desperate to know.

He nodded and smiled and picked up a handful of gauze. She grabbed it, held it to the back of her leg. Blood came through almost instantly and Ethan handed her a fresh one.

The worst of the pain seemed to be retreating, the flush leaving her face like a fever breaking.

After five minutes, the flow became manageable.

After twenty, it had stopped altogether.

Ethan wet one last cotton ball with alcohol and cleaned the incision site while Theresa cringed. Then he pinched closed the gaping wound, ripped the top off the superglue with his teeth, and squeezed out a generous bead, which he extended down the length of her cut.

It was almost dark outside now and growing colder by the second inside the study.

He held the incision closed for five minutes, then let go.

The adhesive held.

Ethan moved around to the front of the chair and put his lips to Theresa's ear.

"I got it out. You did amazing."

"It was so hard not to scream."

"The glue is working, holding it closed, but you should stay put for a little while. Give it time to really set."

"I'm freezing."

"I'll bring you blankets."

She nodded.

He smiled at her.

She still had tears in the corners of her eyes.

She mouthed, "Let me see it."

He lifted the Harpy off the plate and held the end of the blade up to Theresa's face.

The microchip sat in cooling blood that was becoming more and more viscous.

The muscles in her jaw tensed with a flicker of anger. Violation.

She looked at Ethan.

No words spoken, but that didn't matter. He could see them written plainly across her face—*Those fuckers.*

He picked the microchip off the knife, cleaned the blood and tissue with a piece of gauze, and presented it to her. Then he reached into his lapel pocket and lifted out the gold necklace he'd bought that afternoon. It consisted of a thin, braided chain with a heart-shaped locket.

She said, "You shouldn't have."

Ethan opened the locket, whispered, "Keep the microchip inside the heart. Unless I tell you otherwise, you have to wear this necklace at all times."

* * *

It was actually warm in the living room. Ben's cheeks glowed in the firelight. He was sketching the open woodstove. The flames. The blackening wood inside. The pieces of the smashed coffee table scattered around the base.

"Where's Mom?"

"Reading in the study. You need anything?"

"No."

"Let's not bother her for a while, okay? She's had a hard day."

Ethan gathered up an armful of blankets from the stash under the sofa and headed back to the study.

Theresa was shivering.

He wrapped her up.

Said, "I'll make you something warm for dinner."

She smiled through the pain. "That'd be great."

Then he leaned in and whispered, "Come out in one hour, but no matter how much it hurts, walk straight. If they catch you limping on the cameras, they'll know."

* * *

Ethan stood at the kitchen sink, staring into the blackness out the window. Three days ago, it had been the end of summer. Leaves just beginning to take on color. Jesus, fall had been a blink—from August to December in seventy-two hours.

The fruit and veggies in the refrigerator were almost certainly the last fresh things they would eat for months to come.

He filled a pot with water and put it on the range to boil.

Stuck a roomy saucepan beside it, turned the eye up to medium, and poured a spot of olive oil.

They had five vine-ripened tomatoes left—just enough.

A dinner plan percolated.

He smashed a clove of garlic, diced an onion, dumped it all into the oil.

While things sizzled, he chopped tomatoes.

He could've been standing in their kitchen in Seattle. Late Saturday afternoons, he'd put on a Thelonious Monk record, open a bottle of red, and immerse himself in cooking a fabulous dinner for his family. No better way to unwind after a long week. This moment had the feel of those peaceful evenings, all the trappings of normal. Except that a half hour ago he'd cut a tracking chip out of the back of his wife's leg in the one spot in their house that wasn't under constant surveillance.

Except for that.

He added the tomatoes and crushed them into the onions and poured more oil and leaned over the stovetop into the sweet-smelling wafts of steam, trying, just for a beat, to embrace the fantasy.

* * *

Theresa came out as he was rinsing the pasta. She was smiling and he thought he sensed pain in it—a subtle strain—but there was no falter to her gait. They ate dinner as a family on a blanket in the living room, crowded around the woodstove and listening to the radio.

Hecter Gaither was playing Chopin.

The food was good.

The heat enveloping.

And it all passed too quickly.

* * *

After midnight.

Ben slept.

They'd burned through the coffee table in two hours, and now the Victorian was plunging back into the deep freeze.

Ethan and Theresa lay facing each other in bed.

He whispered, "Are you ready?"

She nodded.

"Where's your necklace?"

"I'm wearing it."

"Take it off, leave it on the bedside table."

When she'd done it, she said, "Now what?"

"We wait one minute."

* * *

They dressed in the dark.

Ethan looked in on their son, found the boy out cold.

He walked downstairs with Theresa.

Neither said a word.

As he opened the front door, Ethan raised the hood of his black sweatshirt and motioned for Theresa to do the same.

They went outside.

Streetlamps and porch lights punctuated the darkness.

Frigid and no stars.

They walked out into the middle of the street.

Ethan said, "We can talk now. How's your leg?"

"Agony."

"You're a rock star, babe."

"I thought I was going to pass out. I wish I had."

They moved west toward the park.

Soon they could hear the river.

"Are we really safe out here?" Theresa asked.

"We're not safe anywhere. But at least without our chips, the cameras won't pick us up."

"I feel like I'm fifteen again, sneaking out of my parents' house. It's so quiet."

"I love coming out late. You never crept out before? Not even once?"

"Of course not."

They left the street and wandered into the playing field.

Fifty yards away, the bulb of a single streetlamp shone down on the swing set.

They walked until they reached the end of the park, the edge of the river.

Sat down in the dying grass.

Ethan could smell the water but he couldn't see it. He couldn't see his hands in front of his face. Invisibility had never felt so comforting.

"I shouldn't have told you," he said. "It was a moment of weakness. I just couldn't stand to have this lie between us. For us not to be on the same page."

"Of course you should have told me."

"Why?"

"Because this town is bullshit."

"But it's not like there's something better out there. If you ever dreamed of leaving Wayward Pines, I destroyed that sliver of hope."

"I'll take the truth any day. And I still want to leave."

"It's not possible."

"Anything's possible."

"Our family would be slaughtered in the first hour."

"I can't live like this, Ethan. I thought about it all day. I can't *stop* thinking about it. I won't live in a house where I'm spied on. Where I have to whisper to have a real conversation with my husband. I'm done living in a town where my son goes to school and I can't know what he's being taught. Do you know what they're teaching him?"

"No."

"And you're fine with that?"

"Of course not."

"So fucking *do* something about it."

"Pilcher has a hundred and sixty people living inside the mountain."

"There are four or five hundred of us."

"They're armed. We're not. Look, I didn't tell you what was going on so you'd ask me to blow everything up."

"I won't live like this."

"What do you want from me, Theresa?"

"Fix it."

"You don't know what you're asking."

"You want your son growing up—"

"If burning this town to the fucking ground would make things just a little better for you and Ben, I would've torched it my first day on the job."

"We're losing him."

"What are you talking about?"

"It started last year. It's only getting worse."

"How?"

"He's drifting away, Ethan. I don't know what they're teaching him, but it's stealing him away from us. There's a wall going up."

"I'll find out."

"You promise?"

"Yes, but you have to promise me something."

"What?"

"You won't breathe a word of anything I've told you. Not a single detail to anyone."

"I'll try my best."

"One last thing."

"What?"

"This is the first time we've been together in Wayward Pines without the cameras watching."

"So?"

He leaned over and kissed her in the dark.

* * *

They walked through town.

Ethan felt freezing motes begin to strike his face.

He said, "Is that what I think it is?"

In the distance, the light of a lonely streetlamp became a stage for snowflakes.

There was no wind. They fell straight down.

"Winter's here," Theresa said.

"But it was just summer several days ago."

"Summer's long. Winter's long. Spring and fall shoot past. The last winter went on for nine months. The snow was ten feet deep at Christmas."

He reached down and took hold of her mittened hand.

Not a sound in the entire valley.

Total hush.

Ethan said, "We could be anywhere. Some village in the Swiss Alps. Just two lovers out for a midnight stroll."

"Don't do that," Theresa warned.

"Do what?"

"Pretend we're in some other place and time. The people who pretend in this town go mad."

They stayed off Main, kept to the side streets.

The houses were dark. With no woodsmoke in the valley, the snow-streaked air carried a clean, rinsed quality.

Theresa said, "Sometimes, I hear screams and screeches. They're far away, but I hear them. He never mentions it, but I know that Ben hears them too."

"Those are the abbies," Ethan said.

"Strange he's never asked me what the sound is. It's like he already knows."

They walked south beyond the hospital on the road that purported to lead out of town.

Streetlamps fell behind.

Darkness closed in.

A fragile quarter inch of snow dusted the pavement.

Ethan said, "I paid a visit to Wayne Johnson this afternoon."

"I'm supposed to take him dinner tomorrow night."

"I lied to him, Theresa. I told him this gets better. I told him it was just a town."

"Me too. But that's what they make you say, right?"

"Nobody can make me do anything. It's always a choice in the end."

"How's he doing?"

"How do you think? Scared. Confused. He thinks he's dead and this is hell."

"Will he run?"

"Probably."

At the edge of the forest, Ethan stopped.

He said, "The fence is about a mile straight ahead."

"What are they like?" she asked. "The abbies."

"Like all the bad things you have nightmares about when you're a kid. They're the monsters in the closet, under the bed. There are millions of them."

"And you're telling me we have a *fence* between us and them?"

"It's a big fence. Has electricity going through it."

"Oh, well, in that case."

"And there's a few snipers up on the peaks."

"While Pilcher and his people live in safety in the mountain."

Theresa walked a few steps down the road, the snow collecting on her shoulders, on her hoodie.

"Tell me something. What's the point of all those pretty little houses with white picket fences?"

"I think he's trying to preserve our way of life."

"For who? Us or him? Maybe someone should tell him our way of life is over."

"I've tried."

"We should all be in that mountain, figuring something out. I'm not living the rest of my life in some psycho's model train town."

"Well, the man in charge doesn't share your view. Look, we aren't going to fix this tonight."

"I know."

"But we will fix it."

"You swear?"

"I swear."

"Even if it means losing everything?"

"Even if it means we lose our lives." Ethan stepped forward, opened his arms, pulled her in close. "I'm asking you to trust me. You have to go on like nothing has changed."

"That's going to make my psychiatrist appointments interesting."

"What appointments?"

"Once a month, I go to an appointment, talk to a shrink. I think everyone does. It's the only time we're allowed to open up to another human being. We get to share our fears, our thoughts, our secrets."

"You can talk about anything?"

"Yes. I thought you knew about these meetings."

Ethan felt his hackles rising.

He pushed the rage back down—it wouldn't help him now.

"Who do you see?" he asked. "A man? A woman?"

"A woman. She's very pretty."

"What's her name?"

"Pam."

He closed his eyes, drew in a deep, cold shot of piney air.

"Do you know her?" Theresa asked.

"Yes."

"And she's one of Pilcher's?"

"She's pretty much his second in command. You can't tell her anything about tonight. Or your chip. You understand? Nothing. Our family would be killed."

"Okay."

"Has she ever inspected the back of your leg?"

"No."

"Has anyone?"

"No."

He checked his watch—2:45 a.m. Nearly time.

He said, "Look, I've got someplace to be. I'll walk you home."

"Seeing Kate again?" she asked.

"And her group. Pilcher's dying to know what they're up to."

"Let me come."

"I can't. She's expecting just me. If suddenly you show up too, things could get—"

"Awkward?"

"It could spook her. Besides, she and her people might have killed someone."

"Who?"

"Pilcher's daughter. She was a spy. Point is, I don't know if they're dangerous or not."

"Please be careful."

Ethan took his wife's hand and they turned back toward home.

The lights of Wayward Pines looked hazy through the snow.

He said, "Always, my love."

17

Standing in the forest among the pines, she thought there was nothing prettier than snowflakes falling through night vision.

Ten years ago, there'd been a forest fire three miles from the center of town. She'd stood in the burning trees watching embers rain down from the sky. This reminded her of that day, except the snow glowed green. Burning green. Each flake leaving a luminescent trail in its wake. And the floor of the forest and the road and the snow-covered roofs of the houses in town—they all glowed like LED screens.

The snow that had collected on Ethan's and Theresa's shoulders glowed too.

As if they'd been sprinkled with magic dust.

Pam didn't even have to hide behind a tree.

As far as she could tell, Ethan hadn't brought a flashlight, and it was so dark out here in the woods, beyond the reach of streetlamps and porch lights, that she had no fear of discovery. She needed only to stand in total silence, fifteen feet away, and listen.

She wasn't supposed to be here.

Technically, she'd been sent to observe the new arrival, Wayne Johnson. It was his second night in Wayward Pines, and night two was historically a night for runners. But she was starting to think that Wayne might fall in line faster than the projections. That he wouldn't pose any significant problems. He'd been an encyclopedia salesman after all. Something about the nature of his profession, at least to her, suggested conformity.

So instead, she'd slipped into the empty house across from Ethan's Victorian and dug in behind the curtains in the living room with a straight-on view of his front door.

Pilcher would be pissed that she'd abandoned her mission. There'd be a little hell to pay on the front side of this decision, but on the back—when her boss had finally calmed down and heard her out—he'd be thrilled with the results of her choice.

She'd done it before with Kate Ballinger. Staked out the woman's house at night for two weeks before she finally caught her leaving. But tracking her and her husband had been another story. Pam had lost her soon after when Kate had literally disappeared underground. She'd tried to convince Pilcher to let her devote some real resources, but he'd shot her down since Alyssa was already on the case.

How'd that fucking work out for you?

Her opinion, the old man put up with way too much shit from his sheriff.

She didn't get it. Didn't understand what it was exactly that Pilcher saw in Burke. Yes, Ethan could handle himself. Yes, he had the skill set to run the town, but Jesus, no one was worth the trouble he'd put them through.

If it was her call—and one day it would be—she'd have dealt with Ethan and his family two weeks ago.

Chained Ben and Theresa to the pole beyond the fence.

Let the abbies come for them.

Sometimes, she fell asleep imagining the screams of Ethan's son, picturing Ethan's face while he watched his boy, and then his wife, eviscerated and eaten before his eyes. She wouldn't feed Ethan to the abbies, though. She'd put him in lockup for a month, maybe two. Hell, maybe a year. However long it took. Make him watch and rewatch the abbies devouring his family. Keep the footage rolling on an endless loop in his cell. The screams turned up. And only when the man was broken in every way imaginable, when his body had wasted itself into nothing but a shell for a shattered mind, *then*, only then, she'd release him back into town. Give him a nice little job—maybe a waiter, maybe a secretary—something subservient, boring, soul crushing.

Of course, she'd check in on him each week.

Hopefully, if she'd done it right, there would be just enough of his mind left to remember who she was and all that she had taken from him.

And he would live out the rest of his days as a pathetic scab of a human being.

That was how you dealt with men like Ethan Burke. With men who tried to run. You annihilated them. You made them a horrifying example for everyone to see.

You sure as fuck didn't make them sheriff.

She smiled.

She had caught him.

Finally.

This fantasy that she'd been dreaming about as she lay in her room inside the mountain struck her, for the first time, as achievable.

She wasn't exactly sure of what to do next, of how to use this ammunition to realize that dark, beautiful fantasy, but she would think of something.

It made her so happy.

Standing in the dark between the pines with the burning specks of green falling all around her, she couldn't make herself stop smiling.

18

Ethan stood on the corner of Main and Eighth in front of the double doors that opened into the four-hundred-seat opera house. The building had been locked up for the night, and through the glass, the lobby was dark, none of the framed movie or Broadway posters visible. Performances were held on a semi-regular basis—music recitals, community theater, town hall meetings. Classic movies were shown on Friday nights, and every two years, mayoral and city council elections were held here.

Ethan checked his watch—3:08 a.m.

It wasn't like Kate to be eight minutes late to anything.

He buried his hands deep in his pocket.

The snow had stopped. The cold was merciless.

He shifted his weight between his feet, but the movement did little to warm him.

A shadow appeared around the corner of the building and moved straight toward him, footsteps squeaking in the snow.

He straightened—not Kate.

She didn't move like this and wasn't nearly as big.

Ethan clutched the Harpy in his pocket, thinking, *I should've left when she was five minutes late. That was a sign something was wrong.*

A man in a black hoodie stepped in front of him.

He was taller than Ethan and wide through the shoulders. Wore stubble on his face and reeked of the dairy.

Ethan slowly tugged the folder out of his pocket, working the tip of his thumb into the hole in the blade.

One flick, he'd have the knife open.

One swipe, he'd have the man open.

"That is a very bad idea," the man said.

"Where's Kate?"

"Here's what's going to happen. First. Knife goes back in your pocket."

Ethan slid his hand into his pocket, but he didn't let go of the knife.

He recognized the man from his file photo, but he'd never seen him in town, and in this moment, outside in the cold and his nerves beginning to fray, he couldn't recall his name.

"Second. See that bush?" The man pointed across the intersection of Main and Eighth toward a large juniper. It loomed behind a wooden bench—a bus stop that had never seen a bus. Just one more artificial detail of this place. Once a week, an old woman who was losing her mind sat all day long on that bench, waiting for a bus that would never come.

"I'm going across the street now," the man said. "Meet me behind that bush in three minutes."

Before Ethan could respond, the man had turned away.

Ethan watched him trudge across the empty intersection as the overhead traffic light changed from yellow to red.

He waited.

Part of him screaming that something had come off the rails—should've been Kate here to meet him.

That he needed to go home right now.

The man reached the other side of the street and disappeared behind the bush.

Ethan waited until the traffic light had passed through three cycles. Then he stepped out from under the awning and started into the street.

Crossing, he finally remembered the man's name—Bradley Imming.

Up and down Main, all was quiet.

It unnerved him—the stark emptiness of the street. The dark buildings. The single traffic signal humming above him as it cast alternating swaths of green, yellow, and red onto the snow.

He arrived at the bench, moved around the bush.

Something bad was going to happen.

He could feel it.

A premonitory thrumming behind his eyes like a warning bell.

He never heard the footsteps, just felt a warm push of breath against the back of his neck a half second before the world went black.

His first instinct was to fight, his hand digging back into his pocket, probing for the knife.

The ground hit him hard, the side of his face shoved into snow, the weight of what must have been several men crushing down on his spine.

He smelled the sweet, rich funk of the dairy again.

Bradley's voice whispered in his left ear, "You just settle right on down."

"The fuck are you doing?"

"You didn't strike me as a man who would willingly wear a hood. I read you right?"

"Yep."

Ethan strained, one last-ditch effort to force his arm out from under his chest, but it was no use. He was thoroughly immobilized.

"We're gonna take a little walk around town," Imming said. "Get you good and disoriented."

"Kate didn't say anything about this."

"You wanna see her tonight or not?"

"Yes."

"Then this is how it has to be. These are what you call nonnegotiable terms. Or we could just call the whole thing off right now."

"No. I need to see her."

"We're gonna get up now. Then we'll help you up. You aren't gonna take a swing at me or anything, are you?"

"I'll try to restrain myself."

The weight lifted.

Ethan caught a desperately needed breath.

Hands grabbed him under his arms, hauled him onto his feet, but didn't let go.

They led him out into the intersection of Main and Eighth, Ethan clinging to the sense that he was facing north.

Imming said, "Remember Pin the Tail on the Donkey? We're gonna spin your ass around, partner, but don't worry—we won't let you fall."

They spun him for a good twenty seconds, fast enough that the world went on spinning even after they had stopped.

Imming said to the men, "Let's take him that way."

Ethan was dizzy on his feet, swerving like a drunk stumbling home after last call, but they kept him upright.

They walked a long time, far past the point of Ethan having the foggiest idea of where he was.

Nobody spoke.

There was only the sound of their breathing and their footsteps in the snow.

* * *

Finally, they stopped.

Ethan heard a creaking sound, like something opening on a rusty hinge.

Imming said, "Just a heads-up, this part's a little tricky. Turn him around, boys. I'll go down first. And check the knot on the back of his hood again."

When they'd turned him a hundred and eighty degrees, Imming said, "We're going to lower you onto your knees." The location of his voice had changed, almost like he was underneath Ethan's feet now.

Ethan's knees hit the snow.

He felt the cold bleed through the denim.

Imming said, "I'm taking hold of your boot, putting it on a step. You feel that?" The sole of Ethan's right boot touched the narrow side of a one-by-four. "Now put your other boot beside it. Good. Boys, hold his arms. Sheriff, go on and take another step down."

Even though he couldn't see, Ethan felt as if he were perched over a great height.

He stepped down onto the next rung.

"Boys, put his hands on the top rung."

"How far of a drop is it?" Ethan asked. "Or do I even want to know?"

"You got about twenty more steps to go."

Imming's voice sounded distant, far below him now, and it echoed.

Ethan ran his hands across the rung to gauge its width.

The ladder was rickety.

It shifted and groaned and shuddered with each descending step.

When his boots finally reached the hard, broken surface below, Imming grabbed him by the arm and dragged him several steps away.

Ethan heard the ladder rattling, the other men starting down, and again the grind of that rusty hinge.

Somewhere above, a door banged shut.

Imming moved around behind him and untied the knot.

Off came the hood.

Ethan stood on the most rotten-looking concrete he'd ever laid eyes on. He looked at Imming. The man held a kerosene lantern that muddied his face in a collage of light and shadow.

Ethan said, "What is this place, Bradley?"

"Know my name, do you? How nice. Before we get to what this place is, let's have us a chat about whether or not you'll be breathing long enough to find out. Whether you get to come with us, or if we kill you where you stand."

The sound of shuffling steps spun Ethan around.

He stared into the eyes of two young men in black hoodies, each holding a machete and glaring at him with an intensity that suggested they might actually want to use them.

"You were given a warning," Brad said.

"No chip or don't bother coming."

"That's right. And now we get to see how well you follow instructions. Strip down."

"Excuse me?"

"Get naked."

"I don't think so."

"It works like this. They're going to examine every square inch of your clothes while I examine every square inch of your body. I understand you were chipped when you met with Kate last night. That means we better find a nice, fresh, ugly-as-sin, stitched-up cut on the back of your leg. If we don't, if I arrive at the conclusion you're trying to pull one past us, guess what?"

"Brad, I did exactly—"

"Guess. What."

"What?"

"We're going to hack you to death with machetes right here. And I know what you're thinking. 'That would start a war, Brad.'

That's what you're thinking, right? Well guess what again? We don't give a fuck. We're ready."

Ethan unbuckled his belt, shoved his jeans and briefs down his legs, and said, "Knock yourselves out."

Ethan pulled off his hoodie and handed it to one of the men with a machete. As he came out of his undershirt, Brad knelt down behind him and ran a gloved finger over the incision.

"It's fresh," he said. "You do this yourself?"

"Yeah."

"When?"

"This morning."

"Best keep it clean while it heals. Get your boots off."

"Aren't you gonna buy me dinner first?"

Tough crowd—not even a snigger.

Soon Ethan was standing naked.

The kerosene lantern didn't shed much light as the three men crouched around the glow, inspecting Ethan's clothes and turning them inside out—every sleeve, every pocket.

The walls of the ancient culvert were six feet apart and six feet high. Everywhere he looked, the concrete was crumbling to the point that it barely resembled concrete. This could've been the catacombs beneath some European city, although in all likelihood, it was simply one of the last remaining pieces of infrastructure from the original, twenty-first-century Wayward Pines.

The tunnel ran on a slight incline toward what Ethan figured was the east side of town. It made sense. That big wall of mountains probably drained copious amounts of water during thunderstorms. Massive snowmelt when summer roared in. Even now, a trickle of water meandered through the disintegrating concrete under Ethan's feet.

Brad looked up, tossed his undershirt to him, said, "You can get dressed."

* * *

As they walked up the tunnel, their footsteps splashing in the runoff, a palpable disappointment hung in the cold, dank air—

these farm boys had wanted to kill him, had been aching to dismember him. He just hadn't given them cause.

The ceiling was low enough to force Ethan to walk hunched over.

The tunnel lay in ruin.

Vines trailed down the walls.

Gnarled rebar showed through the concrete.

Roots.

Lines of snowmelt branched down the walls and dripped from the ceiling.

The lantern only showed what lay twenty feet ahead, and the sound of tiny, scurrying footsteps seemed to be perpetually just beyond the light's reach.

They passed through intersections with other tunnels.

By more ladders that ascended into darkness.

Ethan's boots crushed all manner of things.

Rocks.

Dirt.

Debris carried down from the mountains in heavy rainstorms.

A rat's skull.

* * *

He didn't know how long they trudged through that firelit darkness.

It seemed to take both ages and no time at all.

The quality of the air changed.

It had been stagnant and marginally warmer than conditions in town.

Now they were walking into a steady breeze that brought the fresh chill of the world above.

The trickle running down the floor of the tunnel had expanded into a fast-moving stream, and instead of just the noise of their footfalls in the water, a new, more substantial sound had begun to build.

They walked out of the tunnel into a rocky streambed.

Ethan followed the men as they scrambled up the bank.

When they reached level ground and stopped for a breather, he finally identified the noise that was now so overbearing he would've had to shout to be heard.

He couldn't see it in the oppressive, starless dark, but in the near distance, a waterfall was crashing into the ground. He could hear the main cascade pummeling rock with a constant, thudding *splat*, and his face was damp with mist.

The men were already moving on and he followed the glow of the lamp like a lifeline as they climbed into a dense pine wood.

There was no path that he could see.

The white noise of the falls slowly faded away until he heard nothing but the sound of his own respirations in the increasingly thin air.

He had been cold in the tunnel. Now he sweated.

And still they climbed.

Trees clustered so closely that only the faintest dusting of snow had found its way to the forest floor.

Ethan kept looking back down the hillside, straining to see the lights of Wayward Pines, but it was all as black as pitch.

Suddenly there was no place else for the woods to go.

The trees simply ended at a wall of rock.

The men didn't stop, didn't even pause, just walked on, right up the face of it.

Imming shouted back, "It's steep but there's a path. Just step exactly where we do, and be glad it's dark."

"Why?" Ethan asked.

The men just laughed.

The forest had been steep.

This was insane.

Imming hooked the lantern onto a leather strap and slung it over his shoulder so he could use all four appendages.

Because you needed them.

The mountain swept up well beyond the shit-yourself side of fifty degrees. A steel cable had been bolted into the rock and there was some semblance of a path running alongside it—small footholds and indentations in the rock that appeared to suggest a trail. Most were natural. Some looked man-made. It all looked suicidal.

Ethan clung to the rusted cable—it was life.

They ascended.

Nothing to see but the meager patch of lantern-lit rock in their immediate vicinity.

At the first switchback, the pitch steepened.

Ethan had no concept of how high they had climbed, but he had a terrifying sense that they were already above the forest.

The wind kicked up.

Without the protection of the trees below, the rock had collected a quarter inch of snow.

Now it was steep *and* slippery.

Even Imming and his men slowed their manic pace, everyone taking careful steps, making sure each foothold was sound.

Ethan's hands grew stiff with cold.

At this height, the cable had been lacquered with snow, and each new step required Ethan to brush it off before proceeding.

Past the sixth switchback, the cliff abandoned all reason and went vertical.

Ethan was shivering now.

His legs had turned to jelly.

He couldn't be sure, but it felt like the strain of climbing had ripped the stitches at his incision site, a trail of blood running down the back of his leg and into his boot.

He stopped to catch his breath and refortify his nerve.

When he looked up again, the lantern had vanished.

There was nothing above him, nothing below.

Just endless, swimming darkness.

"Sheriff!"

Imming's voice.

Ethan looked up and down again—still nothing.

"Burke! Over here!"

He glanced across the cliff.

There was the light, twenty feet away, but they weren't climbing anymore. They had somehow moved across the sheer face of the cliff.

"You coming or what?"

Ethan glanced down and saw it: one long step away, a single plank, six inches wide, had been bolted into the rock with a smaller cable running parallel above it.

"Let's go!" Imming yelled.

Ethan stepped from the foothold, across two feet of emptiness, onto the six-inch plank. It was coated with slush and the back half of his cowboy boots hung off the edge.

He clutched the cable, went to move his right boot, but its smooth sole lost traction on the icy board.

His feet went out from under him.

The scream he heard was his own.

His chest slammed against the rock, one hand barely gripping the cable as his weight tugged him down, the twined metal biting into his fingers.

Imming was shouting at him, but Ethan didn't comprehend the words.

He was zoned in on the cold, cutting steel as he felt his grip slowly dissolving and his boots beginning to slide off his feet.

He saw himself slipping, imagined the stunning lift in his stomach, his arms and legs flailing. Could there be anything worse than falling in total darkness? At least in the daylight, you'd see the ground rushing up to end you, have a chance, albeit fleeting, to prepare.

He pulled himself up by the cable until his boots touched the plank again.

Leaned into the rock.

Gasping.

Hand bleeding.

Legs shaking.

"Hey, asshole! Try not to die, okay?"

The men laughed and their footsteps trailed away.

No time to regroup.

With meticulous sidesteps, he traversed the rock face.

After five minutes of terror, the lantern disappeared around a corner.

Ethan followed, and to his infinite relief, the trail widened.

No more cable or wooden planks.

Now they walked up a gently sloping ledge.

Maybe it was the exhaustion and the fading overload of adrenaline, but Ethan missed the transition entirely.

From outside to in.

The light of the lantern now shone on rock walls all around him, even overhead, and the air had spiked ten degrees.

Their footfalls made an echo.

They moved through a cavern.

Up ahead—a din of voices.

Music.

Ethan followed the men to the end of the passage.

The sudden onslaught of light burned his eyes.

His guides walked on, but Ethan stopped at the wide, open door.

Couldn't quite grasp what he was seeing.

Couldn't fit it into a previous point of reference.

The room was several thousand square feet—the footprint of a comfortable house. The ceiling dipped low at the corners, vaulted past twenty feet in the center. The rock walls glowed the color of adobe in the abundance of firelight. There were candles everywhere. Torches. Kerosene lamps dangling from wires in the ceiling. It was warm, the heat radiating from a large fireplace in a distant corner—a recess in the room that apparently vented smoke outside. There were people everywhere. Congregating in small groups. Dancing. Sitting in chairs around the fire. Nearby, a trio of musicians played on a makeshift stage—trumpet, stand-up bass, an upright piano that Ethan figured must have been disassembled and hauled up here in pieces. It was Hecter Gaither on the bench, leading the band in some moody jazz thing that would've sounded right at home in a club in New York City. Everyone was dressed to the nines in clothes that couldn't have possibly made the trip Ethan had just endured.

People were smoking.

Talking over the music.

Smiling.

Laughing.

The smell of booze like perfume in the air.

And then Kate was standing in front of him.

She had dyed her hair back to that java brown, and she wore a black, sleeveless number.

Smiling and the glassiness of liquor glistening in her eyes like tears, she said, "Of all the gin joints in all the towns in all the world." She ran her hand down the left sleeve of his hoodie. "Looks like you had a rough hike in. Let's get you into something dry."

She led him through the crowd to the far side of the room. They swung around into an alcove where the clothes the people had worn here hung dripping from wooden racks.

"Forty-two long, right?" she asked.

"Yeah."

She showed him to a black suit hanging from the end of a rack filled with dry, pristine formal wear.

"Looks like your old threads, huh? Shoes and socks right over there. Get dressed and come on out."

"Kate—"

"We'll talk in there."

She left him.

He stripped out of his hoodie, his undershirt, his damp jeans. There was a bench against the wall and he sat down and pulled off his boots and inspected the incision.

A few of the stitches had popped, but he'd brought along extra gauze and tape.

He wrapped his leg tightly enough to stop the bleeding and used his damp undershirt to clean the line of dried blood that trailed all the way down to his foot.

* * *

Walking back into the party, Ethan couldn't deny that he felt like a brand-new man. There'd been a mirror in the changing room, and he'd combed his wet hair over to the side in the style he'd worn back in his g-man days.

Someone had constructed a bar along one side of the cavern.

Ethan threaded his way toward it through the crowd and installed himself on an open stool.

The bartender wandered over.

White oxford, black tie, black vest.

Refreshingly old-school.

He threw a cocktail napkin down on the dark, scuffed wood of the bar.

Ethan recognized him from town. They'd never spoken, but he worked the cash register several days a week at the grocery store.

"What'll it be?" the man asked, no indication that he knew or cared who Ethan was.

"What do you have?" Ethan asked, glancing at the bottles lined up on the wall in front of a mirror. He saw bourbon, scotch, vodka. Brand names he recognized, but they were all nearly empty. Unlabeled bottles of clear liquor seemed to be in ample supply.

The mirror had been framed with dozens of Polaroid photos. One toward the center caught his eye. It was a close-up of Kate and Alyssa, both women dressed like flappers—newsboy caps, bobbed hair, gaudy makeup, and pearls. Their cheeks were pressed together. They looked drunk, in the moment, and irredeemably happy.

The barkeep said, "Sir?"

"Johnnie Walker Blue. Neat."

"Those bottles are actually more for atmosphere and extra special occasions."

"All right. Then what do you recommend?"

"I make a mean martini."

"By all means."

He watched the barkeep pour from various unmarked bottles into a big martini glass, which he set on Ethan's napkin and garnished with a wedge of green apple.

The man said, "Cheers. First one's on me."

As Ethan raised the glass to his lips, he heard Kate's voice: "Now try and keep an open mind."

She claimed the barstool beside him as he sipped.

He said, "Wow. Well at least they got the glassware right. Until now, I've never actually wanted to *untaste* something."

It was odorless, but on the tongue the overwhelming note was burn, followed by a strong citrus pucker, and a finish that was mercifully short, like the flavor had just fallen off a cliff.

He carefully returned the martini glass to the napkin.

"You aren't going to tell me this bathtub gin grows on you."

Kate laughed. "You look good, Agent Burke. I have to say the elegance of the black suit and tie suits you a thousand times better than that woodsy sheriff getup."

In the reflection of the mirror, people were dancing to a slow jazz tune. He spotted Imming and his goons in tuxedoes, passing a mason jar and watching the band.

Ethan reached for the stem of the martini glass, thought better of it.

"Nice digs," he said. "How'd you get all of this up here?"

"We've been bringing things for years. Glad you could make it."

"Well, I barely did, and I still don't understand what it is I made it to. Is this a costume party?"

"Kind of."

"So what's everyone pretending to be?"

"See, that's the thing. Nobody here *is* pretending, Ethan. This is a place to come and be who you really are." She turned in her barstool, surveyed the crowd. "We talk about our past here. Our lives before. Who we were. Where we lived. We remember the people we loved, who we've been separated from. We talk about Wayward Pines. We talk about whatever we want, and we have no fear of anything inside this room. It isn't allowed."

"Do you talk about leaving?"

"No."

"So you've never been to the fence?"

She sipped the foul concoction posing as a martini.

"Once."

"But you didn't go to the other side."

"No, I just wanted to see it. Since we started coming to this cave, we've had three people cross to the other side."

"How?"

She hesitated. "There's a secret tunnel."

"And let me guess."

"What?"

"None of them ever returned."

"That's right." She stepped down off her stool. "Dance with me."

Ethan took her hand.

They walked across the uneven rock into the throng of slow dancers.

He cupped his hand to her back but kept a respectful distance.

"Harold won't mind," Kate said. "He's not the jealous type."

Ethan pulled her closer, their bodies almost touching. "How about this?"

"When I said he's not the jealous type, that wasn't a dare."

But she didn't pull back.

They danced.

He hated how good it felt to touch her again.

"What do all these people think of me being here? They act like they don't even realize the sheriff is in the house."

"Oh, they realize. We had discussions about it. I convinced them you could be trusted. That we needed you. I stuck my neck out."

"You do need me. That's true."

"Question is, do we *have* you?"

"If I say no, will I wind up naked and stabbed to death in the middle of the road?"

He felt Kate's fingernails dig into his shoulder.

There was fire in her eyes.

"Not me, not any of my people laid a finger on Alyssa. We aren't revolutionaries, Ethan. We don't come to this cave to stockpile weapons and plan a coup. We meet here to be in a place where we aren't watched. To feel like human beings instead of prisoners."

He guided her away from the music.

"I've been wondering something," he said.

"What?"

"Two things really. First, how did you figure out that you had a microchip in your leg? Second—how did you know that if you removed the microchip, the cameras wouldn't see you? I don't know how you could possibly have just guessed that."

She looked away from him.

Ethan pulled her out of the main cavern and into the colder passageway.

It had been there always—he saw it now. An embedded suspicion. But up until this moment, until he'd actually voiced the question, the simplicity of the truth had eluded him.

He said, "Kate, look at me. Tell me the truth about Alyssa."

"I did."

God, he'd forgotten how well he knew this woman, how easily he could see straight through her. He thought of the photograph of Kate and Alyssa behind the bar as he caught something else in her eyes that she could no longer hide—pain, loss.

"She wasn't only their spy, was she?"

Kate's eyes filling with tears.

"She was yours too."

They spilled down her cheeks and she let them go.

She said, "Alyssa reached out to *me*."

"When?"

"Years ago."

"*Years*? So you know everything. You've known all this time."

"No. She never told us what was beyond the fence. She said it was for our own safety. In fact, she made it clear that leaving would be death, that all of us, her included, were stuck here. I believed her. Most of us did. I never knew where Alyssa came from. Where she lived when she wasn't in town. How she knew all these things that we didn't. But she hated how we're treated. These conditions. She said there were others like her who felt the same way, and she gave her life to help."

"She was your friend?"

"One of my best."

"So the bell pepper, the secret notes, Alyssa's investigation . . ."

"All for show. They made her investigate us. Maybe they were onto her. Suspected what she was doing."

"Do you know who *they* are? Did she ever tell you?"

"No."

In the cavern, the band was playing a new song, something fast.

People were jitterbugging.

Ethan said, "Was Alyssa even here three nights ago?"

"No, there was no meeting. Too risky. But she'd been here plenty of times before. The night she died, I met her in the crypt. We talked about what she was going to do. They were expecting a full report from her. They wanted her to name names, to turn us all in. So examples could be made."

"What did you and Alyssa decide she should do?"

"Make up an excuse for why she didn't get to see our group. It was the only option."

"What time did you and Alyssa part ways? This is very important."

"As I was walking home, I remember hearing the clock strike two."

"And where was this exactly?"

"Corner of Eighth and Main."

"Where'd she go after you left her?"

"I have no idea."

"No, I mean which direction?"

"Oh. I think she started walking south down the sidewalk."

"Toward the hospital?"

"Right."

"And there's no possible way one of your people killed her? Maybe someone who knew she knew the truth? Who was willing to do anything to get it?"

"Impossible."

"You're absolutely certain? Those boys who brought me here tonight had more than a few rough edges. And machetes."

"Well, they don't trust you. But they loved Alyssa. Everyone did. Besides, it's no secret among my people that there's a tunnel under the fence. Alyssa wasn't stopping anyone from leaving."

"Then what does stop them?"

"The people who left and never came back."

* * *

He got that Johnnie Walker Blue after all.

Kate went behind the bar, requisitioned the bottle and two rocks glasses, and carried them to a small table out of the main current of the noise and the motion.

They drank and watched the crowd and listened to the music, Ethan studying the faces, becoming increasingly floored, because no one in this room was someone he would've expected to *be* in this room.

In Wayward Pines, this crowd walked the line like perfect little townies.

Followed the rules, caused nary a ripple.

He would've pegged most everyone here as full-on converts to everything that life in Wayward Pines entailed, and yet here they were, freed of their microchips, at least for a few hours, drunk and happy and dancing in a cavern.

After the next song, the band quit playing.

The dynamic in the room changed almost instantly.

People found seats at tables, or sat on the floor against the rock wall.

Ethan leaned over to Kate, whispered, "What's happening?"

"You'll see."

Kate's husband walked over to their table.

Ethan stood.

"Harold Ballinger," the man said. "I don't believe we've actually met."

"Ethan Burke."

They shook hands.

"You worked with my wife many years ago."

"That's right."

"I'd love to hear about it sometime."

As they sat down, Ethan wondered if Kate had even told her husband about their time together. He wasn't getting that vibe.

A man was arranging torches in a half circle around the front of the stage.

He stepped down, and a woman in a strapless dress took his place in the firelight.

Only her blond dreads gave her away—it was the barista from the coffee shop.

She was smiling, holding a martini glass in one hand, a hand-rolled cigarette in the other.

There was no microphone.

She said, "It's getting late. I think we only have time for one share tonight."

A man stood, asked, "Okay if I go?"

"Sure. Come on up."

He made his way to the stage in a dark suit that didn't quite fit him—a little short in the cuffs, a little tight across the chest—and as he stepped into the spotlight and the candles lit his face, Ethan realized it was Brad Fisher. He and Theresa had eaten dinner at the man's house just two nights ago.

Ethan scanned the crowd, but he didn't see Mrs. Fisher.

Brad cleared his throat.

Nervousness in his smile.

"My third time here," he said. "Some of you know me. Most of you don't. Yet. I'm Brad Fisher."

The room responded like an AA meeting, "Hello, Brad."

He said, "First of all, where's Harold?"

"Back here!" Harold yelled.

Brad turned slightly so he faced Ethan's table.

"Harold came into my office two months ago, and without going into too much detail, made it possible for me to come here. I don't know how to thank you, Harold. I'm not sure I'll ever be able to."

Harold waved him off and yelled, "Pay it forward!"

Laughter shuddered through the room.

Brad went on, "I was born in Sacramento, California, in 1966. It's funny—the week before I woke up in Wayward Pines, I thought I had finally arrived at the prime of my life. I actually remember thinking those exact words. I had this great new job in Silicon Valley, and I had just married my best friend. Her name was Nancy. We met at Golden Gate Park. Don't know if any of you know San Fran. There's this Japanese Tea Garden. We met on the moon bridge. It was . . ." His face softened at the memory. "So cheesy. One of those high arching bridges. I mean it was something out of a movie. We always laughed about it.

"For our honeymoon, we opted for a road trip instead of a tropical getaway. We'd only known each other six months, and there was something that sounded right about just being on the road together. Driving across the West. We kept it loose. We didn't make plans. It was the best time of my life."

Even from the back of the room, Ethan could see that Brad was steeling himself to go on.

"A week or so into our trip, Nancy and I hit Idaho. Stayed in Boise for the first night, and I still remember that morning over breakfast when Nance picked Wayward Pines off the map. It was in the mountains. She liked the sound of it.

"We checked into the Wayward Pines Hotel. Had dinner at the Aspen House. We ate on the patio, all those white lights strung from the aspen trees twinkling above us. It was one of those nights. You know what I mean, right? You talk about the future over a bottle of wine and everything seems possible and within reach.

"We went back to our room and made love and fell asleep and when we woke up, we were here and nothing has ever been the same. Nance lasted two months and then she took her own life.

"Now I live with a stranger with whom I've never shared a single authentic moment. It's been a lonely couple of years since I woke up in Pines, and that's why meeting Harold and now all of you—people who I can share real moments with—is the best thing that's happened to me in a very long time." He sipped his martini, winced. "It grows on you, right?"

Someone shouted, "Never!"

More laughter.

Brad said, "I know we all have to start the cold walk home pretty soon, but I hope I can get up here and talk more about my wife. My real wife." Now he raised his glass. "Her name was Nancy, and I love her, I miss her . . ." Here came the emotion. "And I think about her every single day."

Everyone in the room stood.

Glasses raised, winking in the firelight.

The room said, "To Nancy."

They drank and then Brad stepped down off the stage.

Ethan watched him walk out into the passageway where the man slid down onto the floor and wept.

Ethan looked at Kate, wondering what her group thought of the striking incongruence of time. Brad Fisher had said he was born in 1966, but the man couldn't have been older than twenty-nine or thirty, which meant he had come to Wayward Pines, Idaho, in the mid-1990s, with Bill Clinton president and 9/11 still five or six years away. No doubt others in this room had come to town before him and after him. What did they make of it? Did they compare and contrast their own views of the world before, searching for meaning in their current existence? Did those who had arrived around the same time seek one another out for the comfort of a shared knowledge of history?

"Imagine it," she said. "First time in two years he's been able to openly speak about his real wife."

People were forming a line to the dressing room.

"What about his Wayward Pines wife, Megan?" Ethan asked. "He couldn't bring her?"

"She's a teacher."

"So?"

"They're true believers. Someone scored him a dose of something that he probably slipped into his wife's water at dinner. Knocked her out cold for the entire night so he could slip out."

"So she doesn't know he's coming to these."

"No way. And she can't ever find out."

* * *

Everyone had left.

Ethan changed out of his black suit and back into the damp jeans and hoodie.

In the main cavern, Kate was blowing out candles and Harold was collecting empty martini glasses and lining them up on the bar.

With the last candle, Kate lit a kerosene lamp for the journey home.

They followed Harold down the passageway.

Outside, the sky had cleared.

Stars blazed down out of the dark and the moon was bright.

Harold took Kate's lamp and slung it over his shoulder and they all moved down the ledge to where the path swung out across the face of the cliff. All of the homeward-bound foot traffic had polished the wooden planks and the cables clean of snow.

Ethan could see Wayward Pines now.

Snow-mantled and silent in the valley below.

White roofs.

Twinkling lights.

He thought of all the people down there.

Those dreaming of their lives before.

Those still awake in the wee hours in their private prisons, wondering what their lives had become, not knowing if they were alive or dead.

The men and women trudging home from the cavern in wet clothes back to a world they knew was wrong.

His wife.

His son.

Kate said, "Ethan, I have to know."

"Know what?"

"How bad was it? What they did to Alyssa. Did she suffer?"

Ethan reached for the cable and took that first, stomach-churning step onto the plank. He told himself not to look down, but he couldn't resist the urge. The forest was three hundred feet below the soles of his boots, the pine trees crowned with snow.

"She died quickly," he lied.

"Please don't do that," Kate said. "I want the truth. How much did they hurt her?"

It had been heady in the cavern, but now the questions came in a rush of mounting heat . . .

Had Alyssa been tortured by Pilcher's people to name the members of Kate's group?

Or killed by Kate's people to stop *her from naming them?*

"Ethan?"

Where had it happened?

"Ethan."

Who had cut her?

Pilcher didn't murder his daughter.

Was Kate playing him?

"What did they do to my friend?" she asked. "I have to know."

He glanced back at the woman he had once loved. She and her husband were standing on the edge of the cliff.

He'd assumed he would come out of this night with a better understanding of what had happened to Alyssa, but he only felt more uncertain.

Plagued with more questions.

Pilcher's words beginning to echo through his head.

You have no idea . . .

What she's capable of.

"They tore her up, Kate," Ethan said. "They tore her up bad."

19

The exhaustion hit him at the intersection of Eighth and Main.

He was alone now, had split off from Kate and Harold several blocks back.

The sky wasn't that deep blue-black anymore.

Stars fading.

Dawn coming.

He felt like he'd been awake forever, couldn't remember the last good night of sleep he'd logged.

His legs ached. His stitches had ripped again. He was cold and thirsty, and just four blocks away, his house beckoned. He would strip out of his wet, freezing clothes, climb under as many blankets as he could amass, and just recharge. Get his head right for—

The noise of an approaching car turned his head.

He stared south toward the hospital.

Headlights raced in his direction.

The sight of them stopped him in the crosswalk under the traffic light.

It was something you hardly ever saw in Wayward Pines—a car actually driving through town. There were plenty of vehicles parked along the streets, and most of them ran. There was even a filling station at the edge of town with a mechanic next door. But people rarely drove. It was mainly set decoration.

For a moment, he imagined the impossible—that it was a minivan heading toward him. Dad behind the wheel. Mom asleep beside him in the front seat, kids in dreamland in the back. Maybe they'd been driving all night from Spokane or Missoula. Maybe they were coming here on vacation. Maybe just passing through.

It wasn't real.

He knew that.

But for a half second, standing in the predawn stillness in the middle of town, it felt possible.

The approaching car was hauling ass down the middle of Main, tires straddling the white line, RPMs in the red. It must have been doing sixty or seventy, the racket of the engine reverberating between the dark buildings, high beams flooding his eyes.

It had just occurred to Ethan that he might want to get out of the road when he heard the RPMs fall off.

The Jeep Wrangler that had taken him up into the mountain so many times before slid to a stop in the crosswalk in front of him.

No doors, no soft top.

Ethan heard the emergency brake engage.

Marcus stared at Ethan from behind the wheel, a grogginess in his eyes hinting that he hadn't been awake for long.

Over the idling engine, he said, "You gotta come with me, Mr. Burke."

Ethan put his hand on the padded roll bar.

"Pilcher sent you to get me at five in the morning?"

"He called your house. No one answered."

"Because I've been out all night doing what he asked me to do."

"Well, he wants to see you right away."

"Marcus, I'm tired, cold, and wet. You tell him I'm going home, taking a shower, and getting some sleep. Then—"

"I'm sorry, but that's not going to work, Mr. Burke."

"Excuse me?"

"Mr. Pilcher said now."

"Mr. Pilcher can fuck right off."

The traffic signal above them threw alternating colors on the Jeep, on Marcus's face, on the gun he was suddenly pointing at Ethan's chest. It looked like a Glock but Ethan couldn't be sure in the twilight.

He studied Marcus—anger, fear, nerves.

The shake in the gun was barely perceptible.

"Get in the Jeep, Mr. Burke. I'm sorry to have to do this, but I got my orders, and they're to take you to Mr. Pilcher's office. You were a soldier, right? You understand that sometimes you gotta do what you're told, and whether or not you like it doesn't matter."

"I was a soldier," Ethan said. "I flew the Black Hawk. Carried men into battles I knew they wouldn't return from. Unleashed hell on insurgents. And yeah, I took orders." Ethan climbed into the passenger seat and stared down the barrel of the pistol into Marcus's stormy eyes. "But I took them from men who had my total trust and respect."

"Mr. Pilcher's got mine."

"Good for him."

"Your seat belt, Mr. Burke."

Ethan buckled his seat belt. Guess he wasn't going to get that recharge after all.

Marcus holstered his weapon, released the emergency brake, and shifted into first.

Popping the clutch, he whipped the Jeep around on the snowy pavement, and floored it up Main Street, the back of the Wrangler fishtailing as the tires sought out traction.

They shot past the hospital doing fifty-five, still accelerating as they approached the darkness beyond the edge of town.

When the road entered the forest, Marcus downshifted into third.

Ethan had been uncomfortable walking home, but at least he'd been moving enough to keep the blood circulating. This was miserable, the wind screaming into the Jeep, chilling him down to his core.

Marcus downshifted again and veered off the road into the trees.

Maybe he wasn't thinking clearly, but the last thing Ethan intended to do was show up for a meeting with Pilcher.

As they neared the boulders, Marcus reached into his parka and pulled out something that resembled a garage door opener.

In the distance, a triangle of light began to spread across the snow.

Marcus brought the Jeep to a stop at the foot of the rock outcropping.

The wide door in the cliff was still opening, sliding up and back into the rock.

Ethan's fingers were so numb he could hardly feel them gripping the knife.

He flicked open the blade and leaned over in one movement.

The curved point digging into the side of Marcus's windpipe before he'd even thought to react.

His right hand slipped off the steering wheel, reaching for the gun.

Ethan said, "I will open you up."

Marcus put his hand back on the wheel.

"Squeeze that wheel like your life depended on it, because it does."

The mountain was wide open now, light shining out from the tunnel onto the snow and the surrounding trees.

Ethan spoke into Marcus's ear.

"Very slowly, take your right hand off the wheel, reach down, and shift into first. Keep your hand on the stick and drive into the tunnel. Once we're inside, turn off the engine. You understand what I'm telling you?"

Marcus nodded.

"I don't want to hurt you, Marcus, but I will. I've killed before. In war. Even in this town. I'll do it again. Don't think I won't just because I know you. That will not be a factor."

Marcus's hand shook as he palmed the gearshift and worked it into first.

He gave a little gas, and they rolled slowly into the tunnel.

Marcus brought the Jeep to a full stop just inside like he'd been told.

As the door lowered behind them, Ethan pulled the gun out of Marcus's holster—a Heckler & Koch USP, chambered for .40 cal.

He wondered if there were cameras watching.

Marcus said, "You're finished. You know that, right?"

Ethan twirled the HK so he gripped it by the barrel. Marcus saw it coming, started to cover up, but Ethan caught him flush on the side of the head with the butt of the composite stock.

Marcus sagged back and would've toppled out of the Jeep but his seat belt caught him. Ethan snatched his identification card off his coat, unbuckled him, and let gravity pull him the rest of the way down onto the pavement.

Then he unbuckled himself and climbed over into the driver seat.

Jammed his foot into the clutch.

Cranked the engine.

Soon, he was hurtling up the road into the mountain.

* * *

The giant, hanging globe lights hummed above him in the massive cavern, but otherwise, the superstructure was quiet.

Ethan checked the load on the HK.

Had to laugh.

Of course there was nothing in the chamber.

He ejected the magazine—empty as well.

Tossing the pistol into the backseat, he stepped down out of the Jeep.

At the sliding glass doors, he dug Marcus's ID card out of his pocket and swiped it through the reader.

The Level 1 corridor was empty at this hour of the morning.

Ethan took the stairwell up to the next floor.

The long stretch of checkered tile gleamed under the fluorescent lights and the corridor echoed with his footfalls. It felt strangely illicit walking these hallways by himself.

Unsupervised. Unchaperoned.

Down toward the end, he stopped at the door leading into surveillance and peered through the glass.

Someone sat at the console scrolling through the camera feeds—mostly shots of people tossing and turning and fucking in their beds, bodies indistinct through the glow of night vision.

He swiped Marcus's keycard.

The door unlocked.

He stepped inside.

The man at the console swiveled around in his chair.

Ted.

Head of surveillance.

The last guy Ethan was hoping to find at the controls.

"Sheriff." There was a note of alarm in Ted's voice. "I didn't know you were dropping by."

"Yeah, I didn't put this one on the schedule."

Ethan moved toward the wall of screens as the door closed after him.

He said, "Show me your hands."

"I don't understand."

"You don't understand what 'show me your hands' means, Ted?"

Ethan took out the knife.

Ted slowly raised his hands.

The room smelled of stale coffee.

Ethan said, "Anyone next door?"

"Two guys," Ted said.

"Any reason to expect your techs might make a surprise visit?"

"I don't think so. They typically keep their noses to the grindstone."

"Let's hope so for everyone's health and safety."

Ethan eased down into the chair next to Ted's. The man's hands shook and this gave Ethan a small push of relief. If he was afraid, he could be controlled. The lenses in the man's glasses were as big as windows and the large, dilated pupils behind them looked bleary and fried.

"You been up all night, Ted?"

"Yes."

"How long until you're off shift? And please understand that lying to me about this is the last thing you want to do."

Ted rotated his wrist so he could see the face of his watch.

"Thirty-four minutes."

"Are you scared, Ted?"

The man nodded slowly.

"That's good. You should be scared."

"Why are you doing this, Sheriff?"

"To get some answers. You can put your hands on your lap, Ted."

The man wiped his brow on his shirtsleeves and placed his palms flat against his cotton pants.

"I just want to make something very clear," Ethan said.

"Yes?"

"I don't know if you have an alarm in here, some sneaky way of notifying people you're in trouble. But if that happens, if you make that mistake, I will kill you."

"I understand."

"I don't care if thirty armed guards show up outside that door. If it opens, I'm assuming you called someone, and the last thing I do before I'm taken down is cut your throat."

"Okay."

"I don't want that to happen, Ted."

"Me either."

"That's up to you. Now let's go to work. Wipe the screens of the current video feeds."

Ted turned slowly in his chair and faced the console.

He tapped at a panel and the twenty-five screens went dark.

"First things first," Ethan said. "I assume there's a live camera feed of the Level Two corridor right outside that door?"

"There can be."

"Bring it up and put it on that monitor in the top right corner."

A long shot of the Level 2 corridor appeared—empty.

"Now I want to see where Pilcher is."

"He isn't chipped."

"Of course he isn't. Are there cameras in his residence or his office?"

"No."

"Does that seem right to you?"

"I don't know."

"How about his number two? Where's Pam, or is she off the radar too?"

"Nope, we should be able to locate her."

A screen in the upper left-hand corner flashed to life.

Ted said, "There she is."

It was a shot of the gym from a camera in the corner.

A room filled with exercise bikes, treadmills, free weights.

The place was empty except for one woman in the center of the frame, doing effortless-looking pull-ups on a bar.

"You just keyed off her microchip?"

"That's right. What's this all about, Ethan?"

Ethan glanced over at the feed of the Level 2 corridor.

Still empty.

Said, "You got a camera down at the entrance to the tunnel?"

Ted's fingers went to work.

The tunnel appeared.

Marcus was sitting up on the concrete, his head hung between his legs.

"Who's that?" Ted asked.

"That was my escort."

"What happened to him?"

"He pulled a gun on me."

Marcus was trying to stand. He made it onto his feet, but his legs suddenly buckled, and he sat back down on the road.

"Let me ask you something, Ted."

"What's that?"

"What'd you do before Pilcher brought you on board?"

"When I met him, my wife had been dead a year. I was homeless, drinking myself to death. He used to volunteer at the shelter where I sometimes stayed."

"So you met him while he was serving you soup?"

"That's right. He helped me clean up. I'd be dead if he hadn't come into my life. No doubt in my mind."

"So you believe he's above suspicion? Can do no wrong?"

"Did you hear me *say* that, Sheriff?"

Up on the screens, Marcus was standing now, attempting to take a wobbling step up the tunnel.

"Ted, last time I was here, you showed me how you could track a microchip. See where someone had been."

"Yep."

"I assume that's not possible with Pilcher?"

"Correct."

"How about Pam?"

Ted turned in his chair.

"Why?"

Marcus was stumbling up the tunnel now.

"Just do it."

"What date range?"

"I want to see where she went three nights ago."

All the screens turned dark.

They merged into a single aerial overview of Wayward Pines, and a red blip appeared overtop of the mountain south of town.

"What's that location?" Ethan asked.

"The superstructure."

"Can you push in?"

"Yeah, but it's just going to zoom in on trees on the mountainside. We have a highly developed aerial grid over town, but not over this complex."

There were numbers—what looked like military time—in the bottom right-hand corner of the screens.

"This is her location at twenty-one hundred hours?" Ethan asked.

"Yeah, 9:00 p.m."

"All right, take us forward slowly."

Time sprinted by—seconds, minutes, hours—but the blip didn't move out of the mountain.

Ted paused everything, said, "We're now at one in the morning."

"And Pam still hasn't left the mountain. Run it forward."

Just before 1:30 a.m., the blip moved out of the mountain, through the forest, and onto the road into Wayward Pines.

Ted pushed in.

The Pam-blip grew larger, now moving quickly down the road toward town.

Ethan said, "Do that thing where it shows all the areas that are covered under visual surveillance." The DayGlo overlay appeared. "Since Pam is chipped, her movement will trigger camera footage, correct?" Ethan asked.

"Yes."

Pam took a backstreet that ran parallel to Main.

"Now what's our time?"

"1:49 a.m."

"Can we actually see her on camera?"

"Weird."

"What?"

"I'm not getting a 'view cam feed' option." Ted pushed in closer. An entire city block filled the twenty-five screens. "Oh, that's why. See? She's standing in a blind spot." Up close, there was a scattershot of dark spaces in the DayGlo, and as the seconds whirled by, Pam seemed to always stay in the black.

"She's good," Ted said. "Knows all the camera placements and where to go to stay out of the footage."

Ethan said, "Run it out to 1:55 a.m."

Ted zipped ahead several minutes.

At 1:55 exactly, Pam's blip hovered on the south side of the opera house at the corner of Main and Eighth.

You were there. The night of Alyssa's death, you were watching when she and Kate split up.

Ted said, "Maybe if you told me what you're looking for, I could help you."

At 1:59, Pam started moving south.

And then you followed Alyssa.

Pam passed into an area of DayGlo.

Ted said, "I have a 'view cam feed' option."

"Let's see it."

The screens changed to a camera view of Main Street.

It was a grainy, night-vision shot, but Ethan could just make out the shadow of Pam walking quickly down the sidewalk.

She passed out of view.

The feed went black.

The screens returned to the aerial map.

"What was she doing in town?" Ted asked.

"At 1:59, Alyssa and Kate Ballinger part ways at the corner of Main and Eighth. Neither woman is chipped, so there's no footage. I'm told that Alyssa headed south, presumably toward the superstructure. Pam follows Alyssa. Keep in mind that several hours later, near the pastures south of town, I'll discover Alyssa. Naked in the middle of the road. Tortured to death."

"The Wanderers killed Alyssa."

"Maybe. Maybe not. Check our three surveillance cams, Ted."

Ted switched back.

Marcus had vanished from the tunnel door cam.

Pam had left the gym.

The Level 2 corridor stood empty.

"Go back to where we were," Ethan said. "Let's see where she goes."

Ted switched to the aerial view of Wayward Pines.

Pam continued south out of town. Where the road curved back, her blip moved into the forest and went all the way to the fence.

Ethan asked, "Can you add my microchip to these screens?"

"You mean for the same moment in time?"

"Exactly."

Ethan's blip appeared.

"So you were there with Pam?" Ted said. "I don't understand."

"I was. Three nights ago at the fence. Peter McCall had just died."

"Oh, I remember that."

"Now run Pam's trajectory again, from 1:59 a.m. until she reaches me and the fence."

Ted replayed Pam's movement.

"I'm not following," Ted said.

"Then run it again."

He ran it three more times, and at the end of the third, said, "What the hell?"

Ted leaned forward in his seat.

His demeanor had changed.

Less fear, more intensity.

More focus.

Ethan said, "Am I wrong, or are there two and a half hours missing from Pam's surveillance on the night Alyssa was murdered?"

Ted rewound the footage.

He pushed in until the blip itself took up four screens.

Then played it over and over and over.

"The time jump is seamless," Ted said. "The only tell is the running clock."

He typed furiously across three keyboards.

An error code flashed on the screens.

Ted stared at it, his head cocked, like it didn't compute.

"What does that mean?" Ethan asked.

"There's a missing data field. From 2:04 a.m. until 4:33 a.m."

"How is that possible?"

"Someone deleted it. Let me try one other thing."

Now the screens showed what Ted was typing—a long, incomprehensible line of code.

It only returned a different error message.

Ted said, "I just ran a system restore, back to sixty seconds before the time jumped ahead."

"And?"

"The surveillance we're looking for has been deep-sixed."

"Which means what exactly?"

"It's been erased."

"Could Pilcher or Pam have done this?"

"Definitely not. I mean not by themselves. The deletion itself would be practically impossible, but to patch Pam's surveillance history back together with a missing data field and make it look so flawless? No way. That took a high level of expertise."

"So who would have helped them? One of your surveillance techs?"

"Only if they were ordered to."

"You weren't asked to do this?"

"No. I swear to you."

"How many on your team are capable of something like this?"

"Two."

Ethan pointed his knife at the door at the end of the massive control panel. "Are they in there now?"

Ted hesitated.

"Ted."

"One of them is."

Ethan started toward the door.

Ted said, "Wait." He pointed at the bank of screens, which had reverted to the live surveillance cameras inside the superstructure.

Pam and Pilcher were coming down the Level 2 corridor, two guards in tow.

Ethan glared at Ted. "You alerted them?"

"Of course not. Sit down."

"Why?"

Ted attacked the touchscreens.

The surveillance cam feeds disappeared.

"Get them back," Ethan said.

"If this means what I think it means, we don't need that on the screen when they walk in here."

Ted pulled an aerial map of Wayward Pines, zoomed down onto Kate Ballinger's house, and exploded the interactive blueprint.

He pushed down into the camera over her bed.

Kate and Harold filled the screens—dawn light coming through their windows as they dressed.

Ethan took a seat. "You're actually helping me?"

"Maybe."

Voices came into range just outside the door.

Then the sound of a lock clicking back.

"You better think of something quick, Sheriff."

Ethan said, "One last thing. If I needed to speak to someone in a pinch in the middle of the day in the middle of town—"

"The bench on the corner of Main and Ninth. Blind spot. Deaf spot."

The door opened.

Pilcher entered first, Pam right on his heels.

He said over his shoulder, presumably to the guards, "Just hang back a moment. I'll let you know."

Pilcher strode into the middle of the room and stared down at Ethan with a bright, focused anger.

"Marcus is in the infirmary with a concussion and a cracked skull."

Ethan said, "Little shit pointed a gun at me. Lucky he's not in the morgue. You give him that authority?"

"I told him to drive into town, find you, and bring you back to me by whatever means necessary."

"Well, then I guess he has you to thank for the cracked skull."

"What are you doing here?"

"What's it look like?"

Pilcher looked at Ted.

Ted volunteered, "He wanted to see some live footage of the Ballinger residence."

On the screens, Kate had moved into the kitchen.

She was running water through a French press, washing out the old coffee grounds.

Pilcher smiled. "What's wrong, Ethan? Didn't get enough face time last night? I'd like to see you in my residence right now."

Ethan stepped toward Pilcher.

He had a good six inches on the man as he stared down at the tip of his nose.

Said, "I'd be happy to accompany you, David, but first I feel the need to share with you that if you ever pull any shit like that again—sending your lackey to fetch me with a gun—"

"Careful," Pilcher cut him off. "The back end of that sentence could be expensive."

He looked around the side of Ethan.

"You sure everything's okay here, Ted?"

"Yes, sir."

Pilcher looked back at Ethan, said, "After you."

Ethan tucked his hands into his front pocket as he walked past Pam. She was smiling like a maniac, her skin still glazed with sweat from the gym.

Outside in the corridor, two large, powerful men stood on either side of the doorframe. They were dressed in plainclothes, but submachine guns dangled on straps from their necks and they watched Ethan with aggressive eye contact.

Pilcher led everyone down the corridor and swiped his keycard at the pair of unmarked doors that accessed the elevator to his residence.

He glanced back at his guards. "I think we've got it from here, gentlemen."

When they were all in the car, Pilcher said, "Marcus tells me you stole his keycard?"

Ethan handed it over.

"Looks like you had a rough night, honey," Pam said.

Ethan glanced down at his hoodie—still damp, streaked with mud, torn in several places.

He said, "I was on my way home to clean up when Marcus intercepted me."

"I'm glad he did." She smiled. "I like you dirty."

When they reached Pilcher's residence, Pam grabbed Ethan's arm and held him back in the car.

She put her lips to his ear and whispered, "I happened to see you and Theresa out on your midnight stroll last night. Oh, don't make that face. I haven't told anyone. Yet. But I just wanted to let you know that I own you now."

* * *

Pilcher showed Ethan and Pam to a circular glass table on the outskirts of an immaculate kitchen. His personal chef was already working up breakfast—the smell of eggs and bacon and ham wafting over from the large Viking stovetop.

Pilcher said, "Good morning, Tim."

"Morning, sir."

"Would you mind bringing out coffee? You can take our orders too. There'll be three of us."

"Of course."

The light coming through the window beside the table was gray and dismal.

Pilcher said, "I hear it snowed last night."

Ethan said, "Just a dusting."

"First snow seems to come earlier every year. It's only August."

A young, clean-shaven man in a chef's coat walked over from the kitchen carrying a tray with three porcelain cups and a large French press.

He set everything on the glass and carefully lowered the plunger.

Filled everyone's cup.

Said, "I know that Pam and Mr. Pilcher take it black. Sheriff? May I get you some cream and sugar?"

"No thanks," Ethan said.

It smelled like good coffee.

It tasted infinitely better than what they served in town.

The way Ethan remembered it from Seattle.

Pam said, "You would've been so proud of our sheriff yesterday, David."

"Oh yeah? What'd he do?"

"He visited with Wayne Johnson. Your first integration, right, Ethan?"

"Yeah."

"Mr. Johnson was having a difficult time, asking the hard questions they all ask. Ethan handled it perfectly."

"Glad to hear that," Pilcher said.

"It was like watching our baby boy take his first steps. Just really beautiful."

Tim took their orders and headed back into the kitchen.

Pilcher said, "So we're dying to hear all about your evening, Ethan."

Ethan stared down at the steam rising off the surface of his coffee. He was in a rough spot. If this man were capable of killing his own daughter, what would he do to Ethan and his family if Ethan refused to name names?

But if Ethan spilled, he was signing Kate's death warrant.

Impossible choices.

And if that wasn't enough, Pam knew that he'd removed Theresa's chip.

"Ethan, tell us everything you saw."

Threatened with her life, Alyssa might not have named names, but she had undoubtedly told her father, or Pam, the truth.

She would've said that Kate's group *wasn't* dangerous.

Weren't planning a revolution.

That they only met to experience moments of freedom.

And still she was murdered.

The truth hadn't helped Kate and her group. The truth hadn't saved Alyssa.

"Ethan?"

In a moment of horrifying, blinding clarity, he understood what he had to do.

Risky. Insane.

"Ethan, for fuck's sake."

But his only play.

He said, "I got in."

"What does that mean?"

Ethan smiled. "I saw the inner circle."

"You were taken to where they meet?"

"They blindfolded me and led me off into the forest. We climbed this cliff to a cavern halfway up the mountain."

"Could you find this place on your own?"

"I think so. I wasn't blindfolded for the return trip."

"I'll want you to draw a map."

"Sure."

"So what did you see?"

"There were fifty or sixty people there."

"Including your former partner and her husband?"

"Oh yes. And Kate and Harold? They were clearly running the show."

"You recognized others?"

"I did."

"We'll need a full list of names."

"Shouldn't be a problem. But you should know something."

"What?"

"I went into last night expecting a harmless gathering. Anytime there are rules in place, it's human nature for people to sneak around them. The speakeasies of the 1920s are a perfect example. But this gathering, these meetings—they aren't harmless."

Pilcher and Pam exchanged a glance, the surprise in their faces unmistakable.

Clearly, Alyssa had told them the opposite.

Ethan said, "Frankly, I thought you were just being a control freak, but you were right. They're actively recruiting new members. And they have weapons."

"Weapons? What kind?"

"Homemade mostly. Hatchets. Knives. Bats. I saw one or two handguns. They're amassing quite the armory."

"What do they want?"

"Look, everyone was very nervous having me around."

"I can imagine."

"But from what I gathered, they want to take control. To turn the entire town. That much is clear. They aren't risking their lives to go to these meetings just to sit around and talk about the good old days before Wayward Pines. They know they're under surveillance. They know there's a fence. Some of them have even gone to the other side."

"How?"

"I don't know yet." Ethan wrapped his hands around his coffee mug to let them warm against the heated porcelain. "I'll be honest. I was skeptical going in," Ethan said. "But you . . . *we* . . . have a serious problem."

"What about Alyssa?" Pam asked.

"Are you asking if *they* killed her?"

"Yeah."

"Well, nobody walked up and confessed while I was there, but what do you think? Look, these people are ultra-paranoid about being discovered. They don't know specifically *who* you are, David, but they know someone like you exists. They know someone is controlling all of this. And they want to stop you by any means necessary. They want a war. Liberty or death and all that shit."

Tim returned carrying a silver tray.

He set down a plate of fresh fruit—certainly the last of it—from the gardens.

"A poached egg on sourdough for you, Mr. Pilcher. Eggs Benedict for you, Pam. And scrambled for you, Sheriff."

He freshened up everyone's coffee and left.

Pilcher took a bite of his egg, studied Ethan for a moment.

He said finally, "You understand, Ethan, that a war between the last several hundred human beings on the face of the earth is something that cannot be allowed to happen."

"Of course."

"What would you propose?"

"I'm sorry?"

"If you were me, what would you do?"

"I don't know. Haven't really had a chance to consider it."

"Why do I find that hard to believe? Pam?"

"Well now. First things first, I would have our super-duper sheriff here write down the names of each and every person he saw last night at the little soiree. Then I would ask me," she pointed at herself, "to put together a small team. We'd roll through town, and in one night, disappear every last motherfucker on that list." She smiled. "Then again, I'm on the rag, so maybe I'm just feeling a bit bloody—no pun intended."

"You would put them all back into suspension?" Pilcher asked.

"Or kill them horribly. I mean, at this point, they kind of strike me as lost causes, don't you think?"

"How many did you say there were, Ethan?"

"Fifty or sixty."

"I can't see sacrificing so many of my people. Call me a hopeless optimist, but I have to think there's a percentage of Kate's group who could be persuaded by means less final than torture and death."

Pilcher dashed a modest helping of salt across his egg.

Took a bite.

Gazed out the window in the rock.

It was a stunning vista through the face of a cliff. A thousand feet below, a forest swept down the mountainside into town.

When Pilcher turned back to the table, he wore a new look of resolve.

He said, "Ethan, it's going to be an interesting night ahead for you."

"How's that?"

"You're going to call your first fête."

"For who?"

"Kate and Harold Ballinger will be the guests of honor."

Pam was beaming.

"What a brilliant idea," she said. "Cut off the head of the snake, the rest of it dies."

Pilcher said, "I know the only fête you've experienced, Ethan, was your own, but I assume you've studied the manual. That you know what will be expected of you."

"Any qualms with overseeing the execution of your former fling?" Pam asked.

"Your sensitivity is overwhelming," Ethan said. "Someday remind me to explain to you what empathy is."

"Perhaps it was poorly phrased," Pilcher said, "but the question is apt. Are you up to this, Ethan? And don't misunderstand me and think that I'm implying you have a choice in the matter."

"I dread it," Ethan said. "If that's what you're asking. I loved her once. But after last night, I understand the need for what's going to happen."

The muscles in Pilcher's face seemed to relax.

"To hear you say that, Ethan . . . nothing would make me happier than for you to be fully on board. The three of us working together. For me to have your complete loyalty and trust. It's so important, and there's so much I haven't told you. So much I want to share. But I have to know you're really with me."

"The Ballingers have to be taken alive," Pam said. "You have to make that clear from the start to the officers or our guests will be killed in some alley. In light of the message we're trying to send, they need to die in the circle on Main Street. It needs to be bloody and awful so all the people in their group understand the price of their disobedience."

"I'll be watching how you run this fête," Pilcher said. "Your performance tonight can go a long way toward building some real trust between us." Pilcher finished off his coffee and stood. "Go home, get some sleep, Ethan. I'll send Dr. Miter into town this afternoon to sew your chip back in."

Pam smiled. "God, I love the fêtes," she said. "Even better than Christmas. And I have a hunch the townspeople do too. You know some of them keep costumes in their closets for the big night? They decorate their knives and rocks. We all need to go a little crazy now and then."

"You consider killing two of our own just going 'a little crazy'?" Ethan asked.

"At the end of the day, it's what we do best, isn't it?"

"I hope that's not true."

Pilcher said, "Personally, I hate the fêtes. But then again, those are *my* people down there, and as hard as it is, I know what they need. Perfection all the time would drive them mad. For every perfect little town, there's something ugly underneath. No dream without the nightmare."

20

Ethan walked into his dark house.

He ran a bath downstairs and went up to his bedroom.

Theresa was sleeping under a mountain of blankets.

He leaned down and whispered in her ear, "Come join me in the bath."

The water in the tub was the only hot thing in the house, but it was gloriously hot.

The room had filled with steam by the time Theresa wandered down.

It coated the mirror over the sink, the window above the tub. Made the plaster look as if it was perspiring.

She undressed.

Stepped into the water and eased down between his legs.

With the two of them in the water, there was only an inch between the surface and the lip of the clawfoot tub. The warm mist so thick he could barely see the sink.

With his foot, Ethan turned the knob just enough to fill the bathroom with the noise of running water. He pulled Theresa back into his chest. Even in the heat, her skin was cool against his. Her ear was right at his lips, and it was such a perfect position to talk to her that he didn't know why it had never occurred to him before.

Steam enveloped them.

He said, "Kate's people didn't kill that woman whose murder I was investigating."

"Then who did?"

"Either Pam, someone else under Pilcher's employ, or the man himself."

"His own daughter?"

"I don't know that for sure, but regardless, there's going to be a fête tonight."

"For who?"

"Kate and Harold."

"Jesus. And as sheriff, you have to run it."

"That's right."

"Can't you stop it?"

"I don't want to stop it."

"Ethan." She turned her head and looked up at him. "What's going on?"

"Better if you don't know."

"You mean in case you don't pull it off?"

"Yeah."

"How real is that possibility?"

"Very. But we talked about it last night. I promised you I'd fix this, even if it meant we took the risk of losing everything."

"I know. It's just . . ."

"A little different when the rubber actually meets the road. Pam knows about us, by the way. That we went out last night."

"Has she told anyone?"

"No, and I'm betting that she won't, at least not before the fête."

"But what happens if she says something after?"

"After tonight, none of this will matter anymore. But look, I don't have to do this. We could fall in line. Live out the rest of our days as good little townies. I'd be sheriff. There'd be perks to that. We have no mortgage here. No bills. Everything provided for. I used to work late every night. Now I'm always home for supper. We have more time together as a family."

Theresa whispered, "There's a part of me that wonders if I could buy into it, you know? Just settle. But it wouldn't be a life, Ethan. Not on these terms." She kissed him, her lips gone soft from the steam and the heat. "So do whatever you have to do, and just know that no matter what happens, I love you, and I've felt closer to you in the last twenty-four hours than in the last five years of our marriage in Seattle."

* * *

The snow was gone by midafternoon.

Under a blue winter sky, Ethan stood just beyond the fence that encircled the school.

Children streamed out of the brick building and down the steps. He spotted Ben walking with two friends, backpacks hanging from their shoulders, talking, laughing.

How normal it all seemed.

Kids getting out of school for the day.

Nothing more.

Ben reached the sidewalk. He still hadn't noticed his father.

Ethan said, "Hey, son."

Ben stopped and so did his friends.

"Dad. What're you doing here?"

"Just felt like picking you up from school today. Mind if I walk you home?"

The kid didn't look like he wanted to be walked home by Dad, but he hid the embarrassment with grace.

Turning to his friends, he said, "I'll catch up with you guys later this afternoon."

Ethan put his hand on Ben's shoulder.

He said, "How about we go to your favorite place in the world?"

They walked four blocks down to Main Street and crossed to a candy store called The Sweet Tooth. Some of the school kids had beaten them there—clusters of boys and girls grazing the hundreds of glass jars filled with gumballs, Spree, Sweet Tarts, Pixy Stix, Cry Baby bubble gum, Jolly Ranchers, Jawbreakers, M&M'S, Starburst, Pez, Skittles, Sour Patch Kids, Nerds, Smarties, Atomic Fireballs—no staple of teeth-rotting goodness absent from the collection. Ethan knew that, like everything else, it had all been stored in suspension. But he couldn't help thinking that if anything could last unchanged for two thousand years, it had to be a Jawbreaker.

He and Ben ended up at the chocolate counter.

Homemade fudge in all its permutations beckoned from beneath the glass.

Ethan said, "Pick out whatever you want."

Armed with hot chocolates and a paper bag heavy with an assortment of fudge, Ethan and Ben strolled the sidewalk.

This was the busiest time of day in Wayward Pines, with school having just let out and the streets wonderfully noisy with the laughter of children.

It never felt more real than this.

Ethan said, "Let's find a place to sit."

He led his boy across the street to the bench on the corner of Main and Ninth.

They sat drinking their hot chocolates and nibbling at the fudge and watching people walk by.

Ethan said, "I remember when I was your age. You're a much better kid than I was. Smarter too."

The boy looked up, fudge crumbs around his mouth.

"Really?"

Between his glasses and the earflaps that hung down from his hunting cap, Ethan thought he bore a strong resemblance to Ralphie from *A Christmas Story*.

"Oh yeah. I was a little shit. Mouthy. Full-on rebellious streak."

This seemed to amuse Ben.

He sipped his hot chocolate.

"School used to be just school," Ethan said. "We had homework. Parent-teacher conferences. Report cards."

"What's a report card?"

"A slip that showed what your grades were for a quarter. You probably don't really remember when you went to school in Seattle. This one's a little different."

Now Ben stared down at the pavement under their feet.

"What's wrong, son?"

"You're not supposed to talk about that." He said it in a grave, quiet voice.

"Ben, look at me."

The boy looked up.

"I'm the sheriff of Wayward Pines. I can talk about whatever the hell I want. You understand, I run this town."

The boy shook his head. "No you don't."

"Excuse me?"

Now Ben's eyes were filling up with tears.

"We can't talk about this," he said.

"I'm your father. There's nothing you and I can't talk about."

"You aren't my father."

A shiv straight into Ethan's gut would've felt better.

He lost his breath.

Saw the world suddenly through a blur of tears.

He barely found his voice. "Ben? What are you talking about?"

"Not my real one."

"I'm not your real father?"

"You don't understand. You never will. I'm going home."

Ben started to stand, but Ethan put his arm around him, held him to the bench.

"Let go of me!"

"Who do you think your real father is?" Ethan asked.

"I'm not supposed to talk about—"

"Tell me!"

"The one who protects us!"

"Protects from what?"

The boy glared up at Ethan, all tears and vitriol, and said, "The demons past the fence."

"You've been beyond the fence?" Ethan asked.

The boy nodded.

"Who took you?"

Stonewall.

"Was it a short, older man with a shaved head and black eyes?"

Ben didn't answer, but it was an answer.

"Look at me, son. Look at me. What do you mean when you say he's your father?"

"I told you. He protects us. He provides for us. He created all of this, everything we have in Wayward Pines."

"That man is not God, if that's what you've been—"

"Don't say that."

Ethan thinking, *If there were no other reason for burning this place to the ground, it's this. They're stealing our children away from us.*

"Ben, there are things in this world that are true and that are lies. Are you listening to me? Your mother's and my love for you—there is nothing truer than that. Do you love me?"

"Of course I do."

"Do you trust me?"

"Yes."

"That man who took you past the fence is not God. He's the furthest thing from it. His name is David Pilcher."

"You know him?"

"I work for him. See him almost every day."

Suddenly, Megan Fisher was standing in front of them.

Ethan hadn't even heard her footsteps.

She'd come out of nowhere.

Kneeling down carefully in her woolen skirt, she put her hand on Ben's knee.

"Everything okay, Benjamin?"

Ethan forced a smile. "We're fine, Megan," he said. "Rough day at school. I'm sure you know how that goes. But nothing a little trip to The Sweet Tooth can't fix."

"What happened, Benjamin?"

The boy was staring down into his lap, literally crying into his hot chocolate.

Ethan said, "It's kind of a private matter."

This snapped Megan's head up.

Gone was the perky, pleasant host who had welcomed him and Theresa into her home several nights ago.

She said, "Private?"

Like she didn't understand the meaning of the word.

Like Ben was *her* son and it was Ethan overstepping his bounds.

"At School of the Pines," she went on, "we believe in a community approach to—"

"Yeah, private. Like mind-your-own-fucking-business private, Mrs. Fisher."

The look on her face—pure shock and disgust—made Ethan fairly confident she had never been spoken to like that before. Certainly not since she'd woken up in Wayward Pines and attained this position of power.

Megan stood straight up and scowled down at him like only a teacher can.

She said, "They're *our* children, Mr. Burke."

He said, "Like hell."

As she stormed off down the sidewalk, Ben launched out of his father's grasp and sprinted away across the street.

* * *

"Afternoon, Belinda," Ethan said as he walked into the sheriff's office.

"Afternoon, Sheriff."

She didn't look up from her cards.

"Any calls?"

"No, sir."

"Anyone been by?"

"No, sir."

He rapped his knuckles on her desk as he walked past, said, "Hope you're in the mood for some big fun tonight."

He could feel her eyes on him as he moved on down the hallway toward his office, but he didn't look back.

Inside, he hung his hat on the coatrack.

Went to the closet, unlocked the door.

He'd only opened it up once before, his avoidance purely psychological. The things inside represented what he hated most about this job, this town. What he'd been dreading since day one.

His predecessor's costume hung from a brass wall hook.

During his own fête, he'd only glimpsed Sheriff Pope from afar, the details of this outfit lost in the midst of Ethan's fear and panic.

Up close, it looked like the cloak of a demon king.

Fashioned out of a brown bear's coat, there was extra fur padding under the shoulders and it tied across the collarbone with a link of heavy-gauge chain. The fur itself clumped in places where Ethan suspected blood had spattered, stuck, dried. But no effort had been made to clean the garment, which reeked like the breath of a scavenger—rotted blood and decay. None of it rivaled the adornments. The scalp of every prior guest of honor had been stitched into the fur. Thirty-seven in all. The earliest resembled beef jerky. The most recent were still pale.

On a shelf above the cloak rested the headdress.

The skull of an abby formed the centerpiece. The jaws were wide open, held in place with metal rods, and a rack of antlers had been screwed down into the top of the brainbox.

A sword and a shotgun lay across brackets in the wall, the rhinestones that covered them glittering under the overhanging lightbulb.

Ethan startled when his telephone rang.

Such a rare occurrence.

He walked out into his office, around his desk, and caught it on the fifth ring.

Answered, "Sheriff Burke speaking."

"Do you know who this is?"

Even though he spoke at barely a whisper, Ethan recognized the voice as Ted's.

He said, "Yes. How'd you know I was here?"

"How do you think?"

Of course—Ted was watching him from surveillance inside the mountain.

"Is it safe for us to talk like this?" Ethan asked.

"Not for long."

"They'll find out?"

"Eventually. Question is, will it matter when they do?"

"What does that mean exactly?"

"I found it."

"Found what?"

"That thing we were looking for. It was buried, hidden deep, but nothing can truly be erased."

"And?"

"Not over the phone. Can you meet me in the morgue in twenty minutes?"

"Sure."

"Dr. Miter just walked into your station. You better get going."

Ethan heard voices in the background, the sudden shuffle of Ted hanging up his phone.

The moment Ethan shelved his phone it rang again.

"Hi, Belinda," he said.

"Sheriff, there's a Dr. Miter here to see you."

To reinsert my microchip.

"I'm kind of in the middle of something. Would you mind getting him a cup of coffee and showing him over to the waiting area?"

"Yes, sir."

Ethan opened the deep left-hand drawer of the desk, lifted out his leather belt and holster, strapped it on.

He turned his attention to the gun cabinets, unlocked the doors and the drawer on the middle one.

From the drawer, he lifted out a Desert Eagle, popped in the magazine, holstered it.

Then he took down the Model 389 Rifle—a camo-stock with a blued assembly and 4x32 scope.

His phone rang again.

He grabbed it.

"Yes, Belinda?"

"Um, Dr. Miter doesn't really want to wait anymore."

"A doctor who doesn't want to wait. Do you see the irony there, Belinda?"

"I'm sorry, sir?"

"I'll be right out."

Ethan hung up the phone and moved to the window beside the gun cabinet. It was a slider. He opened the clasps, forced it open, then pushed the screen completely out of the frame.

Climbing awkwardly over the sill, he lowered himself behind the row of bushes that lined the front of the building.

Fought his way through the grabby branches and jogged down toward the street.

He'd driven the Bronco to work this morning and he pulled open the driver-side door and stowed the rifle on the gun rack.

As he cranked the engine, he could hear the phone in his office ringing again through the open window.

* * *

Ethan pulled his Bronco into an empty parking space on Main and walked over to the storefront glass of Wooden Treasures.

Kate was sitting behind the cash register, staring with a kind of bored, blank intensity into nothing. To go from that brilliant sliver of freedom last night back to the day-to-day enslavement that defined life in Wayward Pines must be a crushing thing, he thought. Figured the days after their secret parties were filled with hangovers and the hard edge of reality. Of what their lives truly were.

Ethan knocked on the glass.

* * *

They sat on the bench on the corner of Main and Ninth.

The downtown had emptied out.

It didn't look real anymore.

Could've been the set of a movie after production had stopped.

Already the light was beginning to fail as the sun slipped behind the western wall of rock.

"We're safe to talk here," Ethan said.

"You look terrible," Kate said. "Have you slept?"

"No."

"What's wrong?"

"I need to know how to find the tunnel under the fence."

"Why?"

"There isn't time to explain. Have you been to it?"

"Once," she said. "Years ago."

"Did you go through to the other side?"

She shook her head.

"Why?"

"Scared."

"How do I find it, Kate?"

"There's a big dead pine stump. As tall as you. Bigger around than anything near it. If it's still standing, you can't miss it. The door to the tunnel is right beside it, in the forest floor. It'll be covered over with pine needles. I don't think anyone's gone to the other side in a long, long time."

"Is it locked?"

"I don't know. Ethan, what's going on?"

He stared at her.

Wanting to tell her.

Wanting to warn her.

He said, "You're just going to have to trust me."

* * *

Ethan parked his Bronco out of sight in the alley behind the hospital.

Slipped in through a service door.

The ground floor stood absolutely silent.

He took the stairs down to the basement and stepped out into the intersection of four vacant corridors, headed toward the windowless double doors at the terminus of the east wing.

The last few fluorescent light panels near the morgue had gone out.

He reached the doors in semi-darkness.

Pushed through.

Ted stood at the autopsy table at an open laptop.

Ethan walked over as the doors swung closed behind him

Said quietly, "We safe to talk here?"

"I killed the surveillance cams to the hospital's sublevel." He glanced at his watch. "But they'll only stay in sleep mode another ten minutes."

"Where's Pam?"

"Upstairs in a therapy session."

Ethan moved around the gleaming table, stood beside Ted.

He glanced at the cold chambers, the sink, the organ scale. Ted had angled the examination lamp away from the table, so it fired one corner with an obscene radiance and left the rest of the morgue to shadows.

The laptop finished powering up.

Ted typed in his username and password.

"Why here?" Ethan asked.

"I'm sorry?"

"Why did you want to meet here?"

Ted pointed at the screen.

The footage rolled.

HD quality.

From a corner in the ceiling, a camera aimed down at Alyssa.

Ethan said, "Fuck."

Strapped with thick, leather restraints to an autopsy table.

To *this* autopsy table.

"No audio?" Ethan asked.

"Didn't have time to find it. Trust me, you'll be glad of that."

Alyssa was screaming something.

Her head lifting off the table.

Every muscle straining.

Pam appeared.

She took a handful of Alyssa's hair and jerked her head down hard against the metal table.

David Pilcher moved into the frame.

He set a small knife on the metal and climbed up onto the table.

Sat astride his daughter's legs.

He lifted the knife.

His lips moved.

Alyssa screamed something back as Pam held her head in place.

Pilcher's lips pursed.

His head cocked to one side.

He didn't look angry.

Wore no expression at all as he stabbed his daughter in the stomach.

Ethan recoiled.

Pilcher pulled out the blade as Alyssa writhed against the restraints.

Black blood began to pool on the autopsy table.

Pilcher's lips moved again as Alyssa's face disintegrated into agony, and when he raised the knife for another strike, Ethan turned away.

He felt sick, swallowed against the taste of iron in the back of his throat.

"I think I get the idea."

Ted leaned down and typed on the laptop.

The screen went mercifully black.

"And it goes on like that," Ted said. "On and on and on."

Ethan felt shaken for having seen it.

Thought of all those black holes in Alyssa's body he'd seen that first day in the morgue.

He said, "So that night, after Alyssa and Kate parted ways, Pam followed Alyssa, somehow got her down here in the basement. Maybe Pilcher was already waiting for them, maybe he came after. When I inspected her body several days ago in this morgue, I wondered how and why she had been drained of blood. Where she had been killed . . ."

"And you were standing at the scene of the crime."

Ethan stared down at the drain beneath his boots.

"You have a copy of this footage, Ted?"

"I made several." Ted reached into his pocket and took out a fingernail-sized memory shard. "This one's for you. It won't play on any device in town, but in case something happens to me and the other copies of this footage, keep it in a safe place."

Ethan slid the shard into his pocket.

Ted looked at his watch. "A few more minutes and we better be gone. What now? I considered just airing this footage on every screen in the mountain."

"No, don't do that. Go back to work. Carry on like nothing has changed."

"I'm hearing there's going to be a fête tonight for the Ballingers. Word's already spreading in the mountain they're responsible for Alyssa's death. What are you going to do?"

"I have something in mind, but I haven't told anyone."

"So just stand by?"

"Yeah."

"Okay." Ted took one last glance at his watch. "We better get moving. The cameras wake up in sixty seconds."

* * *

It was four in the afternoon when Ethan reached the curve in the road at the end of town. He kicked the Bronco into four-wheel low, drove down the embankment and into the forest.

The ground was soft and patches of snow lingered in the shade between the pines.

It was slow going.

A half mile seemed to take forever.

He spotted the first pylon through the windshield, and as he approached, the cables materialized, and then the coils of razor wire along the top.

He stopped the Bronco thirty yards back.

Dark enough to warrant headlights, but he didn't want to risk turning them on.

Sitting behind the wheel as the engine idled, he couldn't escape what a fear-inspiring thing it was to behold.

Just some steel and current.

And considering all that it was expected to keep out of Wayward Pines, and what it was intended to keep safe, it seemed so very fragile.

Hardly like all that was standing between humanity and extinction.

* * *

Kate had been right.

The stump was unmissable.

From a distance, it looked like a great silver bear, standing on its hind legs, the dead, gnarled branches near the top raised high like threatening claws. The kind of ominous shape which, at dusk, might give someone a start.

Ethan parked beside it.

He grabbed the rifle.

Stepped down onto the forest floor.

It was getting dark too fast.

The door slam echoed through the woods.

Then silence rushed in.

He circled the stump.

There was no snow here, just a bed of compressed pine needles, and nothing that would indicate a door.

He opened the back window of the Bronco and lowered the tailgate.

Grabbed the shovel and the backpack.

* * *

A half hour into digging, the head of the shovel struck something hard. Throwing it aside, he fell to his knees, used his hands to tear out the rest of the pine needles—two, maybe three years' worth of accumulation.

The door was made of steel.

Three feet wide, four feet tall, flush against the ground.

The handle was locked down to an eyebolt with a padlock, which years of rain and snow had rusted into oblivion.

One hard blow from the shovel broke off the lock.

He shouldered the backpack.

Loaded the rifle.

Slung it over his right arm.

He drew the big pistol and jacked a .50-caliber hollow-point cartridge into the chamber.

The hinges on the door creaked like fingernails down a blackboard.

Pitch black inside.

The damp-earth smell of a crawlspace.

Ethan tugged the Maglite off his belt, clicked it on, paired it with the Desert Eagle.

Steps had been cut into the earth.

Ethan carefully descended.

After nine, he had reached the bottom.

The beam of light showed a passageway framed up and supported by four-by-fours.

The construction looked makeshift and hurried, confidence not inspired.

Ethan walked under tree roots and rocks lodged in the dirt.

The walls seemed to narrow in the middle, his shoulders brushing against them, and he had to move like a hunchback so his head didn't scrape the ceiling.

Midway through, he thought he heard the fence humming through the ground, thought he felt a tingling in the roots of his hair from his proximity to that astronomical voltage straight above his head.

There was a tightness in his chest, like his lungs were constricting, but he knew that was a purely psychosomatic response to moving through this subterranean space.

Then he was standing at the foot of another set of earthen steps, his light shining skyward onto another steel door.

He could go back, get the shovel, take an awkward whack at it.

Instead, he pulled his pistol, drew a bead on the rusted padlock.

Took a breath.

Fired.

* * *

An hour later, Ethan closed the tailgate and the back hatch.

He returned the rifle to the gun rack.

He draped himself across the hood, saltwater burning his eyes.

The light down here in the gloom of the forest was nearly gone.

It was so quiet he could hear his heart pounding against the metal.

When he could breathe normally again, he stood.

He'd been hot, but now the sweat felt clammy and chilled his skin.

"What the hell are you into?"

Ethan spun.

Pam stood peering through the tinted glass into the back of the Bronco, as if she'd materialized out of nothing.

Wore tight-fitting blue jeans that showed her figure and a red tank top, her hair pulled back into a ponytail.

Ethan studied her trim waistline.

She wasn't armed as far as he could see unless she was packing something compact in the small of her back.

"You checking me out, Sheriff?"

"Do you have a weapon?"

"Oh, right, that's the only reason you're ogling me."

Pam lifted her arms over her head like a ballerina, went up on point in her tennis shoes, did a little twirl.

She didn't have a weapon.

"See?" she said. "Nothing in these jeans but little old me."

Ethan pulled the pistol out of his holster, held it at his side.

Alas, empty.

"That's a big gun, Sheriff. You know what they say about guys with big guns."

"It's a Desert Eagle."

"Fifty caliber?"

"That's right."

"You could kill a grizzly bear with that beast."

"I know what you did to Alyssa," Ethan said. "I know it was you and Pilcher. Why?"

Pam ventured a step toward him.

Eight feet away.

She said, "Interesting."

"What?"

"I've now closed the distance between us. Two steps—two big steps—and I could be all up in your personal space, and yet you haven't even threatened me."

"Maybe I *want* you in my personal space."

"I made myself available to you and you would rather fuck your wife. What's bothering me, the rub if you will, is that you're a pragmatist."

"I'm not following." But he was.

"A man of few words and less bullshit. One of the things about you that make me want you. I'm going to go out on a limb and say that if there were any bullets in that gun, you'd have drawn down on me at first sight and wasted my ass. I mean, that's really your only move at this point, right? Am I onto something?"

She took another step toward him.

Ethan said, "There's something else you haven't considered."

"Oh?"

"Maybe I want you in my personal space for another reason."

"And what might that be?"

Another step.

He could smell her now. The shampoo she'd used this morning.

Her minty breath.

"Shooting is so impersonal," Ethan said. "Maybe instead of that, I want to pin you down and beat you to death with my bare hands."

Pam smiled. "You had that chance before."

"I remember."

"You got the jump on me. Wasn't a fair fight."

"For who? I was drugged, for fuck's sake."

Ethan raised the pistol and pointed it at her face.

She said, "That's a big hole at the end of that gun."

Ethan thumbed back the hammer.

For a beat—hesitation in her eyes.

She blinked.

Ethan said, "Think long and hard. Out of all the moments you've experienced, is this the one you want to be your last? Because it's heading fast in that direction."

She was wavering.

Not exactly fear in her eyes, but uncertainty.

Disdain for a situation she was not controlling.

Then it passed.

That steel resolve returning.

A smirk curled her lips.

She had balls. No way around that fact. She was about to call his bluff.

When her mouth opened, he squeezed the trigger.

The hammer snapped down into the firing pin.

Pam flinched—a split second of *am-I-dead* self-doubt.

Ethan spun the pistol in his hand, gripped it by the barrel, and swung with everything he had, four point five pounds of Israeli-made steel on a collision course with her skull, and it would've smashed it in, but Pam weaved at the last conceivable second.

As the momentum of Ethan's swing turned him sideways, she hooked him in the kidney with a blow of such stunning and direct force it brought Ethan to his knees, a bright release of incendiary pain flashing through his lower back, and before he could even fully appreciate *that* pain, she punched him in the throat.

He was on the ground, face against the forest floor, world askew, and wondering if she'd crushed his trachea because he couldn't draw breath.

Pam squatted down in front of him.

"Don't tell me it was that easy," she said. "I had this all built up in my mind, you know? But two shots and you're asphyxiating on the ground like a little bitch?"

He was fading, his vision igniting with oxygen-deprived pyrotechnics.

There.

Finally.

Right on the cusp of uncontrolled panic, something gave.

A trickle of precious air slid down his throat.

He tried not to let on.

Made his eyes bug out as he inched his hand into his back pocket.

The Harpy.

"As you lay there suffocating, I want you to know something."

Ethan worked his thumb into the hole in the blade.

"Whatever you were trying to pull off, you failed, and Theresa and Ben . . ."

He produced a wet, choking sound that made Pam smile.

"What I do to them will make what we did to Alyssa seem like a day at the spa."

He flicked the blade open and shoved it straight into Pam's leg.

It was so sharp, he only knew he'd aimed well when she gasped.

He turned his wrist, turned the blade.

Pam shrieked and jerked back away from him.

Blood darkened her jeans, ran down over her shoe, into the pine needles.

Ethan struggled to sit up.

Came painfully to his feet.

His kidney was throbbing but at least he could breathe again.

Pam was dragging herself away from him with her good leg, seething, "You're dead! You're fucking dead!"

He picked up the Desert Eagle and followed her.

As she screamed at him, he bent over and brought the heavy pistol down on the back of her head.

The forest was quiet again.

The evening gone deep blue.

He was fucked.

Absolutely fucked.

How long could Pam be AWOL before Pilcher sent out a search party? Strike that. There wouldn't even be a search. He'd just dial in on her chip and come right to the fence.

Unless . . .

With the Harpy, Ethan cut out a large swath of Pam's jeans, exposing the back of her left leg.

A shame she couldn't be conscious for this.

21

Superstructure
Wayward Pines, Idaho
New Year's Eve, 2013

Pilcher closed the doors to his office behind him.

Giddy.

Practically vibrating with energy.

Moving past the architect's miniature of the future Wayward Pines, he opened the closet, where a pristine tux hung from the rack.

"David?"

He turned, smiled.

"Sweetheart, I didn't see you there."

His wife sat on one of the couches that faced the wall of screens.

He started unbuttoning his shirt as he walked toward her.

Said, "I thought you'd be dressed by now."

"Come sit with me, Dave."

Pilcher took a seat beside her on the plush leather.

She put her hand on his knee.

"Big night," she said.

"Does it get any bigger?"

"I'm really happy for you. You did it."

"*We* did it. Without you, I—"

"Just listen."

"What's wrong?"

Her eyes welled up. "I've decided to stay behind."

"Stay?"

"I want to see the end of my story in the present. In this world."

"What are you talking about?"

"Please don't raise your voice with me."

"I'm not, I just . . . tonight, of all nights, you choose to tell me this. How long have you felt this way?"

"A while. I didn't want to disappoint you. There were so many times I almost said something."

"Are you scared? Is that it? Look, that's totally normal."

"It's not that."

Pilcher leaned back into the cushion and stared at the blank screens.

He said, "Our entire life together has been building toward tonight. It's all been about tonight. And you're walking away from it?"

"I'm sorry."

"This means you're walking away from your daughter."

"No, it doesn't."

He stared at her. "How does it not? Explain that to me."

"Alyssa is ten years old. Middle school is right around the corner. I don't want her first dance to be in this town that's not even built, two thousand years from now. Her first kiss. University. Seeing the world. What happens to those moments?"

"She can still have them. Well, some of them."

"She's already sacrificed so much since we've moved into the superstructure. Her life, my life, is here and now, and you don't know what the future holds. You don't know what this world will be like when you come out of suspension."

"Elisabeth, you've known me for twenty-five years. Have I ever done or said anything that would lead you to believe I would allow you to take my daughter away from me?"

"David."

"Please just answer that."

"It's not fair to her."

"Not fair? She's getting an opportunity no human being has ever been given. To see the future."

"I want her to have a normal life, David."

"Where is she?"

"What?"

"Right now. Where is my daughter?"

"In her room, packing. We'll stay through the party."

"Please." The desperation in his voice surprised him. "How do you expect me to be separated from my daughter—"

"Oh, fuck off." A flash of pent-up fury. "She barely knows you as it is."

"Elisabeth—"

"*I* barely know you as it is. Let's not pretend all this hasn't been your obsession. Your first love. Not me. Not Alyssa."

"That's not true."

"This project has consumed you. The last five years, I've watched you change into something deeply unpleasant. You've crossed more than a few lines, and I wonder if you fully even know what you've become."

"I've done what I had to do to reach tonight. I make no apologies. I said from the beginning there was nothing that was going to stop me."

"Well, I hope it's all worth it in the end."

"Please don't do this. This should be the greatest night of my life. Our lives. I want you there on the other side when we all wake up."

"I can't do it. I'm sorry."

Pilcher took a long breath in, let it slowly out.

"This must have been difficult for you," he said.

"You have no idea."

"You'll at least stay on through the party?"

"Of course."

He leaned over and kissed her on the cheek.

Couldn't remember the last time he'd done that.

"I should talk to Alyssa," he said.

"After the party, we'll say our goodbyes."

She stood.

Gray Chanel dress.

Wavy silver hair.

He watched her move gracefully toward the oak doors.

When she was gone, Pilcher went to his desk.

Lifted the phone.

Dialed.

Arnold Pope answered on the first ring.

* * *

It would've been the best champagne Hassler had ever tasted if he could appreciate it, but the nerves were getting to him.

This place was unreal.

Word was it had taken thirty-two years to complete the tunneling, the blasting, the excavation. The price tag must have been north of fifty billion. An entire fleet of 747s could've fit inside that cavernous warehouse, but he had a hunch the real money had gone into the room where he now stood.

It was the size of a grocery store.

Hundreds of drink-machine-sized units stood hissing and beeping as far back as he could see. Some of them vented white gas, the vapor hovering ten feet above the floor. It was like walking through a cold, blue fog. The ceiling invisible. The cold air pure and ionized.

"Would you like to see her, Adam?"

The voice startled him.

Hassler turned, faced Pilcher.

The man looked dapper in a crisp tuxedo, champagne flute in one hand.

"Yes," Hassler said.

"Right this way."

Pilcher led him down a long row toward the back of the room, and then up another aisle of machines.

"Here we are," he said.

There was a keypad, gauges, readouts, and a digital nameplate:

THERESA LIDEN BURKE
SUSPENSION DATE: 12/19/13
SEATTLE, WA

Down the front of the machine streaked a thick pane of glass, two inches wide.

Through it, he saw black sand and a patch of skin—Theresa's cheek.

Hassler involuntarily touched the glass.

"We're about to get started," Pilcher said.

"Is she dreaming?" Hassler asked.

"None of our testing—and there's been plenty of it—indicates any level of sentience during suspension. There's no brainwave activity. The longest we've put any of our test subjects under has been for nineteen months. No one reported any sense of time while they were down."

"So it's like a light switch going off?"

"Something like that. Did you get a chance to read the memorandum in your room? Everybody got one."

"No, I just finished the medical exam and came straight here."

"Ah, well, you'll be in for a few surprises."

"Is everyone on your team going under tonight?"

"A small group has been chosen to stay behind for the next twenty years. They'll continue to gather provisions. Make sure we have the latest technology. Tie up a few loose ends."

"But you're going under."

"Of course." Pilcher laughed. "I'm not getting any younger. I'd rather bank my time in the world to come. We should get back out there."

Hassler followed him out into the cavern.

Pilcher's people were waiting—everyone dressed to the nines.

Men in tuxes, women in little black dresses.

Pilcher climbed up onto a crate and looked out over the crowd.

He smiled.

In the light of a giant globe that hung down from a cable in the rock above, Hassler thought he saw Pilcher's eyes turn glassy with emotion.

He said, "Tonight, we come to the end of a journey thirty-two years in the making. But like all endings, it's also a beginning. As we say goodbye to the world we know, we look forward to the world to come. The world that waits for us, two thousand years from now. I'm excited. I know you are too. And maybe you're also afraid, but that's okay. Fear means you're alive. Pushing boundaries. No adventure without fear, and my God are we all on the brink of one hell of an adventure." He raised his glass. "I would like to propose a toast. To each and every one of you who've come this far with me and are about to take this final leap of faith. I promise you, the parachutes will open." Nervous laughter flickered through the crowd. "Thank you. Thank you for your trust. For your work. For your friendship. Here's to you."

Pilcher drank.

Everyone drank.

Hassler's palms had begun to sweat.

Pilcher glanced at his watch.

"It's 11:00 p.m. It's time, my friends."

Pilcher handed his champagne flute to Pam. He untied his bow tie and flung it away. He removed his jacket and dropped it on the rock. People began to applaud. He slid off his suspenders and unbuttoned his pleated shirt.

Now the others were beginning to undress.

Arnold Pope.

Pam.

All the men and women near Hassler.

The cavern became quiet.

Nothing but the sound of clothes sliding off and dropping to the floor.

Hassler thinking, *What the hell?*

But pretty soon, if he didn't join in, he was going to be the sole clothed person in the room, and somehow that seemed worse than undressing with complete strangers.

He pulled off his bow tie and followed suit.

Within two minutes, a hundred twenty people stood naked in the cavern.

From his pedestal, Pilcher said, "I apologize for the cold. It couldn't be helped. And I'm afraid where we're going it's even colder."

He climbed down off the crate and moved in bare feet toward the glass door that opened into suspension.

Within thirty seconds of walking inside, Hassler was shivering uncontrollably—part fear, part cold.

Lines were forming down the aisles, men in white lab coats directing traffic.

Hassler approached one, said, "I don't know where to go."

"You didn't read the memo?"

"No, I'm sorry, I just got—"

"It's fine. What's your name?"

"Hassler. Adam Hassler."

"Come with me."

The lab technician showed him to the fourth row and pointed down the corridor of machines, said, "You should be halfway down on the left. Look for your nameplate."

Hassler followed four naked women down the aisle. The vapor seemed thicker than before and his breath was pluming in the cold, the metal grating over the stone like ice to the soles of his feet.

He passed a man who was climbing *into* a machine.

Now the fear really kicked up.

He realized as his eyes scanned each nameplate that he had never imagined this moment. Never prepared. Sure he'd known it was coming. Known he was voluntarily submitting to this. But somehow, he'd subconsciously pictured something akin to general anesthesia. A mask descending toward his face in a warm operating room. Lights dimming out in a state of drug-induced bliss. Certainly not tramping around naked with a hundred other people.

There.

His nameplate.

His—*holy fuck*—machine.

ADAM T. HASSLER
SUSPENSION DATE: 12/31/13
SEATTLE, WA

He studied the keypad.

An incomprehensible collection of symbols.

He looked up and down his aisle but the others had already disappeared into their machines.

Another lab tech was approaching.

Hassler said, "Hey, can you help me out?"

"Didn't you read the memo?"

"No."

"It explained all this."

"Can you just help me please?"

The tech typed in something on the keypad and moved on.

There was a pneumatic hiss, like pressurized gas escaping, and then the front panel of the machine opened several inches.

Hassler pulled the door open the rest of the way.

It was a cramped, metal capsule. There was a small seat made of black composite, armrests, and an outline of human feet on the floor.

A small, quiet voice in the back of Hassler's mind whispered, *You are out of your goddamn mind to be climbing into this thing.*

He did it anyway, stepping inside and easing his buttocks down onto the freezing seat.

Restraints shot out of the walls, locked around his ankles, his wrists.

His heart rate skyrocketed as the door thundered shut, and for the first time, he noticed a plastic tube curled up on the wall tipped with a needle of horrifying girth.

He thought of Theresa's bloodless face and thought *fuck*.

A sound like a pressure leak kicked in overhead. He couldn't see the gas, but he suddenly smelled something like roses and lilac and lavender.

A feminine, computerized voice said, "Please begin breathing deeply. Smell the flowers while you can."

Through that two-inch stripe of glass, Pilcher appeared.

The computerized voice said, "Everything will be okay."

Pilcher was shirtless, smiling proudly, giving a thumbs-up.

Hassler was no longer cold.

No longer afraid.

As "Dream Weaver" by Gary Wright poured through the speakers, his eyes slammed shut. He'd meant to pray, meant to fix his thoughts on something beautiful, like the future and the new world and the woman he would be sharing it with.

But like every important, defining moment in his life, it had all roared by too fast.

* * *

Pam was waiting for him in the cavern.

She'd slipped into a robe and she held another one for Pilcher, draped over her arm.

"My daughter?" he asked as he pushed his arms through the sleeves.

"All tucked in."

He looked around at the cavern.

"It's so quiet now," he said. "I sometimes think of what this place will be like while we're all under."

"David!"

Elisabeth marched toward them across the stone floor.

"I've been looking all over," she said. "Where is she?"

"I sent Alyssa down to my office before the clothes came off."

Pam said, "Hi, Mrs. Pilcher. You look lovely tonight."

"Thank you."

"I was sorry to hear you won't be joining us."

Elisabeth stared at her husband. "When are you going under?"

"Soon."

"I don't want to stay here tonight. You'll have someone drive Alyssa and me back to Boise?"

"Of course. Whatever you want. And you can take the jet."

"Well. I guess it's probably time to . . ."

"Right. Why don't you head on down to my office. I'll join you in a minute. I just need to see about one last thing."

Pilcher watched his wife walk back across the cavern toward the Level 1 entrance.

He wiped his face.

Said, "I should not be shedding tears tonight. At least not these kind."

* * *

Elisabeth stepped off the elevator.

Their suite was silent. She had never liked it. Never liked anything about life inside this mountain. All claustrophobia. A sense of isolation she had never come to terms with. Her soul felt hunched over from the sheer, crushing weight of living with this driven, single-purposed man. But tonight, finally, she and her daughter would be free.

The doors to David's office were open.

She walked in.

"Alyssa? Honey?"

No answer.

She crossed to the monitors. It was late. Her daughter had probably curled up on one of the couches for a nap.

She reached them.

No.

Empty.

She made a slow scan of the room.

Maybe Alyssa had wandered back upstairs? They could've missed each other, although that seemed unlikely.

Her eyes caught on David's desk.

He always kept it immaculate. Free of clutter. Free of anything at all.

But now, a single sheet of white paper lay in the center.

Nothing else.

She walked over, pulled the page toward her across the polished mahogany so she could read it.

Dear Elisabeth, Alyssa is coming with me. You can see the end of your story on your own. What's left of it. —David

Elisabeth had a sudden strong sense of a presence behind her.

Turned.

Arnold Pope stood just within reach. He'd shaved for the celebration. Tall, broad-shouldered. Short blond hair and almost handsome. It was his eyes that killed the deal. Something in them a touch too cruel and dispassionate when they held your focus. She could smell the champagne on his breath.

She said, "No."

"I'm sorry, Elisabeth."

"Please."

"I like you. Always have. I will make this go as fast as possible. But you have to work with me."

She looked down at his hands, half-expecting to see a knife or a wire.

But they were empty.

She felt weak and sick.

"Can I just have a moment please? Please?"

She met his eyes.

They were cold, intense, and sad.

Revving up for something.

And she knew, a half second before he came at her, that she wasn't going to get that moment.

IV

22

Tobias warmed his grimy hands in the heat of the fire.

He was camped riverside, deep in the mountains of what had once been Idaho.

From where he sat, he could stare down the canyon and watch the sun falling into the V.

So close.

Earlier in the day, he'd caught a glimpse of the jagged cirque that formed the amphitheater on Wayward Pines's eastern wall.

The only thing stopping him from reaching the fence was a thousand-strong swarm of abbies in the forest that bordered the southern edge of town. Even two miles away from their position, he could smell them. Assuming they moved on overnight, he'd be in the clear to go home.

The temptation to sleep on the ground was strong.

Something about sleeping on the soft pine needles seemed massively appealing.

But that would be stupid.

He'd already fixed his bivy thirty feet up in one of the overhanging pine trees. He'd slept off the ground he didn't know how many nights running. One more wouldn't kill him.

And tomorrow night, if all went as planned and he didn't get himself eaten his last day in the wilderness, he'd have a warm bed to crawl into.

Tobias opened his rucksack, shoved his arm to the bottom.

His fingers touched the cloth bag containing his pipe, a book of matches from the Hotel Andra in Seattle, and the tobacco.

He laid everything out on a rock.

It was strange. He'd thought about this moment so many times.

Built it up in his mind.

His last night in the wilderness.

He'd brought a pound with him—all the weight he could justify—and burned right through it in those first months, saving only enough tobacco for one last smoke if he made it this far. There were so many nights when he'd almost smoked it anyway.

The rationalizations plentiful and compelling.

You could die at any time.

You'll never make it back.

Don't get eaten still holding on to what could've been a half hour of pipe-joy.

And still, he'd held out. It made no sense. His chances of returning were nil. But as he opened the plastic baggie and breathed in the smell of the aromatic blend, it was unquestionably one of the happiest moments of his life.

He took his time filling the bowl.

Then tamped it down with his finger, making sure each sprig was lovingly nestled.

The tobacco took the flame beautifully.

He dragged on the stem.

God, the smell.

Smoke clouding around his head.

He leaned back against the trunk of what he hoped was the last tree he would ever have to sleep in.

The sky had turned pink.

You could see the color of it on the river.

He smoked and watched the moving water and felt, for the first time in ages, like a human being.

23

At 8:00 p.m., Ethan was back behind his desk in the station.

His phone rang.

When he lifted the receiver, Pilcher said, "Doctor Miter is more than a little angry with you, Ethan."

The image of Pilcher climbing up on that autopsy table and stabbing his daughter surfaced in the back of Ethan's mind.

You monster.

"Do you hear that?" Ethan asked.

"Hear what?"

For five seconds, Ethan was silent on the line. "That's the sound of me not giving a fuck."

"You're still unchipped, and I don't like that."

"Look, I didn't feel like going under the knife again so soon. I'll come up to the mountain tomorrow first thing and get it over with."

"You haven't run into Pam, have you?"

"No, why?"

"She was supposed to be in the mountain thirty minutes ago for a meeting. Her signal still shows her down in the valley."

After returning to town, Ethan had walked to Main Street and slipped Pam's bloody microchip into the purse of a woman he passed on the sidewalk. Sooner or later, Pilcher was going to start studying camera feeds. When Pam's chip pinged a camera but Pam herself was mysteriously absent, Pilcher would know something had happened.

"If I see her," Ethan said, "I'll tell her you're looking for her."

"I'm not too worried. She tends to go on walkabouts from time to time. At the moment, I'm sitting in my office with a bottle of very nice scotch, watching my wall of screens, ready for the show to begin. Do you have any questions?"

"No."

"You've looked over the manual? You understand the sequence of calls? The instructions you're about to give?"

"Yes."

"If Kate and Harold are killed in the forest, if they're killed anywhere other than Main Street, center of town, I'm going to hold you personally responsible. Keep in mind they have underground support, so give the first wave of officers a little extra time."

"I understand."

"Pam delivered the phone codes to your office earlier in the day."

"I've got them here on my desk beside the manual, but you can see that, can't you?"

Pilcher just laughed.

"I know your history with Kate Ballinger," he said, "and I'm sorry if that's going to put a shadow over tonight for you—"

"A shadow?"

"—but fêtes don't come along all that often. Sometimes a year or two passes between them. So in spite of everything, I hope you'll try to enjoy yourself. Much as I hate them, there's something truly magic in these nights."

In his previous life, Ethan had developed the bad habit of flipping off the phone when he didn't like the person or the message on the other end of the line. He somehow, and wisely, found the strength to restrain himself.

"Well, I'll let you go, Ethan. You've got lots to do. If you don't have too bad of a hangover in the morning, I'll send Marcus down to pick you up. We'll have breakfast, talk about the future."

"Looking forward to it," Ethan said.

* * *

Belinda had gone home.

The station was silent.

It was 8:05 p.m.

It was time.

Hecter Gaither's piano came through the tube radio beside the desk. He was playing the Rimsky-Korsakov edition of *A Night on Bare Mountain*. The frantic and terrifying section had concluded, and he was entering the slow, calming-down movement that conjured up the feeling of daybreak after a night in hell.

Ethan's thoughts were with Kate and Harold.

Were they sharing a quiet dinner at this very moment, with Gaither's piano in the background?

Utterly blind to what was about to happen?

Ethan picked up his phone and opened the folder Pam had left with Belinda.

He looked at the first code and dialed.

A female voice answered, "Hello?"

There was a ping.

The ringing continued.

Each time someone answered, there was another ping.

Finally, a voice that sounded computer-generated said, "All eleven parties are now on the line."

Ethan stared down at the page.

The script had been typed out for him beneath the code.

He could still just hang up.

Not do this.

There were so many ways for it all to go so badly.

None of the ten residents of Wayward Pines on the other end of the line breathed a single word.

Ethan began to read: "This message is for the ten officers of the fête. A fête has been scheduled to begin in forty minutes. The guests of honor are Kate and Harold Ballinger. Their address is Three-Forty-Five Eighth Avenue. Make your preparations immediately. Of critical importance is delivering Kate and Harold to the circle at the corner of Eighth and Main alive and unharmed. Do you understand what I've just said to you?"

A series of yeses tripped over one another coming through the line.

Ethan hung up the phone and started the timer on his watch.

The officers *lived* for the fête.

They were the only residents allowed to keep actual weapons in their homes—machetes issued by Pilcher. Everyone else resorted to makeshift instruments of death—kitchen knives, rocks, baseball bats, axes, hatchets, iron pokers from a fireplace set, anything with heft, a point, or an edge.

He had wondered all afternoon what this block of time would feel like—the forty minutes between setting everything in motion and making that final phone call.

And now that he was *in* it, it screamed past with unimaginable velocity.

He wondered if the last meal of a death row inmate felt something like this.

Time moving at the speed of light.

Pulse rate accelerating.

An eerie, emotional review of all that had led to this moment.

And then he was watching the last ten seconds wind down on his watch, wondering where the time had gone.

He silenced the alarm.

Lifted the phone.

Punched in the second code.

That same computer-generated voice advised, "Please record your message after the tone."

He waited.

The tone came.

He read off the second script: "This is Sheriff Ethan Burke. A fête begins now. The guests of honor are Kate and Harold Ballinger. They are to be caught, brought unharmed to Main and Eighth . . ." He struggled with the final words. "And executed in the circle."

After a long pause, that CG voice said, "If you are satisfied with your message, press one. To review your message prior to sending, press two. To rerecord your message, press three. For all other options, press four."

Ethan pressed one and shelved the phone.

He got up.

On his desk, the nickel plating of the Desert Eagle gleamed under the lamp.

He reloaded and holstered it and walked over to the closet where he took down the headdress and the bearskin cloak.

Three steps from the door, the ringing started.

The first one bled through the radio.

The piano playing stopped.

He heard the bench squeak—Gaither standing.

The man's footsteps trailing away.

The sound of him lifting the phone.

Saying, "Hello?"

Then Ethan's voice—the message he had just recorded—came quietly through the speakers.

Gaither whispered, "Oh God," and then the radio transmission cut to static.

Ethan moved down the hallway, thinking only of Kate.

Did your phone ring?

Did you answer it and listen to my voice ordering your death?

Do you think that I've betrayed you?

He passed Belinda's desk, made his way through the dark lobby.

Outside, there was no moon, just a sky chock-full of stars.

He'd heard this sound before, as his own fête was beginning, but tonight it seemed more sinister because he fully understood the implications.

Hundreds and hundreds of telephones simultaneously ringing—an entire town receiving instructions to murder one of its own.

For a moment, he just stood listening with a kind of horrified wonder.

The sound filled the valley like haunted church bells.

Someone ran past on the street.

Several blocks away, a woman screamed, though whether from excitement or pain, he couldn't tell.

He walked down to the sidewalk and peered through the large glass windows of the Bronco. They were tinted, and considering the only light source was a streetlamp across the road, it was impossible to see anything inside.

Carefully, he opened the driver-side door.

No noise.

No movement.

He tossed the cloak and headpiece into the passenger seat and climbed in behind the wheel.

* * *

It was like driving through his old neighborhood in Seattle on Halloween night.

People everywhere.

On the sidewalks.

In the streets.

Staggering around clutching open mason jars.

Torches.

Baseball bats.

Golf clubs.

The costumes had been ready and waiting.

He cruised past a man in an old bloodstained tuxedo, carrying a two-by-four carved down into a handle at one end, the other embedded with shards of metal like a mace.

The houses had all gone dark, but there were points of light appearing everywhere.

Flashlights sweeping through bushes and alleyways.

Cones of light shining into trees.

Even from behind the wheel, Ethan could see the divisions in the gathering crowd.

How some people saw the fête as nothing more than a chance to dress up, get drunk, go a little crazy.

How others carried an angry purpose in their visage—a clear intent to do harm, or at the very least, drink their fill of watching violence done.

How some could barely stand it, tears running down their face as they moved toward the center of the madness.

He kept to the side streets.

Between Third and Fourth, the headlights struck a pack of children thirty strong running across the road, bubbling with deadly laughter like hyenas, all costumed, knives gleaming in their little hands.

He kept a lookout for the officers—they'd be dressed in black and wielding machetes—but he never saw them.

Ethan turned onto First, headed south out of town.

In the road beside the pastures, he stopped the Bronco.

Turned off the car, stepped outside.

The phones had stopped ringing, but the noise of an assembling crowd was growing.

It dawned on him that it was in this exact spot, four nights ago, that he'd discovered Alyssa Pilcher.

God, how quickly it had all come to this.

Wasn't quite time for him to make his appearance, but soon it would be.

Are you still running, Kate?

Have they caught you?

Are they dragging you and your husband toward Main Street?

Are you afraid?

Or on some level, have you been long prepared for this?

Ready for this nightmare to finally end?

On the outskirts of Wayward Pines, it was cold and dark.

He felt strangely isolated.

Like standing outside a stadium and listening to the noise of a game.

In town, something exploded.

Glass bursting.

People cheering.

He waited fifteen minutes, sitting on the hood of the Bronco with the warmth of the engine coming through the metal.

Let them gather.

Let them go mad.

Nothing would be done without him.

No blood would be spilled.

* * *

When Pam opened her eyes, it was dark.

She was shivering.

Her head throbbing.

Left leg on fire, like something had ripped a chunk out of it.

She sat up.

Where the fuck was she?

It was freezing and dark and the last thing she remembered was leaving the hospital after her final therapy session of the day.

Wait.

No.

She'd spotted Ethan Burke's Bronco heading south out of town. Followed him on foot . . .

It all came back.

They'd fought.

She'd lost apparently.

What the hell had he done to her?

When she stood, the pain in her leg made her cry out. She reached back. A large piece of her jeans had been cut away, and a nasty, open wound oozed down her left thigh.

He'd cut out her microchip.

That fucking motherfucker.

The rage hit like a shot of morphine. She felt no pain, even when she started running away from the fence, back toward town, faster and faster through the dark forest, the electrified hum dwindling into silence.

The sound of screams in the distance stopped her.

Abby screams.

Many, many abby screams.

But something wasn't right.

How could there be screams coming from straight ahead?

Wayward Pines lay straight ahead.

In fact, she should've reached the road by—

Shit.

Shit.

Shit.

She didn't know how long she'd been running, but she'd been running hard, running right through the pain. She'd come a mile at least from the fence.

Not far ahead, in addition to the screams of what sounded like a massive abby swarm, she heard movement coming her way—limbs breaking, sticks snapping.

And she could swear she even smelled them, an eye-watering, carrion stench growing stronger by the second.

In all of her years, she had never wanted to cause someone pain so badly.

Ethan Burke hadn't just cut her microchip out.

He'd somehow stranded her on the other side of the fence, out in the mean, wild world.

* * *

Ethan climbed back into the Bronco, fired up the engine, floored the accelerator.

Tires squealed on the pavement as he launched forward.

He sped into the forest, took the big looping curve that brought him back on a trajectory toward town.

The speedometer read eighty as he blasted past the welcome sign.

He took his foot off the gas, let the RPMs die.

On Main Street now, and still a quarter mile from his destination, but already he could see flames in the distance, the buildings all aglow with firelight and the kinetic shadows of the crowd.

He passed the hospital.

Four blocks from the intersection of Eighth and Main, he was steering around people in the road.

Something had been thrown through the storefront glass of The Sweet Tooth and kids were looting the candy.

This was all acceptable and expected.

The crowd became denser.

An egg broke across the passenger-side window, yolk running down the glass.

He was barely moving now, people constantly in the way.

Everyone costumed.

He steered through a group of men dressed up in drag, lipstick garishly applied, wearing their wives' bras and panties over long johns, one of them armed with a cast-iron skillet.

An entire family—including children—had ringed their eyes with dark eye shadow and painted their faces white to resemble the walking dead.

He saw devil's horns.

Vampire teeth.

Fright wigs.

Angel wings.

Top hats.

Sharpened canes.

Monocles.

Capes.

Vikings.

Kings and queens.

Executioner masks.

Whores.

Now the street was wall-to-wall.

He laid on the horn.

The sea of people begrudgingly parted for him.

Inching along between Ninth and Eighth, he saw other storefronts vandalized, and up ahead—the source of the flames.

People had pushed a car into the middle of Main and set it on fire. Its windows now littered the pavement, shivers of glass glittering in the firelight, flames licking out of the windshield, the seats and the dashboard melting.

Above it all, the traffic signal cycled on obliviously.

Ethan shifted into park and killed the engine.

The energy on the other side of the windshield was dark and volatile—an evil, living thing. He studied all the ruddy faces in the firelight, eyes glassy with whatever bathtub gin had been stockpiled and passed around.

The strangest thing was that Pilcher had been right. Clearly, the fête spoke to them. Met some deep, consuming need.

He glanced into the back of the Bronco and checked his watch.

Soon.

Wool padding had been stitched into the inside of the headpiece, and it fit him snugly. He reached over and locked the passenger door, although he doubted that would make any difference in the end. Grabbing the stinking cloak and the bullhorn, he opened his door, locked it, and stepped out into the fray.

Broken glass crunched under his boots.

The smell of liquor spiced the air.

He donned the cloak.

Pushed his way into the crowd.

People around him began to clap and cheer.

The farther he ventured toward the traffic signal, the louder it grew.

Applause, shouts, screams.

And it was all for him.

They were calling his name, slapping his back.

Someone thrust a jar into his right hand.

He went on.

Bodies packed so tightly it was almost warm between them.

He finally broke through into the eye of the storm—a circle that couldn't have been more than thirty feet in diameter.

He stepped just inside it.

The sight of them closed his throat with grief.

Harold lay on the pavement, struggling to get up, bleeding from several blows to the head.

Two black-clad officers held Kate, the woman he had once loved, each clutching one of her arms to keep her upright.

While Harold appeared stunned, Kate was fully present and staring straight at him. She was crying and he felt the tears sliding down his face before he even registered the emotion. Her mouth was moving. She screamed at him, screamed questions and disbelief, no doubt pleading for her life, but the noise of the crowd drowned her out.

Kate wore a shredded nightgown, and she stood in bare feet, shivering, her knees stained with grass and dirt, one of them skinned to the bone, blood running down her shin, and her left eye swelling shut.

A scene began to form.

She and Harold had gone to bed early—probably still hungover from the night before. The officers burst in. There hadn't even been time to dress. Kate had gone out a window, possibly made a break for the drainage tunnels under town. That's what he would have done. But the ten officers had her house surrounded. They'd most likely run her down within a block or two.

He wanted more than anything in his life to go to her.

Take her in his arms, tell her everything would be okay.

That she would survive this.

But instead he turned his back to her and made his way once more through the crowd.

When he reached the Bronco, he climbed up onto the hood and scrambled the rest of the way up the windshield.

He stood on the roof, the metal dipping under his weight, but it held.

The crowd descended into frenzy again, screaming like their rock star had just walked onstage.

Ethan could see everything from where he stood—the firelit faces crammed between the buildings, the burning car, the circle where Kate and Harold waited to die. He didn't see Theresa or Ben and this gave him some small piece of comfort. He'd warned his wife not to come. Had instructed her to take their son, against his will if need be, and ride out the fête from the relative safety of the crypt.

He lifted the questionable mason jar of hooch into the air.

The crowd reciprocated—hundreds of glass bottles raising, catching the bonfire light of the burning car.

A toast in hell.

He drank.

They all drank.

God-awful.

He smashed the bottle into the street, drew the Desert Eagle, and fired three shots into the sky.

It kicked like a motherfucker and the crowd went crazy.

He holstered the pistol and took the bullhorn, which dangled from a strap on his shoulder.

Everyone hushed.

Everyone but Kate.

She was screaming his name, screaming *why for God's sake why are you doing this to me I trusted you I loved you why?*

He let her go, let her finish, let her scream it all out of her system.

Then he raised the bullhorn.

"Welcome to the fête!"

Screams and cheers.

Ethan forced himself to smile as he said, "I love it even more from *this* side of the bullhorn!"

That got a big laugh.

The manual had given specific guidance for how the sheriff should handle this moment when everyone had gathered and the time for the execution was at hand.

While a handful of residents may have no issues with killing their neighbors, or even relish the job, when it actually comes time for the execution to begin, most people will feel uneasy about spilling blood. This is why your job as leader of the fête is so critical to its overall success. You set the tone of the celebration. You create the mood. Remind them why the guests of honor have been singled out. Remind them that the fête ultimately preserves the safety of Wayward Pines. Remind them that deviation from the rules is a slippery slope, which could easily result in any one of them landing in the circle next time around.

Ethan said, "You all know Kate and Harold Ballinger. Many of you would call them friends. You've broken bread with them. You've laughed and cried with them. And maybe you think that makes tonight a tough pill to swallow."

He glanced at his watch.

It had been more than three hours.

For fuck's sake. Any time now.

"Let me tell you about Kate and Harold. The *real* Kate and Harold. They hate this town!"

The crowd erupted in aggressive boos.

"They go out at night in secret, and here's the worst of it—they meet with others. Others just like them who despise our little slice of paradise." He drummed up some rage. "*How could anybody hate this town?*"

For a moment, the noise was deafening.

He waved everyone quiet.

"Some of those people, the secret friends of the Ballingers—they're here with us tonight. Standing in this very crowd. Dressed up and pretending to be just like you."

Someone shouted, "No!"

"But in their hearts, they hate Wayward Pines. Look around you. There are more of them than you think. But I promise you—we will root them out!"

It was slight, but as the crowd roared again, Ethan felt the Bronco shift imperceptibly on its shocks.

"So the question arises—*why* do they hate Wayward Pines? We have everything we need here. Food. Water. Shelter. Safety. We lack for nothing, and still, some people feel this isn't enough."

Something struck the metal roof under Ethan's boots.

"They want more. They want the freedom to leave this town. To speak their minds. To know what their children are being taught in school."

The boos continued but with a measurable lessening of conviction.

"They have the audacity to want to know where they are."

The boos stopped altogether.

"Why they're here."

The crowd dead silent, heads cocked and brows beginning to furrow as they sensed the sheriff's speech taking an unexpected turn.

"Why they aren't allowed to leave."

Ethan screamed through the bullhorn, "How dare they!"

Thinking, *Are you watching this, Pilcher?*

The Bronco shook under his feet and he wondered if the crowd could hear the noise.

Ethan said, "Almost three weeks ago, on a cold, rainy night, I watched from that window"—he pointed at the apartment building that fronted Main—"while you people beat to death a woman named Beverly. You would've killed me. God knows you tried. But I escaped. And now I stand up here under the guise of *leading* this celebration of depravity."

Someone shouted, "*What are you doing?*"

Ethan ignored this.

He said, "Let me ask you all something. Do you love life in Wayward Pines? Do you love having cameras in your bedrooms? Do you love knowing nothing?"

No one in the crowd dared answer.

Ethan spotted two officers shoving their way through the people, no doubt coming for him.

"Have all of you," Ethan asked, "resigned to Wayward Pines? To life in this town in the dark? Or do some of you still lie in bed at night beside your wife or your husband who you barely even know, wondering why you're here? Dreaming of what lies beyond the fence."

Blank, stunned faces.

"Do you want to know what lies beyond the fence?"

An officer broke out of the crowd and ran toward the Bronco, machete in hand.

Ethan pulled the Desert Eagle, aimed it at his chest, said through the bullhorn, "Fun fact. The shockwave alone from a fifty-caliber round will stop your heart."

The rear left window of the Bronco exploded, glass showering everyone who had crowded up against the side of the vehicle.

Finally.

Ethan glanced down, saw a taloned arm sticking through the hole in the window.

It disappeared and punched through again.

The crowd retreated.

A scream that no one could have mistaken for human ripped out from inside the Bronco.

Gasps rippled through the crowd.

Those closest to the Bronco were clambering back while those who couldn't see were fighting their way toward the front of the line.

The abby was going berserk inside, talons shredding the seats as it struggled against the chain Ethan had tied around its neck.

He was still aiming the Desert Eagle at the officer, but the man wasn't even watching the gun. He stared instead through the Bronco's windshield at what was trying to get out.

Ethan said into the bullhorn, "I want to tell you all a fairy tale. Once upon a time there was a place called Wayward Pines. It was the last town on earth, and the people who lived there were the last of their kind."

Ethan didn't hear the chain jingling anymore.

The abby had broken free and climbed into the front seat.

"They had been preserved for two thousand years in a sort of time capsule. Only they didn't know this. They were kept in the dark. By fear. Sometimes by force. They were led to believe they were dead or dreaming."

The abby was trying to break through the windshield.

"Some of the residents, like Kate and Harold Ballinger, knew in their hearts that something was very wrong. That none of this was real. Others chose to believe the lie. Like good humans, they adapted. Made the best of a fucked-up situation, and tried to just live their lives. But it wasn't a life. It was nothing more than a beautiful prison, run by a psychopath."

A large chunk of the windshield broke out and hit the hood.

"Then one day, a man woke up in town named Ethan Burke. He didn't know it, the people of Wayward Pines didn't know it, and the sick fuck that built this town sure as hell didn't know it, but he had come to pull the wool away from their eyes. To show them the truth. To give them the chance to live like real human beings again.

"And that's why I'm standing here right now. So tell me. Do you want to know the truth?"

The abby was breathless underneath him, furiously attacking the glass.

"Or do you want to keep living in the dark?"

Its head broke through.

Snarling.

Livid.

Ethan said, "It's two thousand years later than you think it is, and our species has devolved into the monster that's inside my car."

Ethan pointed the pistol at the abby's head.

It disappeared.

There was a long beat of silence.

People just staring.

Jaws dropped.

Buzzes slayed.

It came through the windshield, talons scraping down the metal hood, and crashed into the officer standing at the bumper before he even thought to raise the machete.

Ethan put a bead on the back of the abby's head and fired.

It went limp, the man underneath it screaming and flailing against the weight as two of the cross-dressed men helped drag the abby off him.

The officer sat up, drenched in gore, his forearms torn up, skin hanging in tatters where he'd tried to protect his face.

But he was alive.

Ethan said, "Is this too much for you to handle? Want to go back to killing two of your own? Or do you want to walk into the theater with me right now? I know you have questions. Well, I have answers. I'll meet you there in ten minutes, and I swear to God if any one of you so much as lays a hand on Kate or Harold, I will shoot you where you stand."

Ethan pulled off the headpiece, sloughed off the cloak.

He jumped onto the hood, and then stepped down to the street.

The crowd parted, giving him a wide, respectful berth.

He was still holding the Desert Eagle and his blood was hot, simmering for a fight.

Shoving one of the officers aside, he stepped into the circle. Harold was sitting up in the street in his pajamas, two officers still clutching Kate.

Ethan aimed at the one on the right.

"Did you not hear what I just said back there?"

The man nodded.

"Then why the fuck are you still touching her?"

They released her.

Kate crumpled.

Ethan ran to her, knelt down in the street. He took off his parka and wrapped it around her shoulders.

She looked up at him.

Said, "I thought you had—"

"I know. I'm sorry. I'm so sorry. There was no other way."

Harold was out of it, in another world.

Ethan lifted Kate in his arms.

He said, "Where are you hurt?"

"Just my knee and my eye. I'm okay."

"Let's get you fixed up."

"After," she said.

"After what?"

"After you tell us everything."

24

Ethan led the town into the theater.

The dead abby was laid out onstage for everyone to see.

Every seat in the house was filled and there were people in the aisles and sitting on the edge of the stage.

Ethan looked down at his family in the front row, but he couldn't get Pilcher out of his mind. What would the man do? Was he sending his men into town right now? Would he come after Ethan? Theresa and Ben? The town itself?

No. The news was out. And in spite of everything, how many times had Ethan heard Pilcher refer to the town as "my people." They were still, after everything, his greatest assets. He might retaliate against Ethan, but the residents of Wayward Pines now knew the truth, and that was that.

Someone turned on a spotlight.

Ethan stepped into the beam.

He couldn't see the faces now.

Only the harsh, blue-fringed light blazing out of the back of the theater.

He told them everything.

How they had been abducted, suspended, and imprisoned in this town.

How the aberrations had come into existence.

About Pilcher and his inner circle in the mountain.

A few walked out—couldn't stand to hear the truth or didn't believe.

But most people stayed.

He could feel the mood in the room shift from disbelief, to sadness, to anger as he described how Pilcher filmed and scrutinized their every private moment.

When he told them about the microchips, a woman jumped up and raised her fist, shouting at what she perceived to be a hidden camera in the ceiling, "Come down here! *Are you watching this?* Come answer for yourself, you son of a bitch!"

As if in answer, the lights in the theater dimmed.

A projector in the back kicked on and cast an image onto the pearlescent movie screen behind Ethan.

He turned, stared at the heavy white vinyl as David Pilcher appeared.

The man was sitting at his desk in a pose vaguely suggestive of a presidential address, forearms on the surface, hands clasped.

A hush fell upon the theater.

Pilcher said, "Ethan, would you mind stepping aside, letting me have a word?"

Ethan backed out of the limelight.

For a moment, Pilcher just stared into whatever camera was filming him.

He said finally, "Some of you know me as Dr. Jenkins. My real name is David Pilcher, and I'll keep this short and sweet. All the things your dear sheriff just told you are true. If you think I'm here to explain myself to you, or to apologize, let me disabuse you of that notion. Everything you see, *everything*, I created. This town. This paradise. The technology that made it possible for you to be here. Your homes. Your beds. The water you drink. The food you eat. The jobs that occupy your time and make you feel like human beings. You draw breath for no other reason than I allow it. Let me show you something."

Pilcher was replaced with an aerial view of a vast plain, where a swarm of several hundred abbies crossed the rolling grasslands.

Pilcher's voice filled the theater over the images of the swarm.

He said, "I see you have one of these monsters, dead onstage. You should all take a good look at it, and know that there are millions and millions of them outside the safety of Wayward Pines. This is what a *small* swarm looks like."

Pilcher returned, only now he was holding the camera himself, his face taking up the entire movie screen.

"Let's be clear. For the last fourteen years, I'm the only God you've known, and it might be in your best interest to keep acting like I still am."

A rock hurled out of the darkness and struck the screen.

Someone in the crowd shouted, "Fuck you!"

Pilcher looked away, watching everything unfold on his wall of monitors.

From the wings, Ethan watched as three men climbed up onto the stage and began to tear down the screen.

Pilcher started to speak, but someone in the back of the hall pulled the projector out of the wall and smashed it into pieces.

* * *

Pilcher sat alone at his desk.

He picked up the bottle of scotch.

Drained it dry, threw it at the screens.

He had to hold onto the desk as he dragged himself onto his feet.

Swaying.

He'd been drunk.

Now he was annihilated.

Staggered away from the desk across the dark hardwood floor.

Vincent van Gogh watched him from the wall, his face shaven, his right ear bandaged.

Caught himself from falling on the large table in the center of the room. He stared down through the glass at the architectural miniature of Wayward Pines, tracing his finger across it to the intersection of Eighth and Main.

His fist went through on the first try and flattened the intricate model of the opera house.

His hand caught on the jags of glass as he pulled it out.

He punched his bloody fist through another part of the glass.

And another.

His hand was bleeding profusely by the time he'd broken out all of the glass, the tiny shards and pebbles littered across the town like the wake of a biblical hailstorm.

He stumbled alongside the table until he came to Ethan's yellow Victorian.

Crushed it.

Crushed the sheriff's station.

Crushed the house of Kate and Harold Ballinger.

It wasn't nearly enough.

He grabbed hold of the table, bent his knees, lifted, and flipped it upside down.

* * *

Even after Ethan had told them everything, after the movie screen had been pulled down, people stayed in their seats.

Nobody would leave.

Some sitting catatonic. Stunned.

Others weeping openly.

By themselves.

Or in small groups.

Into the shoulders of spouses they'd been forced to marry.

The emotion in the room was staggering. Like the hushed devastation of a funeral. And in many ways, that's exactly what it was. People mourning the loss of their previous lives. All the loved ones they would never see again. All that had been stolen.

So much to process.

So much to grieve.

And so much still to fear.

* * *

Ethan sat with his family onstage behind the curtain, holding them tightly.

Theresa whispered in his ear, "I'm so proud of what you did tonight. If you ever wonder what your best moment was, you just lived it."

He kissed her.

Ben was crying, said, "The stuff I said to you earlier today on the bench . . ."

"It's okay, Son."

"I said you weren't my father."

"You didn't mean it."

"I thought Mr. Pilcher was good. I thought he was God."

"It's not your fault. He took advantage of you. Of every kid in that school."

"What happens now, Dad?"

"Son, I don't know, but no matter what, from this moment on, our lives are our own again. That's all that matters."

* * *

People began coming up to see the dead aberration.

It wasn't a large one, just a hundred twenty pounds. Ethan figured its small size had kept the effect of the tranq dart going longer than he'd planned for.

It was past midnight, and he was looking out over all the people whose lives he had just immeasurably changed when he heard the sound of a phone ringing in the lobby.

He climbed down off the stage and moved up the aisle, pushing through the doors leading out of the theater.

The ringing was coming from the box office.

He sat down behind the ticket window, lifted the receiver to his ear.

"How you doing, Sheriff?"

Pilcher's voice sounded whiskey-thickened and uncharacteristically happy.

"We should meet tomorrow," Ethan said.

"Wouldyouliketoknowwhatyou'vedone?"

"I'm sorry?"

Pilcher spoke more slowly, deliberately. "Would you like to know what you've done?"

"I think I've got a pretty good idea."

"Do you now? Well, I'll tell you anyway. You just bought yourself a town."

"I'm afraid I don't know what that means."

People were coming out of the theater and gathering around the ticket window.

"You don't know what that means? Means they're yours now. Each and every one of them. Congratulations."

"I know what you did to your daughter."

On the other end of the line—silence.

Ethan said, "What kind of a monster—"

"She betrayed me. Me and everyone in this mountain. She put the residents of Wayward Pines in danger. She didn't just tell people about the blind spots in town. She created them. Sabotaged everything I—"

"Your daughter, David."

"I gave her every opportunity to—"

"Your *daughter.*"

"It had to be done. Maybe not the way it was done, but . . . I lost my head."

"I've been wondering—why have me investigate her murder? Find her body in the road? I assume you orchestrated that. What did you possibly hope to gain?"

"Alyssa never gave up Ballinger's group. I didn't think you'd really investigate your former partner unless you thought she'd actually killed someone. And you should've come to the conclusion it was Kate. You would've if you'd searched her house. I had Alyssa's murder weapon stowed in a toolbox in Kate and Harold's shed. You were supposed to find it, but you never even searched, because I guess you never really thought she did it. Well, doesn't matter now."

"How do you sleep at night, David?"

"Because I know that no matter what I've done, it's all been in the service of creating Wayward Pines. Of protecting Wayward Pines. And there's nothing more important. So I sleep just fine. I have a new nickname for you, by the way."

"We need to meet," Ethan said. "We need to talk about what comes next."

"Light-bringer. That's my new nickname for you. Translated from the Latin, Lucifer. Do you know the mythology of Lucifer? It's quite apt. He was an angel of the Lord. The most beautiful creature of them all. But his beauty? It deluded him. He started to believe that he was as lovely as his maker. That perhaps *he* should be God."

"Pilcher—"

"Lucifer led a band of angels in revolt against the Almighty, and I want to ask you a question now . . . how'd that turn out for them?"

"You're a sick man. These people deserved their freedom."

"I will share with you that it did not turn out well at all. Do you know what God did to them? He cast them out. He created a place called hell for Lucifer and all his fallen angels."

Ethan said, "And who am I in this fairy tale? Lucifer? And I suppose that makes you God?"

"Very good, Sheriff." He could hear Pilcher smiling through the telephone. "And if you're wondering where to go to find this place of everlasting torment that I'm about to create for you, I would say look no further."

"What are you talking about?"

"Hell is coming to you."

A dial tone blared for two seconds in Ethan's ear.

Then all the lights winked out.

25

1040 Sixth Street
Wayward Pines
Three Years, Seven Months Ago

On their last day together, she prepared his favorite meal.

All afternoon in the kitchen—slicing, stirring, mixing.

The simple act of keeping her hands busy somehow carrying her from one moment to the next.

But she had to focus, because the second she dropped her guard, it all came crashing down on her.

Three times, she'd lost it.

Crumbling to her knees.

Her sobs filling the empty house.

It had been so hard here.

Scary and lonely, and ultimately, hopeless.

But then he'd arrived. Like a dream.

They'd found comfort in each other, and for a time, everything had been better. She'd actually been happy in this strange little town.

The front door opened, closed.

She set the knife down on the cutting board.

Dried her eyes on a dish towel.

Turned to face him.

He stood across from her at the kitchen island.

Said, "You've been crying."

"Just a little."

"Come here."

She went to him, wrapped her arms around him and cried into his chest as he ran his fingers through her hair.

"Did you talk to them?" she asked.

"Yeah."

"And?"

"No change."

"It's not fair."

"I know."

"What if you just said—"

"I don't have a choice in the matter."

"Can't you—"

"Don't ask me. Please." He lowered his voice and whispered into her ear. "You know I can't talk about it. You know there are consequences."

"It kills me not to understand."

"Look at me." He held her face in his hands and stared down into her eyes. No one had ever loved her like this man. "We'll get through this."

She nodded.

"How long?" she asked.

"I don't know."

"Is it dangerous?"

"Yes."

"Are you coming back?"

"Of course I am. Is he upstairs?"

"He's not home from school yet."

"I tried to talk to him about it, but—"

"He's gonna have a real hard time."

He put his hands on her waist.

Said, "Look, it's done, and there's nothing we can do about it, so let's enjoy the time we do have. All right?"

"Okay."

"Should we go upstairs for a little while? I'd like a little something to remember you by."

"I don't want to burn dinner."

"Fuck dinner."

* * *

She lay in bed, in his arms, watching the sky darken through the windows.

"I can't even imagine what it'll be like," she said.

"You're strong. Stronger than you give yourself credit for."

"What if you don't come back to me?"

"Then know this. The time I've spent with you here in this valley, in this house, has been the best of my life. Better than all my time in the world before. I love you, Theresa. Madly and forever and—"

She kissed him and pulled him on top of her.

Into her.

She was crying again.

"Just be right here," she said. "I love you. God, I love you so much, Adam, don't leave me, please, don't leave me . . ."

V

26

In the last shreds of daylight, Tobias opened his leather-bound journal and read the first page inscription for possibly the thousandth time.

When you come back—and you will come back—I'm gonna fuck you, soldier, like you just came home from war.

He flipped the pages three-quarters of the way through the volume to where he'd last left off.

The pencil was down to its last inch.

The pipe was getting low.

He crushed down the ashes and took a deep draw, collecting his thoughts as the river murmured past.

From where he sat, the sun had left the building, although it still struck the summit of the mountain across the river, a half mile above him.

That swarm of abbies appeared to be on the move.

He could hear them screeching and screaming as they pushed on up the valley, leaving him a clear path to home.

Tobias wrote:

Day 1,308

I'll keep this short and sweet. My last night in the wild and so many emotions. I can see the mountains that surround Wayward Pines from my camp, and with any luck, I'll come out of the cold tomorrow afternoon. There are so many things I'm looking forward to. A warm bed. A warm meal. To speak to another human being again. To sit down with a glass of whiskey and tell people everything I've seen.

I alone have the key to what will save us all. I'm literally the one man in the world who can save the world. I carry that knowledge on my shoulders, but none of it really matters.

Because the closer I get to Wayward Pines, all I can think about is you.

Not a single day has passed when I haven't thought about you. About our time together. About how it felt to hold you that last night.

And now, tomorrow, I'll see you again.

My sweet, dear angel.

Can you feel that I'm close? Don't you know it in your bones somehow, that in a matter of hours, we'll be together again?

I love you, Theresa Burke.

Always.

Never thought I'd get to write these words but . . .

This is Adam Tobias Hassler . . .

Signing off.

27

The torched car was still smoking. The traffic light was dark and the streetlamps had gone out. Absent a single light in operation in the entire valley, the stars burned down with a vivid, icy intensity.

Ethan walked out into the middle of the street, Theresa clinging to one arm, Kate on the other side of him. If it irked Theresa for the three of them to be so close, she didn't show it. Truth be told, Ethan wasn't sure how *he* felt walking between them.

So much love and passion and pain.

Like he was caught between repelling forces.

The same poles of two magnets in dangerous proximity.

People were beginning to filter out of the theater.

Ethan handed Kate the bullhorn, said, "Do me a favor. Keep everybody here. I need to go check on something."

"What's happening?" Theresa asked.

"I'm not entirely sure."

He pulled away from her and headed toward the Bronco.

The abby had wrecked it. There was a large hole in the center of the windshield and the front seats were covered in glass and eviscerated, foam padding spilling out. He couldn't even see through the windshield, so he climbed up on the hood and stomped out the rest of the glass.

He drove south up Main, wind streaming through the open window frame and his eyes watering against it.

When he reached the curve, he veered off the road and followed the tire tracks from his last foray into the forest, high beams shooting through the trees.

He found his way back to the dead pine stump and turned off the engine.

Stepped out into the dark forest.

Something was wrong, and as he approached the fence, he realized it was the silence that unnerved him.

It shouldn't be this quiet.

Those conductors and studded cables should be humming.

He walked west beside the dead fence.

Began to jog.

Then run.

After a hundred yards, he came to the gate—a thirty-foot, hinged section that provided egress from the valley. It was how nomads left, and—rarely—returned. Pilcher sometimes sent trucks through it into the wild to harvest firewood or obtain short-range reconnaissance.

Until this moment, Ethan had never actually experienced the terror of seeing it locked wide open.

As he stood staring through the gate into the unimaginably hostile country beyond, he was gripped with the cold, sinking conclusion that he had misread Pilcher completely.

A scream rose up out of the woods.

No more than a mile away.

Another scream answered.

Then another.

And another.

The noise expanding and growing until the ground seemed to tremble with it, as if all of hell was running through the forest.

Toward the dead fence.

The open gate.

Toward Wayward Pines.

For two seconds, Ethan stood frozen, a single question looping through his head as the panic and the fear and the terror swelled inside of him.

What. Have. You. Done?

And he began to run.

WAYWARD PINES

AND NOW A SNEAK PEEK FROM *THE LAST TOWN*, THE THIRD BOOK IN THE WAYWARD PINES SERIES, COMING IN 2014 FROM THOMAS & MERCER

Ethan sprinted back to the Bronco, the panic growing with every stride, every desperate breath, already trying to see a way out, a way to fix this.

But that quiet fence.

The open gate.

It was pure and simple death.

He drove too fast through the trees, pushing the suspension package to the limit, jarring the last few jags of glass out of the windshield.

Up the embankment, onto the road.

He pinned the gas pedal to the floorboard.

* * *

The entire town was waiting for him out in front of the theater.

Four hundred and something people standing around in the dark like they'd been kicked out of a costume ball en masse.

Ethan thinking, *We don't have a prayer.*

The noise of the crowd was overwhelming.

People emerging from their disbelief and shock, beginning to talk to one another, in some ways, for the first time.

Kate came over. She'd procured real clothes and someone had done a fast stitch job on the gash above her left cye.

Ethan took her over to the car, out of earshot.

He said, "Pilcher killed the power."

"Yeah, I figured."

"No, I mean he killed the power to the fence. He also opened the gate."

She stepped back, studied him.

As if trying to process exactly how bad a piece of news she'd just received.

"So those things," she said. "The aberrations . . ."

"They can walk right in now. And they're coming."

"How many do you think?"

"No telling. But even a small group would be devastating."

Kate glanced back at the crowd.

The conversations were dying out, people edging closer to hear the news.

"Some of us have weapons," she said. "A few have machetes. We'll defend ourselves."

"You don't understand these things."

"And you're looking at me like you don't know what to do."

"Any ideas, partner?"

"Can't you reason with Pilcher? Call him up? Change his mind?"

"I don't think that's possible."

"Then we should get everyone back inside. There are no windows. Just one exit on either side of the stage. Double doors leading in. We'll barricade ourselves in the theater."

"And then what? What if we're under siege for days? No food. No heat. No water. And there's no amount of barricading that would keep the abbies out indefinitely. You understand what would happen if just one of those things got in?"

"Then what, Ethan? What do you propose?"

"I don't know, but they're coming, and we can't just send people back to their homes."

"Some have already gone."

"I told you to keep everyone here."

"I tried."

"How many?"

"Fifty, sixty."

"Jesus."

"Ethan, we'll get through this."

"You don't understand what's coming. When I escaped several weeks ago, I was attacked by one of them. A small one. I came this close to getting ripped apart."

"So what are you saying? This is a death sentence? We're all going to die and that's just how it goes?"

Ethan saw Theresa and Ben moving toward him.

He said, "If I can get into the superstructure, if I can show the people inside who the man they serve really is, then we might have a chance."

"So go. Go right now."

"I'm not leaving my family. Not like this. Not without a real plan."

Theresa reached him.

They embraced.

She kissed him in front of Kate.

Kissed him showily, he thought.

"What did you find?" Theresa asked.

"Nothing good."

"Wait," Kate said.

"What?"

"We need to be somewhere safe while you break into the superstructure."

"Right."

"Somewhere protected. Defendable. And already stockpiled with provisions."

"Exactly."

She smiled. "I might actually know of a place like that."

* * *

Ethan stood on the Bronco's roof, bullhorn in hand.

"We're splitting into four groups of around a hundred each. Harold Ballinger will lead the first. Kate Ballinger, the second. Dave and Anne Engler the third and fourth. There isn't time to explain everything, but please believe me when I say we are all in imminent danger."

Someone shouted, "I have a question!"

They were answered with a single, distant scream.

The crowd had been murmuring.

Everyone went suddenly silent.

The sound had come from south of town—a fragile, malignant wail.

Nothing that could be explained or described, because you didn't just hear it.

You *felt* its meaning.

And its meaning was this: *death is coming.*

* * *

Brad Fisher sat awkwardly in the destroyed front passenger seat of Ethan's Bronco, clutching the handle on the door as Ethan sped through town.

Brad said, "We were in the theater. You were talking. Then I looked over and she was gone."

Ethan was trying to get ahead of his own thoughts, his own fear, fighting to see an endgame that didn't involve mass casualties.

But the man was crying.

Ethan said, "She probably feared for her life, considering what she was doing with the children. Figured people would see her as a traitor." He looked over at Brad. "How do you feel about Megan?"

This seemed to throw the man, to catch him off guard.

"I don't know. I never really felt like I knew her or that she knew me. But we lived together. We slept in the same bed. Sometimes we slept together."

"Sounds like a lot of real marriages. Did you love her?"

Brad sighed. "It's complicated."

The high beams fired across the dark sheriff's station.

Ethan steered over the curb and took the Bronco right up the sidewalk, tires straddling the pavement. He brought it to a stop a few feet from the entrance. Climbed out, clicked on a flashlight as he and Brad reached the double doors.

Ethan unlocked them, propped one open.

"What are we grabbing?" Brad asked as they ran through the lobby and turned down the corridor to Ethan's office.

"Everything."

Brad manned the flashlight as Ethan pulled guns out of the cabinet and matched up the ammunition.

He set a Mossberg 930 on the desk and pushed in eight slugs.

Fed thirty rounds into the magazine of a Bushmaster AR-15.

Topped off the mag for his Desert Eagle.

There were more shotguns.

Hunting rifles.

Glocks.

A sig.

A .357 S&W.

The tranq gun he'd used earlier in the day.

He got two more handguns loaded but it was all costing too much time.

It took seven trips to haul the firearms and ammo-laden rucksack out to the Bronco.

Each time Ethan walked back outside with an armload, he heard new screams to the south of town.

Louder.

Closer.

Brad was shoving the bag of ammo through the busted back window as Ethan jumped in behind the wheel.

He checked his watch.

They'd burned seventeen minutes.

"Let's go!" Ethan said.

Brad yanked the door open and climbed onto the broken seat.

Headlights blazed through the glass doors into the lobby.

Ethan glanced in the rearview mirror. Through the reddish glow of the taillights, a pale form streaked past.

He shifted into reverse.

They shot down the sidewalk and Ethan's head hit the ceiling as the tires launched off the curb and slammed the suspension down onto the pavement.

He braked hard, brought it to a dead stop in the middle of the road, shifted into drive.

Something struck the passenger side door and a screech shook the interior of the Bronco.

Brad's legs disappeared through the empty window frame.

He screamed.

Ethan couldn't see the blood in the dark, but he could smell it—a strong, sudden waft of rust in the air.

He pulled his pistol, but the screams had gone silent.

All he could hear was the fading scrape of Brad's shoes dragging across the pavement.

Ethan grabbed the flashlight, which Brad had dropped between the seats.

Shined it out into the street.

The beam struck the abby.

It was crouched on its hind legs over Brad, its face buried in his throat.

Ravenous.

Tearing.

It looked up, mouth blood-dark, and hissed at the light with the venomous warning of a wolf protecting its kill.

A little ways beyond it, the light showed more pale figures coming down the middle of the street.

Just fucking go. He's gone.

Ethan punched the gas.

In the rearview mirror, a dozen abbies were scuttling toward the car on all fours. The one out in front came up alongside his door. It leapt at Ethan's window, would've come through, but the Bronco accelerated just enough that it missed, hit the side of the car instead, and bounced off.

Ethan watched it tumble across the street and forced the pedal into the floorboard with everything he had.

When he looked back through the windshield, a small abby stood twenty feet ahead of the grille, frozen in the headlights, teeth bared.

He braced.

At contact, the bumper blasted the abby straight back thirty feet. He ran it over and dragged it for half a block, the Bronco jarring so violently he could barely keep his grip on the steering wheel.

The undercarriage spit it out.

Ethan sped north.

The rearview mirror showed a dark, empty street.

He breathed again . . .

IN CASE YOU MISSED IT, PINES, BOOK ONE OF THE WAYWARD PINES SERIES, IS NOW AVAILABLE IN PRINT, AUDIO, AND EBOOK

Secret Service agent Ethan Burke arrives in Wayward Pines, Idaho, with a clear mission: locate and recover two federal agents who went missing in the bucolic town one month earlier. But within minutes of his arrival, Ethan is involved in a violent accident. He comes to in a hospital with no ID, no cell phone, and no briefcase. The medical staff seems friendly enough, but something feels . . . off. As the days pass, Ethan's investigation into the disappearance of his colleagues turns up more questions than answers. Why can't he get any phone calls through to his wife and son in the outside world? Why doesn't anyone believe he is who he says he is? And what is the purpose of the electrified fences surrounding the town? Are they meant to keep the residents in? Or something else out? Each step closer to the truth takes Ethan further from the world he thought he knew, from the man he thought he was, until he must face a horrifying fact—he may never get out of Wayward Pines alive. Intense and gripping, *Pines* is another masterful thriller from the mind of best-selling novelist Blake Crouch.

ACKNOWLEDGMENTS

David Hale Smith, Richard Pine, Alexis Hurley, Nathaniel Jacks, and everyone at Inkwell Management: Thank you for the support and counsel.

Angela Cheng Caplan and Joel VanderKloot: You're rock stars. So grateful to have you in my corner.

A very special thanks to Jacque Ben-Zekry for a world-class edit on this book.

And Jenny Williams for an amazing copyedit on both *Pines* and *Wayward*.

David Vandagriff: Thank you. You know why.

To the team at Thomas & Mercer and Amazon—Andy M.F. Bartlett, Alan Turkus, Daphne Durham, Vicky Griffith, Jeff Belle, Danielle Marshall, Jon Fine, Sarah Tomashek, Rory Connell (gone but never forgotten), Mia Lipman, Paul Diamond, Amy Bates, Reema Al-Zaben, Kristi Coulter, Philip Patrick, Sarah Gelman, and Jodi Warshaw: What can I say? Everyone brings their A-game every day. It is a pleasure and a privilege to have your rocket engines strapped to my books.

Joe Konrath, Barry Eisler, Marcus Sakey, Jordan Crouch, Jeroen ten Berge, and Ann Voss Peterson: Thanks for the cheerleading, ass-kicking, and friendship.

Brian Azzarello: I should've thanked you last time for giving me the title *Pines*. So thank you!

Will Dennis at Vertigo: You helped immeasurably in the early stages of this series and gave me a sense of how big a world it could be.

The home team, Rebecca, Aidan, Annslee, and Untitled Crouch #3: Love you, guys. I hope you know how much.

ABOUT THE AUTHOR

Blake Crouch is the author of over a dozen best-selling suspense, mystery, and horror novels. His short fiction has appeared in numerous short story anthologies, *Ellery Queen's Mystery Magazine*, *Alfred Hitchcock's Mystery Magazine*, *Cemetery Dance*, and many other publications. Much of his work, including the Wayward Pines series, has been optioned for TV and film. Blake lives in Colorado. To learn more, follow him on Twitter, Facebook, or visit his website, www.blakecrouch.com.

BLAKE CROUCH'S FULL CATALOG

THE WAYWARD PINES SERIES

Pines

Wayward

THE ANDREW Z. THOMAS/LUTHER KITE SERIES

Desert Places

Locked Doors

Break You

Stirred (with J.A. Konrath)

THE STAND-ALONE NOVELS

Run

Abandon

Snowbound

Famous

Eerie (with Jordan Crouch)

Draculas (with J.A. Konrath, Jeff Strand, and F. Paul Wilson)

THE SERIAL SERIES (WITH J.A. KONRATH AND JACK KILBORN)

Serial (short story)

Bad Girl (short story)

Serial Uncut (novella)

Killers (novella)

Birds of Prey (novel)

Killers Uncut (novel)

Serial Killers Uncut (double novel)

THE LETTY DOBESH SERIES

The Pain of Others (Letty Dobesh #1) (novella)

Sunset Key (Letty Dobesh #2) (novella)

Grab (Letty Dobesh #3) (novella)

THE SHORT STORIES, NOVELLAS, AND COLLECTIONS

Hunting Season (with Selena Kitt)

*69 (short story)

Remaking (short story)

On the Good, Red Road (short story)

Shining Rock (short story)

The Meteorologist (short story)

Unconditional (short story)

Perfect Little Town (horror novella)

Four Live Rounds (collected stories)

Six in the Cylinder (collected stories)

Fully Loaded (complete collected stories)

THE BOX SETS

Thicker Than Blood
(The Complete Andrew Z. Thomas Series)

The Fear Trilogy
(*Run, Snowbound, Abandon*)

The Letty Dobesh Chronicles
(*The Pain of Others, Sunset Key, Grab*)